ON THE WAY
TO THE SKY

DOUGLAS KENT HALL

ON THE WAY TO THE SKY

McCall Books

New York

c.1

Published simultaneously in Canada by

Doubleday Canada Ltd., Toronto

Library of Congress Catalog Card Number: 73-160059

ISBN 0-8415-0125-4

McCall Books

A Division of SRI Book Company

230 Park Avenue, New York, N.Y. 10017

PRINTED IN THE UNITED STATES OF AMERICA

Design by Margaret F. Plympton

BL NOV 3 '72

To Kaja, Keli, and David

PART ONE

1

Apogee . . . and the Descent

✦✱✦✿✱✦✿✱✦✿✱✦✿✱✦✿✱✦✿✦✿

1944

Three boys, growing from childhood
to early manhood, learn with and from
one another.

1.   Geo had worn his war bonnet, a scraggly fence of
matched guinea fowl feathers sewn in a denim band, which ran
around his narrow forehead and trailed like a strange fin down
between the galluses that crossed his naked back. He was skinny,
his spidery legs warping easily over the ribs of his bold horse. He
rode slowly toward the green stuccoed house where that morning
a moving van had left the new people's furniture.

Geo could see the new boy all right. But he did not think the
new boy could tell he was looking at him. Because his face was
dwarfed behind the Army Air Force flight goggles his Uncle Jed
had brought him on his last furlough. And so, as long as he did
not move his head, he could turn his eyes and look through the
blue lenses without being noticed. He figured this was a whole
lot like being invisible. Except for the pain. The rubber band
that held the goggles on had snapped and he had replaced it
with a double strand of stiff baling wire which, under the weight

of the heavy rubber frames, cut into the tops of his ears. The price he had to pay.

The new boy was not looking either. He was probably scared. Geo nodded to himself. The new boy was standing on the garage roof, down close to the eaves, where the age-blackened shingles curled up like scales on a dead carp. He had hold of a long bamboo pole and acted as if he were trying to get it set in precisely the right spot on the lawn below. A breeze caught at his Batman cape—a square of bed-worn sheet, the stencil design done in either watercolor or black crayon; and as it flapped away from the new boy's body, Geo saw that he was wearing real Levi's (the twisted galluses hooked to the copper buttons on his own bib overalls began to torture the summer's first sunburn on his shoulders).

About the time the shadow of Geo's horse went jolting across the lawn toward the garage, the new boy gave his cape an extravagant flip and, gathering his feet under him like some kind of bird, left the roof.

Geo snickered to himself. He strained his eyes around to see until he felt something pull in his head.

The new boy described a slow arc, gliding out, slowing, coming to a standstill, straight up. He hung there. It was impossible to tell whether he would continue over and down or fall back. Wiggling helplessly, he looked like a bug with bad wings clinging to the end of an upright straw. Geo wanted to give him a push.

Then he went down—swiftly. He crashed out beyond the shadow of the horse. The bamboo pole, vibrating brassily, tangled with his legs, tripped him, and sent him into a sprawling heap. He rolled over a couple of times, got up, and—with a faked nonchalance—gave his cape another casual flip. He started to strut back to the garage, obviously trying not to limp.

By that time, Geo (having first to jerk his head around and snap his mouth shut) had passed: his horse was a good walker. No matter if it did balk at most ditches and run to the bottom of the field and cause him all sorts of other misery when he wanted to catch it. He lowered his goggles, letting them hang about his neck, while he rubbed at the purple creases the stiff baling wire had cut in the tops of his ears. He snorted to himself. The new boy, he decided, was just trying to be different.

He rode on to a thick clump of Patowatomie bushes; hiding there (his legs and most of the horse still visible), he peered back through the leaves. He did not see anyone. The blossoms had all dropped off the branches, leaving only the brittle yellow prongs of the pistil and stamen. The new little plums, hard as dusty green beads, hung in tight clusters. He plucked a few and stuffed them in his pockets. He might need them sometime. To throw or something. He sat there for another few minutes, waiting. His body rolled forward and back, limply in rhythm with the horse's breathing. He felt the foamy sweat off its back soaking through his overalls, the denim sticking to his legs.

Suddenly, the new boy's head poked past the side of the garage. And then, cape swinging, the new boy walked out into the road. He took long, measured strides, sort of sneaking looks in the general direction of the plum bushes. He opened and shut the door on the metal mailbox. Finally, he raised the red tin flag, without leaving a letter. "Stupid!" Geo hissed, his lips tight. That would get him in real trouble. But the new boy left it up. He crossed the road, going behind the garage again, out of sight.

Then there was nothing. Lazy heat. The hanging dust of summer. The end of a tin can sparkling hazily in the barpit. The shimmering road turning gently out of sight around the hill on the face of which Geo's house stood, sheltered by elm and box elders, patches of the galvanized roof shining dully through thick green summer leaves.

Kicking with his bare heels, Geo woke his old horse from its dream of oats and raised his blue goggles again, setting his teeth against the pain of the wires. He started back past the green stuccoed house. He knew he should keep going the other way, toward the creek, where he was supposed to be. But he was curious. The green house had been vacant for a year, vacant long enough that he and Little Benny Westlake had broken in last Halloween and found for certain that it was haunted: they had scurried away from the first creaking door hinge and the sound of a supernatural rustling. And now he was curious to know what kind of kid would come to live in a haunted house.

Standing in the middle of the lawn, the new boy lifted a Red
Ryder BB gun to his cheek. Geo reasoned that it was not loaded:
he had not heard any BBs roll in the barrel when the new boy
cocked it. All the same, he did not much like the idea of the
thing being pointed at him. He pulled up the reins and leaned
ahead—pretending to check the bridle—and took a quick glance
through the fringe of coarse hair under his old horse's jaw. The
muzzle of the BB gun was pointing high into the branches of a
Chinese elm. For some reason, Geo felt disappointed, cheated.

The new boy discovered he was being watched. He lowered
the gun deliberately down past Geo, down past his horse, until
the barrel was beside his leg, pointing at the ground. Then he
pulled the trigger. The discharge blasted a brief ring of dust out
of the grass.

Long after the dust had settled, Geo and the new boy continued to look at each other. The wires on Geo's heavy flight goggles were now almost unbearable to his ears. But he did not
touch them. He held his teeth tight together and let his eyes
smart. He had endured a lot worse. Like the time an old Jersey
had tromped on his foot for a full minute (till it moved from its
own personal discomfort or boredom) and he had not yelled because he had not wanted his pa to know he had been dumb
enough to let it just step on him in the first place.

A couple of sparrows darted out of the elm and sailed under
the eaves of the house. Cocking rapidly, the new boy squeezed
off one shot and then made a desperate *kee-ooo!* sound of a second shot with his mouth. Both birds flew safely away.

"That ain't loaded," Geo declared, speaking slowly. He leaned
forward for emphasis and felt the guinea feathers brush at his
back. "That gun ain't loaded."

"You think those birds'd still be flying if it was?"

With that statement, the new boy shouldered his gun and
marched out to the road. His body was slight, narrow through
the chest. The hand cupped under the butt of the BB gun was
small and white. He had dark hair, no longer combed but still
neatly separated high on the left side by a part like a severe scar.
There was a hint of insolence in the creases at the corners of his
mouth. But it was his gray eyes that caught Geo's fascination.
Something secret or fierce seemed to lurk in them.

To mask his uneasiness, Geo lifted one bare foot and planted it on the point of the horse's withers, bracing his hands behind him on its moist flat rump. Then the weight of the goggles fell on the bridge of his nose and on his cheeks, relieving his ears. But his cheeks and nose and forehead were sweating and gradually the blue glass began steaming over.

The new boy squinted hard at the horse. But Geo could tell he was an inexperienced judge. He seemed to be sort of looking through the animal. The way a person might look at a bike. Or maybe a wagon.

A couple of seconds went by in lethargic silence. Up the road about a quarter of a mile, Geo's old orange tomcat crept out of the weeds, slunk its belly low across the gravel road, and disappeared. The road was empty again. Waves of heat rising off the gravel. Hazy blue lenses growing dimmer and dimmer.

The new boy shoved his hand in his pocket and brought it up brimming with marbles. He leaned his gun against his leg, selected three marbles, and dumped the others back, chittering, into his pocket. He stooped, laying down the gun, and with his finger drew a ring in the dirt. He let a drop of spit fall in the center of the ring, gathered and firmed dirt around the cotton-white blob of foam, forming a peak, and spotted a marble on it. Knuckling up confidently, he shot and knocked the marble out of the ring, his whole manner and style bespeaking a suave urban perfection.

In a counter-display of catlike grace and agility—dangerous and foolish because it did not always work—Geo shifted his weight and slid torpidly down the ribs of the horse, landing on his feet. He touched the ring with his dirty toes.

"Goose egg," he commented laconically.

"You make it."

Geo accepted the challenge. He rubbed out the first ring with the ball of his foot, abrasive yellow calluses scratching like sandpaper, and drew it bigger—although nonetheless lopsided.

"Okay," the new boy crowed. "Put in!" He dropped a peewee, cherry-red, clear as punch, into the ring.

Digging for his own marbles, Geo encountered one of the small, hard green plums. He tossed that casually into the ring. The new boy said nothing. He simply picked up the plum and, without even stopping to inspect it, shot it off into the weeds. He stood looking impassively after it. Geo selected a chippy—one that would still pass—and threw that in.

With his shoe toe the new boy plowed one short straight line, then a second, ten feet apart. "Lags for first."

Geo could see all right at close range, good enough to aim and shoot in the ring. But he had to cock his head at an angle and squint pretty hard through the fog and finger smudges on his blue goggles to make out the lag line. Aiming, he threw his luck-iest agate taw; it hit and rolled, going past the mark. The new boy produced a big steely; it plopped in front of the lag line and did not budge. Still—it looked close. Perhaps a tie. They meas-ured. Geo was two spans, three fingers. The new boy was ex-actly two spans and a hair. His shot.

Geo could tell from the expert way the new boy fitted his forefinger on his taw and twisted his wrist down so the cords on the underside stood out white that he planned to spin in and clean the pot on the very first shot. "Vence spinners!" he declared firmly.

The new boy relaxed. He took a deep indulgent breath. He switched to a lavender steamroller. He shot. The big marble bludgeoned across the ring, barely ticking his peewee.

Geo nudged the peewee off its peak.

"Anys!" Supporting his shooting hand solidly on his left wrist, the new boy fired. The cherry peewee leaped out of the ring (Geo's heart dropped a good six inches in his chest) and the new boy's taw stayed, spinning, burrowing a round hole in the soft dirt.

"One finger!"

Pointing his finger, without as much as a glance, the new boy shot awkwardly down from his knuckles and missed. Geo had known he would.

"You fudged!" the new boy accused on Geo's next turn.

"I slipped," Geo insisted. "Overs." They argued about it. Fi-nally, the new boy shrugged and relinquished. Geo shot again. He missed again.

A smile twisted at the corners of the new boy's mouth. It was, Geo noted privately, the kind of smile adults sometimes made when they said they were not smiling at the one thing he knew they were but at something else instead. Then, the line of his mouth straightening, the new boy cleaned the pot.

Geo leaped on his horse, as though it meant nothing to lose a marble. Well, anyhow, it had only been a chippy. And almost a plum.

"My name's Geo," he announced from that height.

"Don't you have a last name?"

"Doesn't everybody?"

"Normal people do. What's yours?"

"Seagram. George Albert Seagram. I was named after the Prophet."

"What prophet?"

"The Mormon Prophet. What else?"

"You're one of those, huh?" For a second, the new boy stared at him; then he stuck out his hand. "My name's Louis Light."

It was the first time Geo had ever shaken hands with another kid. So he figured Louis Light surely must have come from the city somewhere—Salt Lake, or even Vernal—where they wore shoes most of the time and did things like shaking hands. It gave him an odd pompous feeling that made him want to giggle. All the same, there was something important about it—important, though he could not give a name to what it was or say why it should seem so.

Looking up, he saw the mailman swing away from their mailbox and start down the hill. He always sat in the middle of the car seat, making it appear that he was being held hostage between two invisible people—driver, gunman. Geo did not like this mailman, who was fat and kept a shoe box full of rocks in the seat to throw at dogs. Often he had watched the invisible figures drive the mailman away and had pretended they were taking him off to suffer a slow, gory death through a mixture of Apache and Jap methods. He considered telling Louis Light about the tin flag. He knew what would happen. His friend Little Benny Westlake had had his backside tanned till it blistered for pulling the same trick. Then, however, remembering the marble he had just lost and that uppity business with the handshake, he said simply, "Car coming up the road." He shut his mouth tight with defiance. It would serve Louis right. A marble was a marble.

Louis picked up his Red Ryder BB gun and sauntered off to the side of the road.

The brakes on the old long-nosed Dodge ground, steel on steel, the sound traveling the length of Geo's spine, tingling, raising the short hairs on the back of his neck. The door on the box squawked down; the mailman's fingernails scratched on the bare metal; the door slammed shut.

Scowling, the mailman shoved his fat yellow face out the window at them. "All right. Which one of you little farts put that flag up?"

"What flag?" Louis asked.

The mailman glowered. "The red flag on the side of that mailbox. Don't you know that it's a federal offense to tamper with the United States mail? Huh? This little stunt alone could get you a good stretch in the clink. You the one that did it?"

"Not me," Louis replied, with exaggerated innocence.

"You—huh?" The mailman peered up at Geo.

"No . . ." Geo felt his crotch tighten. His voice went all shaky.

Giving a final warning that he had had enough monkey business, the mailman drove away, his Dodge spitting gravel.

"I better get going," Geo said, almost as if he were repeating words a wise, silent voice had just spoken to him. He had the distinct feeling that if he stayed much longer, Louis Light was going to get him in some real trouble. Because something about this new kid, something about Louis and the way he handled himself in situations, left Geo with the feeling of being in the immediate proximity of more trouble than he had ever known before in his life. So he swung his horse around.

"Hey! How come you're taking off?"

"I've got to work."

"Work? Doing what?"

"Herding cows. They're feeding over along the creek."

"You work, huh?"

Geo enjoyed the look that flickered on the new boy's face. "Yeah. I've been working for years now. Pa gives me jobs. I do chores. It ain't bad." He did not know why he said what he said next, but he did:

"You want to come?"

"Maybe."

"Well, I ain't got all day."

"Okay. I'll ask Grandma."

"Don't you have to ask your ma?"

"No. She's in California. My folks are split up." Louis swung his BB gun on something in the distance, leveling his eye along the sights. Still squinting, he said, "The court gave me to my Grandma and Grandpa Fulton."

"I thought your name was Light."

"It is. Fulton used to be my mother's name."

"The court, huh?"

"Yeah. Judges and all."

"Just split up?"

"Un-huh."

Geo was not quite sure what Louis Light meant by split up. Maybe someone was killed—or maimed. At least. Of course Louis had said nothing about hospitals and graves. But court. That was bad enough. It meant trouble. He did not ask any more questions.

2.   "Well, well." Leon laughed, stretching his neck and making a final plunge with his forefinger to complete his four-in-hand. "Look at Louis."

Louise Fulton crossed the living room cluttered with covered furniture she would spend the next few days stripping and trying to arrange. Leon stood at the window, looking out. Louis was in the road, talking to a new boy, a funny, thin boy on a horse, a boy ridiculously outfitted in feathers and blue goggles that nearly masked his whole face.

"He's making friends pretty fast," Leon observed, deftly finishing the knot in his tie and drawing it up between the points of his shirt collar.

"Yes," Louise replied matter-of-factly. "Or at least getting acquainted with someone he can fight."

Leon's reply, typically, was a dry chuckle. Then, kissing her lightly, he left the house, heading for his office in town. She watched him back the green Plymouth out of the garage and saw Louis turn from his new friend to call to his grandpa. Leon was probably right: a boy should grow up in the country. Even if it meant leaving the home she had spent so many years putting together. And the extra miles of driving every day would not make it any easier to stretch the gas stamps. And she found herself thinking of the coincidences that had left her with children she had not borne. With Louis; with Leon's daughter.

She and Leon had found each other following the wreckage of each of their previous marriages. Leon's first wife, a woman he had loved to the point of distraction and aching despair, had died in childbirth, leaving him a living daughter. For almost one entire year he could not bear to give the girl a name of her own. But he had managed. He always managed. A small man, he seemed heavy as a stove on his short legs. Not fat. Round, solid. He was of a gentle disposition. He had a finely tempered persistence and an enduring patience, as well as the adequate common sense and good judgment to know when he was biting off all he could chew. He rarely took less. Never more.

In this respect, Leon Fulton was true to his pioneer breeding, the strong Mormon blood that coursed his veins. His family had migrated to Utah with the Saints. He had been born here, in the valley, and spent his life in Vernal. And he had gone along with the Church, professing—or more accurately, acknowledging—his inherited Mormon beliefs and doctrines until one Sunday morning late in the month of October when the bishop—a man named Carter—spent a substantial part of the service tutoring the congregation on the dubious merits of one candidate for President of the United States. Alf Landon! Leon snorted to himself. Materialism and politics! Standing abruptly, he made his way along the sharp row of knees to the aisle, and straight out of the chapel. He had never returned.

Leon Fulton maintained that if Joseph Smith were to come upon the Saints today, his horror would be so great he would immediately invent a new gospel. And Brigham Young, a grizzled man of action, would not allow the sun to set once before he had organized a new Mormon Battalion to march upon this wayward people, scourging ward after ward until he had purged the whole tribe of its foulness and pollution.

But Leon was not bitter. That would have gone against his nature. The evening Bishop Carter paid his annual visit to "settle up" on tithing, that ten percent of everything which Leon had always scrupulously paid—paid, that is, right up to the October .morning when he had quit (taking solace when Carter's man, Landon, had lost, and lost badly), he refused to make either the payment or a simple statement of why he had fallen away. He refused, too, to join the bishop on his knees in a prayer concerning the two hundred dollars in question. He simply let the man kneel in front of his chair, pray his most persuasive prayer, talking himself hoarse in the process, then leave, shaking his head sadly at the stubbornness and what he imagined to be the state of sin to which he had just been witness.

Basically, Leon Fulton was a calm man. His most vociferous moments were spent over the washbasin each morning. He seemed to attack the cold water, cupping up handfuls and splashing it in his face, snorting and hissing furiously. When he finished, the pores on his nose would be textured like a ripe strawberry. He dried roughly and fastened on his bifocals. Then, folding the towel carefully over the rack, he would have quieted enough to face his solid world of order and precision.

"Grandpa," Louis called. "Can I go herd cows?"

Leon smiled. "It's all right by me. But I think you'd better run ask your grandma."

Louise Fulton. Her own history was vaguely southern. That is to say this: she was born in Missouri (an element of her being which would, in moments of memory and poignancy, let her voice go soft and syrupy). At the age of eleven she came west, to Wyoming. There, on her father's remote ranch, she grew to be an excellent horsewoman and matured, almost unnoticed, into a robust beauty who needed neither rouge nor cosmetic coloring for her lips. One of the first single men to see her, a young veterinarian named Jim Foster, who had ridden out to doctor a prize mare, returned the next afternoon and proposed marriage.

Months later she finally accepted, thinking she saw fire in his soul. And she allowed him the first kiss for which he had been hungering and pleading. But the horse doctor (which was the way she referred to him now, refusing to remember him as Jim or James Foster or even just Foster) turned out to be merely fiery and impetuous. His fits of drinking and jealousy and violence finally drove her away. Taking her three-year-old daughter, Gloria, she rode by horseback to the railroad station, caught a train, then a stage, crossed the mountains into Colorado, crossed the sagebrush flats into Utah, and chose to stop and live in Vernal. First, because of the arid beauty of the Ashley Valley; second, because that was as far as her savings would take her.

At the General Mercantile Company, where she found her first job, men spoke to her in the most flattering terms. But she was too full of hate and fear and bad memories of the horse doctor to accept any of their offers of courtship. None, that is, prior to the one Leon Fulton proposed the day he crossed the street from Utah Freight and Storage, which he managed and in which he held considerable stock. Looking her squarely in the eye, fingering the gold watch chain on his vest, he told her he was a serious man, a widower with a daughter just past two years old, and knew that she needed a decent home for herself and for her own daughter and suggested that they start things off by dining together that evening. At six. And she had simply stood there and said yes. Though she had wanted to laugh. Glancing at his fingers, which seemed to be methodically counting the links on the opulent loop of gold chain, she had simply said yes—duplicating even his tone and inflection. Gradually, the practicality of Leon's bold offer was consumed by an undying passion and a growing tenuous love. The first, she knew, had been a façade for the second (for he had spoken like a man offering a lady flowers and saying he was doing it because there was a surplus in his garden).

In direct contrast to the happiness they found with each other, Leon and Louise had been forced to stand back and watch their two children make blustery bad starts at life. Leon's daughter, who was finally called Joleen (replacing Baby, her name during the first long year of Leon's sorrow) had been killed with her boyfriend in a spectacular automobile accident: both had been found naked—a fact not openly publicized in the predominantly Mormon town. Then, a year later, Gloria had run off and married Willie Light, had, in fact, phoned collect from Elko, Nevada, to announce it—circumstances supposedly explaining the rest. And while Willie was away in the Army, where he still was—and damn well could stay for all of her—that marriage had disintegrated. So Leon and Louise had become father and mother as well to Louis Light, each hoping (without admitting it) that they would do a better job with him than they had with Jo and Gloria.

Paradoxically, the turbulence of her early years and the failure and futility she had been forced to witness and then accept had left relatively few marks visible on Louise Fulton. Age had come to her gently, as if it were merely a gilded frame that had been away to be measured and mitred. Still beautiful (Leon did not often tell her, but the fact was always evident in his eyes), with full features, strong cheekbones, high and cleanly shaped, a slender nose with small flared nostrils, a close mouth that retained the soft red blush of her youth, brown hair gone ashen, and an olive tinge to her skin that kept it supple and smooth, she looked as though she had lived easily. A life of pamper and plenty . . .

Louis crossed the porch and let the screen door bang.

"Grandma, can I go herd cows with that kid?"

"We'll see."

"He needs to know now."

Louise led Louis back out on the porch. She looked at the boy who had ridden his horse halfway up the path.

"What's his name?"

"I don't know."

"Didn't you ask?"

"He's only a kid. Can I go?"

"I told you my name!" the boy on the horse shouted. "It's Geo."

Louise thought Louis was going to laugh. But he did not. He said, "His name's Geo. He was named after some prophet."

"The Mormon Prophet," Geo emphasized. "George Albert Smith. But my name's not Smith—it's Seagram."

Louise smiled. "You can go for an hour."

Louis started down the steps toward the horse.

Sometimes she wanted so badly to sweep him up in her arms,

to hold him, to coax him to say what he was thinking, to say what it was that kept him so silent, so secretive. But Louis, it seemed, had never wanted to be loved. Or even touched. There were times when he actually made her flinch. His eyes were so oddly penetrating. They had the gray sheen of gun steel and seemed to possess a wisdom far beyond his age. She had never seen anything like it in Gloria, who had always had a deceptive sweetness, a veneer that rarely allowed anything from beneath to show through. Louise saw this quality as contemptible and, although she would afterward be ashamed of it, there were times when she read certain false passages in Gloria's letters and caught herself actually hating her own daughter. She shook her head. No, it was obvious that Louis had inherited his eyes from Willie Light.

Louise realized then that she had gone rigid. She held her hands fisted against her sides. She was trembling. Maybe it was silly. But it embittered her to have to acknowledge that they were raising a boy whose name would be Light. She only hoped that he had somehow acquired from Leon Fulton the common decency to be a credit to the human race—and not to carry on in what she had had the misfortune to learn to call the Light Tradition.

3.   "Ain't you on *yet?*" Geo asked, faking impatience. In his artless attempt at mounting, Louis Light had almost dragged him off. Geo wondered if the kid had ever been on a horse before. "City slicker," he muttered under his breath.

"Yes," Louis said. He was trying futilely to hold back his heavy breathing.

Geo wanted to mock him, but he did not. He was still mad about Louis saying he had forgotten his name. He had not forgotten: that was a dirty lie.

Gently rocking in the swale of the horse's back, they rode to the corner, past old man Carlson's place, and turned down the lane. Two dusty ruts unspooled through the tough saltgrass. Milkweed pods had started to show white beards. The stalks of sunflowers were beginning to stretch above the tops of cedar posts along the roadway. They found the Jerseys, shaded up, black jaws hinging, swinging, shutting on pulpy cuds, tails switching languidly at flies. They rode on.

"There!" Geo pointed. He felt a sudden swelling of pride and importance he could hardly contain. "That's the hideout."

Louis got off the wrong side of the horse. Geo clapped one hand to the side of his head. City slicker! he accused again, to himself, *Any*body would know better. Silently, holding his lips tight so he would not giggle at Louis's lack of horse sense, he slid down the embankment and led the way into the clean hollow beside the creek, which ran in shallow ripples over the golden stones. The place was grassy, overshadowed by willows and cottonwood saplings. Along the edges of the creek stood spears of jointweed, which could be popped apart and put together again in ceremonial necklaces. Buttercups grew in masses of dense clusters, as yellow as rich traces of sulphur. Geo plopped down on the grass, flattening his skinny body against the moist cool soil.

"What's it like?" he asked, finally blurting out the thing that had been bothering him since Louis first mentioned it.

"What?" Louis looked at him curiously.

"I mean is it the same?"

"What?"

"Not having folks."

"I've got folks."

"I mean real ones. Is it the same?"

"I don't know."

"You don't?"

"No. I never lived with my folks—not that I can remember."

"Don't you wish you could?"

Louis was silent a moment. Then he said, "No."

A little while later, sitting up as casually as he could, Geo pulled a page of folded newspaper from his bib pocket. He tore off two squares and showed Louis how to strip and shred cedar bark for a smoke. Then, while they sat puffing at the hot, fast-

burning cigarettes, he told Louis all about Little Benny Westlake, who owned half interest in the hideout.

"Sometimes Little Benny swipes smokes from his pa, real ones,
and we have a fine time down here. Benny's got him a bottle of
carbide, too. We use that to make cold water bombs."

"Carbide?" Louis's voice was quick with interest. "Where'd he
get that?"

"His pa sometimes works out at the gilsonite mines. The min-
ers all burn carbide in their lamps. Benny's pa doesn't work out
there a whole lot though. He's a musician."

"A musician?" Louis repeated, squinting.

"Yeah. A cowboy musician, like you're always hearing over the
radio. I guess Little Benny's fixing to be one, too. At least he's got
a guitar."

"You like cowboy music?" Louis asked.

"I like it fine. But I don't get to hear it much—except out at
Little Benny's." Geo paused, then he resumed seriously. "I
haven't figured everything out yet. But something crazy's going
on around our house. It's like this—Ma listens to cowboy music
when Pa's out of the house. And Pa listens to it when he's driving
somewhere in the pickup. But they don't ever listen to it together. And when I ask if we can hear some, Ma says it's cheap.
And Pa, he just nods his head."

"Sometimes," Louis said, taking a calculated drag on the butt
of his cedar-bark cigarette, "adults are a real puzzle."

"Yeah," Geo agreed. Then Louis added, "And that makes it
sort of hard on us kids."

4.   "Hell, I been playing in our band since I was big enough
to reach around them strings. Ain't nothing wrong with that."

"Except that maybe being up all those nights stunted your
growth some," Geo suggested, no malice intended.

"Nope," Little Benny Westlake objected, giving his head a firm twist. "Mozart was making up songs when he was still just a kid. Ma," he explained to Louis in a quick aside, "told me all about Mozart. And I don't believe he was stunted. I ain't no midget myself. Neither. My body's just taking its sweet time about sprouting up. That's the way Pa puts it. And Pa's probably right."

Little Benny had hair as white as washed wool. His small round face looked like a miniature of someone else's face. His pants were cinched in bunches under a wide leather belt studded with big nickel spots and glass jewels. The belt was too long; the surplus snaked down into his left front pocket. He wore cowboy boots that were badly run over at the heels and had holes scrubbed through the points of the curled toes.

"Whew!" Benny cried. "I'm aching for a smoke." He produced a pack of Camels he had smuggled down in his shorts and passed them around. "Damn!" he said, slapping at his pockets. "I never brought no matches."

"I've got some," Louis spoke up. He pulled out a brass bullet casing, removed a wooden stopper, and shook a few blue-tip matches into his palm.

"You smoke?" Louis asked Geo.

"I did yesterday. You saw me."

"I mean cigarettes. Cedar bark like we had yesterday doesn't count. These are real cigarettes. I thought you were a Mormon."

"Yeah," Little Benny joined in with a gleeful giggle. "Named after the prophet."

"It doesn't matter much yet," Geo said. "Not till after I'm baptized. When I'm eight. Then I've got to watch out."

They all lit up and squatted in the grass, where they could blow smoke and spit in the creek. Covertly, Geo and Little Benny both considered the polished city skill Louis Light employed in handling his cigarette—sucking in mouthfuls of smoke, letting them pour out, while he just looked straight ahead, squinting, pensive. Pretty soon, they were all smoking with a studied squint and a mean droop to their mouths.

"You ever shot off any bombs, Louis?" Little Benny inquired.

"Some." Louis let a little smoke seep out his nostrils and stifled a cough. "I suppose you guys are still only making cold water bombs."

Little Benny daubed his ash idly at a stone. His forehead wrinkled seriously. "Ain't no other." He watched Louis's face and waited.

"Says who?"

"What others?" Little Benny challenged starchily.

"Fire bombs."

"What's that?" Geo said sarcastically. "A *city* bomb?"

Louis Light just looked at him. It seemed he could not be insulted.

Louis built the fire. Geo and Little Benny, both coughing from the stench, created a potent mixture of carbide and creek water in a fruit jar. Louis constructed a simple chute of peeled willow sticks and set it up so the jar would drop directly into the coals. The carbide was mixed; the white willows were set. They were ready.

The very instant Little Benny saw Louis's fingers let go of the jar, he knew something was about to happen. He was petrified. And he could not jump away.

There was an interminable icy silence while the bomb slid down the sharp incline of the chute. It dropped. One minute it was in the air. The next it was in the fire. It seemed to float briefly in the flames. Until it exploded. A shrapnel of shattered glass and smoldering sticks shot out, smoking in the grass, hissing in the creek.

Little Benny's round face knotted-up, going as white as his hair. His mouth contorted in a bluish ring around a soundless scream which gradually grew audible. Then piercing. His hands dropped to his leg. His overalls were ripped. An ugly shard from the bottle had speared his flesh. Blood ran on the slick surface of the glass, pushing along a gray, bubbling froth of the carbide solution. Geo grabbed the glass and yanked it out, hoping it would not even leave a cut. Little Benny let out a fresh scream.

"Come on," Louis ordered in a cool voice. "Let's get him loaded on your horse."

Geo leaped on. Louis hoisted Little Benny up behind him. Little Benny's teeth were bared in pain, and each time he moved he howled harder. His leg was spewing thick red blood. Geo felt it flowing out hot and wet on the back of his leg and running down his calf to his heel. He started getting sick to his stomach.

Louis slapped the horse on the rump. "Hurry!"

Geo reined it up. "Come on, Louis."

"That old horse can't carry the three of us."

"This here horse'll carry ten of us. And anyhow, I ain't going up there alone. Now come on, Louis. We can't just let Little Benny bleed to death here."

Little Benny renewed his howl and buried his blubbering lips against Geo's naked back, dripping slobber down his spine.

"You can't let me die!"

Geo winced. But he held firm. They were not going to pin this on him. "Louis, I'm not going without you."

"Oh, god," Benny gurgled.

"Louis—" Geo cried. "He's bleeding like a stuck hog."

"Louis, you can't let me die."

In one amazingly agile movement, Louis leaped on the horse— from the right side this time. He drove his sharp shoe heels deep into its flanks, kicking it into a farting lope. He grabbed Little Benny so he would not roll backwards off the horse's rump.

"Let go of me!" Little Benny screeched. "I can't breathe! Don't touch me."

But Louis did not let go.

"I can feel the life running right out of my leg," Little Benny cried piteously. "It's numb and buzzing like the beginning of death."

"You'll be all right, Benny," Geo assured him. "Won't he, Louis?"

Louis did not say anything.

"No, I won't neither. Oh, lord, I'm going fast."

Geo kicked the horse harder. And they raced, the three of them bobbing on the old horse's spine, along the graveled road toward the Westlake house.

The closer he got to home (growing increasingly more confident that he would actually make it alive, and probably even conscious) the more Little Benny wanted to cry. And the more he detested the feel of Louis Light's fingers clamped on his shoulders. Louis was the only person who had ever given him any real fright. He tried to figure it out. But he did not know why.

Goddam you, Louis Light, Little Benny said to himself, repeating over and over the one word his pa would not tolerate. Goddam you goddam you goddam you. . . .

5.   Julie Volks watched them come up the hill, Little Benny howling at the top of his voice. Julie was a pretty child. Seven. Well formed. Except in the knees, where she retained the dimpled plumpness of a baby. Then, too, her stomach tended to protrude when—as now—she forgot to stand as she knew a lady should stand. Her lower lip pushed out, she seemed completely absorbed, as though she were anticipating and maybe even enjoying the approaching catastrophe. It was not until the last possible moment that she turned, cupped her hand against the screen wire, and called, almost casually:

"Aunt Belle, I think there's something the matter with Little Benny. He's crying."

Belle Westlake, wide red face blazing with kitchen heat, her naturally curly hair all screwed tight to her head from the steam, burst out on the porch. A bunch of string beans hung out of the fisted end of her left hand like fat worms, and in her right hand she held a foggy Mason jar she had been stuffing full for the pressure cooker, a pinch of salt already starting to melt in the bottom.

The instant Little Benny caught sight of her, he yowled with added agony and tumbled down off the horse, grasping his injured leg.

"Lord, boy!" Belle scolded, bustling down to where he lay theatrically thrashing about on the grass. "What's got into you? Benny? Benny? You get up from there and shush that blabbermouth. Right now! Hear? You shush or I'm going to box your ears."

"Ma!" Little Benny blubbered against her leg. "I don't want to die."

"Shush up that foolishness! Lord, Benny, what've I done?

Raised you up to be a boobie? What if your brother Hartt was to come home from the Army and catch you carrying on like this? With no more shame than one of them Japs he's over there having to kill." She planted herself firmly in front of him. "Now come on in the house and we'll wash that cut and paint it with some red medicine."

Still clutching the string beans and the jar, Belle Westlake gathered Little Benny under her arm and, like a broadtailed red hen brooding a runt chick, ushered him into the house.

Julie stayed outside. There was a pool of blood on the edge of the sidewalk. Stooping, she flattened her palm, first splaying her fingers in a wide fan, and pushed it down into the blood. She lifted her hand and pressed a print of it onto the dry concrete.

She stood up, holding the bloody hand away from her body, and watched the two kids who had brought Benny ride off down the hill. She opened the screen door and started in the house—to wash her hands and then to go to her Aunt Belle's mirror, which covered an entire door. She would stand in front of it and brush her hair, using the sparkling rhinestone-backed brush she had to sneak out of a drawer. She would draw the short white bristles through her sandy blond hair until the ringlets shone and crackled with electricity.

She paused long enough to watch the boys turn the corner toward the hideout. Momentarily, her lower lip stood out. She would see them again. And they would let her in the hideout. She started to smile. Then, she slipped on into the living room, the screen door slamming behind her.

6.   "I won't be a cripple for life or nothing like that—it's just a bit stiff yet. And they's a scab on it as long as your finger." Little Benny showed his scab, with no accusations or expectations of apologies. "I gotta keep it covered up. Because I keep having this here bad urge to pick it off." He pried lightly at the edges of the red scab with one dirt-mooned fingernail.

"Benny!" Julie scolded. "Don't you touch that scab!" Reaching ahead, she gave him a sharp slap on the hand and yanked his pants down to shield the scab. She was on the horse behind Little Benny. Her pink panties showed from under her short dress.

I see London, I see France, Geo thought and then turned away, trying to stop the singsongy verses that kept right on going inside his head.

Julie slipped down from the horse and sat on a tree stump, crossing her legs one way, then the other, and fooling with her dress. She had a funny way of talking that embarrassed Geo. She said things like "how very peculiar" and "what a darling little place." And when she spoke, she nodded like a quick bird balancing on a wire.

"What's *she* doing here?" Louis demanded.

Little Benny did not reply (he was still scared of Louis) except to let his shoulders start up in a shrug.

"Do you have some ordinance against ladies?" Julie questioned. Her voice was brittle. "Geo, is there any conceivable reason why I shouldn't be here?" She cocked her head. "Is there?"

"Ask Louis." Geo could not talk to her. Not at all. She made him feel strange, sort of all haywire inside. He kept wanting to bump into her.

"Louis?" she repeated. "I was under the distinct impression that half of this hideout belonged to you, Geo, and the other half belonged to Little Benny."

"It does," Geo stated, giving an affirmative nod. "Yes—and the other half belongs to my friend Louis Light."

"But that's impossible!" Julie cried. "There isn't any *other* half."

"There is so. Louis's got it," Geo maintained. "The last half is his. We made a deal." He touched his pocket, which still bulged with most of Louis's marbles. He could settle up with Benny later.

"I don't care what deal you made. You can't have three halves, you ninnies! You can only have three thirds."

"Nope," Louis spoke up, thumbs pronged in his front pockets. "Three halves is what we've got. *You* probably can't see that— since you're a woman. But this institution happens to be a men's club and we do our figuring according to men's rules. It's like my

Grandpa Light always says: you can't expect a woman to understand anything, because women've got a private way of looking at things that makes them think they're right all the time."

After a while, Geo did bump into Julie. He and Louis and Little Benny (limping) all began chasing her and grabbing her and falling with her and rolling like puppies with her in the damp grass along the cool creek. Finally, played out, they sprawled beside the water and looked up at the sky, where fat summer clouds sailed east towards Colorado.

Languorously, Julie reached out and plucked a buttercup. She just loved the way the tight little petals stood up.

"I'll bet I can tell if you like butter." She grinned. "I just hold this blossom under your chin. If your skin looks yellow, that's a sign you do."

First, she stuck the flower under Little Benny's chin. "Oh, my! Yellow as yellow ever was!"

"Yeah. Hell, I can eat butter right off the dish," Little Benny bragged. "You know that, Julie."

"Hold still now!" Julie ordered. Geo, who had been slowly backing away from her flower, froze.

"Yes, you like it too." Seeing a bashful blush cross his face, she giggled. "My!"

Louis stared at her. "I don't like butter," he stated bluntly.

According to the flower, his statement was true to the letter. But something prompted her (she could not resist) to crush the petals up under his chin, leaving him smudged with a whirl of color. "You do so!"

"You bitch!" Louis spat.

She giggled and watched while he wiped at the yellow stain with the back of his hand.

"I'll bet none of you have ever played nasty," she said suddenly.

The grassy cove grew silent. Julie smirked. She had said it to get even with Louis Light.

"Julie," Little Benny whispered, his voice full of pain and betrayal.

Although he did not quite know what she meant, Geo could not bring himself to look at Julie. Suddenly, he wanted a drink. He crawled to the creek. A water snake slowly unwound itself from the rocks and grass in the shallows and curled away, head up, shimmying harmlessly across the water to the other bank. Geo waited for the idea of it swimming there to wash on downstream and then pushed his mouth down into the water.

"Well," Julie said. She glanced at Louis and saw him formulating his speech.

"Sure," he said smoothly. "I've done it. Plenty of times."

"I'll bet." Julie sneered.

"Want me to prove it?"

"You have to give me something first—all of you."

"What?"

"A dime."

Nobody had a dime. Nobody even had a nickel.

"Tomorrow, then," she said. It was almost a question.

7.   "Where you going to get your dime?"

Geo gazed at Louis in mute disbelief. He could still hear the faintly haunting tittup of Little Benny's pinto. Carrying her away. Tittup-tittup. Was Louis going to do it? Geo hedged the question, "Where'll you get yours?"

"Come on."

"Huh?"

"Come on."

They rode to the corner. Geo tied his horse to a willow and followed Louis, who was already pushing through the brush to the creek. They crossed the weir and entered old man Carlson's yard. Geo hesitated. He was afraid of Carlson. He saw him at Sunday school. But he knew he hid whiskey in his barn and swore all the time—worse than Little Benny, who was no Mormon. Louis jerked his head. Geo followed. Creeping close to the side of the house, they peered around the corner. Louis pointed to a row of pop bottles, washed and standing on the back porch. Just inside the railing.

"How'd you know about them?"

"I knew," Louis said. "Let's get them."

"Steal?" Geo gasped.

"We can get them tonight—easy."

"Steal?" Geo breathed, unable to push himself beyond the word. It seemed to tighten in his soul, like a piano wire. Pluck! Jeff Seagram had always warned him that according to the laws of God, Stealing (*Pluck!*) was the next worse thing to Adultery. (*Pluck!*) Which was a word he had never explained, but which Geo sort of figured had something to do with being a bad adult —a concept abstract enough to inspire awe and fear. (*Pluck!*) And Adultery (*Pluck!*) was right next to Murder (*Pluck!*). All three were sins against man (directly) and against God (in principle). A lot of which Geo could not even start to understand.

"What do *you* think we ought to do?" Louis asked. "Since you think you're so smart."

"There's plenty of bottles along the barpit."

"Sure."

"There are. I've seen millions."

"If there's not, you promise to help me get these?"

"Only if there ain't that many in the barpit."

"Promise?"

"Okay."

"Say it."

"I promise."

They spent two hours hunting. They scuffed through crotch-deep grass and weeds on both sides of the road and turned up one Coca-Cola bottle and one Orange Crush bottle that was partly filled with dirt. Geo remembered a Squirt bottle they had used to feed bum lambs; he sneaked that out of the barn—the scaly black rubber nipple still intact. Louis found a Dad's bottle containing kerosene in his grandpa's garage. He poured the kerosene over a pile of sticks and dropped a match from his bullet shell on them. While the fire blazed, he and Geo totaled up their find. Four bottles: eight cents. Which would not buy Julie for even one of them.

"We've got to get those bottles."

"Steal?" Geo moaned. (*Pluck!*)

"Tonight."

"Steal?"

"We won't get caught."

"That won't make it right."

"Maybe not," Louis said. "But it's better."

Geo moaned silently inside. For most of the day, he had been withholding something. Now, he just had to say it, "Louis, how come you want to play that with her when you went and called her what you did?"

"Called her what, Geo?"

"That," he swallowed. "Bitch."

"That's what she is."

"How do you know?"

"I can tell," Louis said, nodding sapiently.

"Is it because she's one of those girls from town?"

"Yes. They're all like that."

"I hate them," Geo decided, although with the exception of Julie Volks he had never known any girls from town.

"We'll meet tonight and get those bottles."

"I ain't allowed off the place after dark."

"Sneak off—I'm going to."

Geo shuddered. Sneaking (*Pluck!*) And Stealing (*Pluck!*). Those two, he reasoned, along with *honor thy father* (*Pluck!*) might well make this as serious a sin as Adultery (*Pluck!*). Maybe he would find himself confessing and bawling and carrying on right in church like some of the adults who kept saying in Testimony Meeting how awfully sorry they were about being sinners. And he wondered if that was not a pretty good way to tell who had committed Adultery—the bad adults. But Geo had never had a friend like Louis Light, so he listened to every word of his plan.

Old man Carlson did his milking in the cool of the evening. "Some folks call me lazy," the old man had said one time to Geo's father. "But I maintain it don't matter one iota to them cows." Which made it simple to know when he was out there: a light burned from a tall pole over the corral. When he was finished choring and was ready to head for the house, he turned off the light.

That, Louis explained, would be their signal of warning.

8.   The Seagrams were quiet, pious people. Jefferson and Cora had both been born here in the valley, of Mormon stock. They met at a Stake Conference, talking under the trees for a long time after the church meetings were over; they courted at the socials, dances, and picnics sponsored by the Mormon Mutual Improvement Association, and stayed true to every law set forth by their religion. They were married for all of eternity— sealed to each other—in the secret rooms of the Mormon temple in Salt Lake City. They shared a healthy fear of the Mormon God and his two subordinates, Jesus Christ and the Holy Ghost, and made themselves ready to meet them each day (and as Mormons, living the Good Life, they were confident they would achieve eternal bliss and be allotted a portion of the uppermost Kingdom of Heaven, the Celestial Kingdom, where the initial binding entrance requirement was to be a baptized, confirmed, and faithful full-tithe-paying Mormon). Before each meal they knelt down on the kitchen floor; at night they knelt at the foot of their bed. And had each other as witness of what transpired thereafter. They waited years for Geo. His mother said he had come as a blessing. She could have no more. And his coming had committed them further to God and the Church. They believed what the Prophets had taught them and were convinced that, as it was prophesied, a time was close at hand when the war would end and the leaders of the Church would also become the leaders of the nation and all America would be as righteous and wholesome as a Mormon Sunday school, a veritable showplace of Charity, Virtue, and Love. This, of course, was God's will.

The evenings of their six working days were identical: Jeff, tired after the long hours in the fields, would untie his shoes and read the Deseret *News*, while Cora sewed, the vibrating onrush of the foot treadle rattling the lid on an empty, glass candy jar in a knickknack shelf nearby. At seven o'clock, they would turn on the radio and listen through the static for news of the war. When something of special interest was reported, the sound of the treadle and the dull punching of the needle and the rattling of the candy jar would cease. In that order.

On the night of the robbery, Geo listened for the radio. He heard it. Finally. The big speaker buzzing behind the fancy wooden grille. He lowered his blue goggles into place (wads of toilet tissue cushioning his sore ears from the wires) and left the house via his bedroom window. He sneaked through an alfalfa field to the road. He met Louis near a culvert. A huge summer moon the color of platinum rolled up out of Split Mountain Gorge, balancing on the top of the purple mountain like an opulent eye. The sea-blue sky held clouds like churned foam. And a few stars.

"I can see you plain as day—almost," Geo said. "And I'm wearing these goggles."

Louis started walking.

"We'll get caught."

Louis kept walking.

Geo sighed.

They stopped at a weir. Water in the creek bubbled over the rotting moss-slick boards. They sat down above the spillway, shredded fresh cedar bark, and rolled smokes, cupping the spitting, yellow match flames close in their palms. The hot tindery smoke, parching his mouth and throat, made Geo feel big. He relaxed a little. His joints seemed to swing easier. He did not shake much until they were standing next to the house. Then he had to hold his mouth shut tight and clench his fists to keep his teeth from snapping together.

Out in the corral there was a commotion: a stool banging, a bucket, a cow kicking, old man Carlson's voice rising in a steady blue streak that made Geo's ears burn.

Louis crawled ahead. His shoe scraped across the wooden door that opened down into the cellar. He froze. Geo bumped into him.

"Damn!" Louis whispered. "Wouldn't you know it."

"What?"

"Look."

The head and shoulders of Mrs. Carlson's shadow stretched onto the porch, bobbing and flitting across the bottles and shuttling along the spindles in the wooden railing. Supper dishes clunked in the sink.

Crouching there at the edge of the porch, Geo felt a chill go shuddering through him and a hackle of hair raise up on the back of his neck.

"Let's get out of here," he whispered urgently through his teeth.

"No," Louis hissed, grabbing his sleeve. "We'll wait."

"We can get them bottles some other time," Geo insisted, though he knew they needed them for the next day. He panicked: he knew something bad was about to happen. The taste in his mouth was no longer smoke but the acrid tinning of fear. He could not help thinking that what he was doing, the combination of the three sins—honor thy father (*Pluck!*), Sneaking (*Pluck!*), Stealing (*Pluck!*)—was more serious than Adultery (*Pluck!*). The next to the worst sin.

"There," Louis sighed.

The shadow was slipping off the porch. The row of pop bottles glistened in the crepuscular light. Louis grabbed Geo's hand and yanked him around in front of the porch.

"Hold that!" Louis ordered, shoving a gunny sack into his hand.

Louis could not get the bottles to fit through the narrow spaces between the spindles.

"Come on, Louis. We can't get them," Geo sighed.

"Shut up!"

Louis climbed onto the porch, crouching, holding himself against the spindles. Reaching over the top of the railing, he grabbed a bottle. One . . . two . . . three, Geo counted silently. Four . . . five . . . six. He sighed again. "Louis—that's enough!" He gasped. Louis was reaching for another one. He jerked at the leg of his Levi's. "Six was all we needed!"

Seven.

The light on the pole above the corral suddenly snapped out. Geo could hear the milk pails—two, full—advancing through the stiff weeds beside the path. He could almost see the green seeds sifting into the foam, seeds that would get caught in the straining cloth. He let out a sob. He could not help it. If his father ever found out (*Pluck!*) he would draw the wide leather belt out of his pants and tan him within an inch of his life. He thought of the heavy, square nickel buckle, the sharp tongue. He imagined the sound of the leather cutting through the air.

Eight. Louis lifted that bottle above his head.

"Shut your mouth, Geo, or I'll clobber you."

"I hate you, you dirty stealer!" Geo sobbed. He bit his soft bottom lip and held his breath. He followed Louis to a place in the shadows against the porch and huddled there. Louis, his eyes like stars, raised the bottle threateningly. Geo bit harder.

The gate squawked, opening, then sprang shut. The two cast-iron cogs and the big derrick pulley clanked on the chain. Old man Carlson's steps on the hollow porch sounded ponderous and heavy as drumbeats. Geo thought maybe he had been nipping on his whiskey, getting meaner and meaner. The old man set the pails down, pails ringing dully. In his mind, Geo could see his wizened face as he squinted to count his bottles. His heart was beating so hard that it hurt his throat.

The old man, who had a bad back, grunted. He scraped his shoes, cracked, acid-eaten leather, speckled cork soles. He dragged them hard across the hoe blade nailed to the edge of the porch. Manure, in dry flakes and damp clods, rained down on the two thieves.

Geo's eyes, enclosed in the stifling figure eight of his blue goggles, were shut. His nervous sweat clouded the lenses. He was praying, sending up an earnest prayer of repentance. He begged for forgiveness, for deliverance. He asked for a miracle. Anything. He halted long enough to hear the old man go inside the house. His prayer had been answered. But he could not open his eyes. He heard the tinkle of bottle glass muffled in the gunny sack. It grew fainter. He could not move. Huddled there, he prayed again. He explained to God that he had only held the gunny sack, that Louis Light had, in fact, done the real stealing. He prayed that he was sorry he liked Louis. But he did. Even though Louis was a city slicker. And full of the kind of devilment you learned in town. He felt that the world was whirling about him. That he was the worst sinner in the whole history of man.

Louis scrambled back and gave him a fierce shake. "Come on, dummy! You're going to get caught. Then you'll squeal."

"I ain't scared."

"What?"

"I ain't scared."

"Then what're you doing?"

"Praying."

"Oh, brother! Come on."

"I ain't scared."

"Then get the lead out!"

"I ain't scared, Louis," Geo repeated. But he could not move.

Louis grabbed him by one of his galluses and gave a hard yank which lodged the crotch of his overalls up into his crack, making it hard for him to walk straight. Louis dragged him out to the road.

"Geo, you called me a dirty stealer," Louis reminded sternly, giving a couple of more threatening jerks on the gallus, wedging his overalls tighter in his crack.

"I never really meant it, Louis. Honest I never."

Louis stared at him for a long time, his lips curling with contempt. Again, Geo thought he could see stars in Louis's eyes. They were as cold as his hand had been. Then they flattened till they were like two icy coins.

"All right," Louis said finally. "Just to prove it, you've got to take your horse to the store tomorrow so we can cash in the bottles."

"I can't do that," Geo said feebly.

Louis tightened his grip on the gallus. "*What?*"

Geo's pants were so tight now it was hard for him to even swallow.

"What?"

"My pa'd whale the living daylights out of me." He saw Louis start to turn away in disgust. "But I'll do it, Louis."

9·   It was a mile and a half to the Maeser store, a country center at a principal crossroads. According to Geo's calculations, they could make it there and back in an hour. And maybe his father would not be any the wiser. As an added precaution, he wore his goggles, double layers of chalky cottonwood leaves folded under the wires, and bent low over his horse's neck, trying for as much incognito (a thing his Uncle Jed had said you could get from colored glasses) as he could manage.

They took twelve bottles in the gunny sack. They found one more on the way. Which made twenty-six cents. They each ended up with a dime, two fingers of licorice, and a bubble gum. It was easier than Geo had thought. They had not had to lie or anything. The woman in the store simply counted the bottles, not noticing the ones they had swiped from Carlson, and laid the money out on the counter.

Looking ruefully at his three cents' worth of licorice and gum, then over at the bright dime in his other hand, Geo proposed, "Maybe we just ought to buy ourselves a slug of candy instead. We could forget that—" he wanted to say bitch, the way Louis had, but he could not—"girl, that Julie."

"No," Louis vetoed, clamping his teeth on one of his licorice sticks, stretching it out till it broke. "We've got to be honest."

"Honest?" Geo was flabbergasted. "We stole them bottles."

"That's all the more reason not to make it worse by going back on our promise." His eyes narrowed. "You chicken?"

Geo flared up. "I ain't chicken of no girl!" His thin face hardened seriously. He adjusted his goggles. "But I don't care for them a whole lot." That was honest too.

"Okay."

Geo had to hurry back and check on his cows. He pictured what it would be if his father found out he was here. He saw the belt come sliding out of the loops. He started his horse off at a trot. He was on the point of kicking it up into a lope when he realized that Louis Light was slipping all over the place, his legs slapping like noodles.

"What's wrong, Louis, can't you ride a horse?"

"I'm doing okay," Louis shouted, his jouncing cheeks breaking the words into strange syllables. "You've got the mane to hang onto."

"I ain't a hold of no mane," Geo shouted, showing Louis both hands.

Stubbornly, he held his horse at the same stiff trot until he himself started getting a stabbing side ache and the baling wire on his goggles had cut through the leaves and was beginning to torture his ears. Then he gave a gentle nudge with his bare heels and eased the horse into a comfortable lope. He felt Louis rock and fall against his back, letting out a little grunt of pent up pain each time he hit.

Little Benny and Julie Volks were out on the front lawn. Julie was steeping tea for her dolls in a china pot, light blue and barely large enough to fill the thimble-size cups. Little Benny sat on a codfish box and strummed his guitar, which was so fat he could just reach his right arm around to the strings.

"If I had the amplifier out here," Little Benny chuckled, "I'd sure set up one hell of a racket."

"Why don't you come on down to the hideout," Geo blurted. "You . . . and *her*."

"Can't come right now. I'm getting in practice for the big dance tonight. I've got to put in a full hour on a new tune."

"This for your family band?" Louis asked.

"Yep. Course, now, our whole band ain't exactly intact no more. Not since they took Hartt off and put him in the war."

"My dad's in it too," Louis announced. "He's in France."

Geo looked away, trying to ignore them and hide his bitterness at the same time. Why hadn't his pa gone?

"So's Hartt," Benny was saying. "France. That's overseas, ain't it. I remember just before Hartt went across he came home and we all played a big war bond benefit. Lord, that Hartt! He played like moonlight."

"I've never heard moonlight," Louis charged evenly.

"No, and it's likely you won't be hearing none neither before Hartt gets home to play it for you."

"That right?"

"Yeah."

Louis dug in his pocket and flipped his dime into the air, shutting off the conversation. He held the coin out to tantalize Julie, keeping it barely beyond her reach.

"I've got one too," Geo stated.

"Oh?" Julie cried. "*Well.*" She pursed her lips, as if to spread a fresh coating of lipstick. "I might be down after lunch." She spun, giggling, her dishwater hair flowing silkily over the straps of her lime-colored sunsuit. She did a prissy strut all the way up the walk to the house.

Little Benny imitated her wiggle with a hot lick on his guitar.

"Women," Louis Light muttered, in a tone that both Geo and Little Benny tried secretly to repeat to themselves.

10.
Where was Louis? Maybe he had had to stay home to hoe weeds. Or to mow the lawn. Or maybe (and this thought was exhilarating) . . . maybe Louis Light was just plain scared. Geo said this over and over to himself and clapped his hands.

Still, every few minutes, he would slip out of the hideout and take a look up the lane. Each time he did, he told himself he would not look again. What did he care if Louis came or not? What did he care?

He struck what he considered a nonchalant pose against a tree trunk. He did it mostly to convince himself that he did not need Louis. That he was wholly at ease. But a moment later, hearing a high giggle, he lost all composure. He dashed out. Julie, in a bright pink pinafore, was coming down the lane. Bigger than life. Little Benny was right behind her, one knee in the bed of his wagon, one foot pushing.

Frantically, Geo remembered something: Louis was the one who had told her he knew how to play it. The one who had called her a bitch. And ought to know. Because he came from town.

Spinning, he ran down to the creek. He peed in the water, watching the warm yellow stream pound up white clusters of bubbles that gathered and spun in the dimpled places over the green stones, then zipped quickly out of sight under the low willows. Scrambling up the bank to mount his horse (only to go check the cows, not because he was scared, not because he was running) he heard the sound and stopped.

Smash-clank, smash-clank, smash-clink . . .

All of them were coming in parade. Louis had appeared from somewhere, as though by some previously planned maneuver. He had tin cans clamped to the soles of his shoes and was banging up a lot of dust. Julie had climbed in the wagon. She held herself in a stylish magazine pose, one white pump braced out on the side of the wagon. Little Benny was pulling her, limping jerkily along on his bad leg. Geo leaped on his horse, lowered his goggles in place, and raced up the lane to meet them.

Holding herself gracefully erect in the jiggly wagon, Julie inclined her head in majestic bows toward the willows and saplings on one side of the road and the shaggy cedar posts on the other, every inch of her regal seven-year-old body warm, glowing. This was not the first attention she had received from boys. She was very popular on her block in Vernal: she had allowed boys to watch her bathe in thick bubbles, bought before the war, and she had played under blankets with them. Today, however, it all seemed distinctly different; it seemed very special. Her entourage might have been a full orchestra—the wagon rattling and bumping beneath her, the broken syncopation of the horse's three shoes ringing on the patina of cobbles crusted in the lane, and Louis Light, his squashed tin cans clattering like an anxious drum, marching out in front. Louis was really cute. Julie knew Geo and Little Benny were jealous of him. And she could see why. She just loved the mysterious way he acted, sort of talking without saying words. Waiting till exactly the right time to say the right thing in words. The right words. Exactly.

Two dimes. (She certainly could not charge Little Benny.) She had never taken money before. Candy some of the time. And once she had (and could not for the life of her remember the reason now) actually refused a nickel.

"Isn't it perfectly sweltering!" she cried.

The wagon stopped. The three boys looked at each other, grinning sheepishly.

"And the dust! Ugh!" She gesticulated, fanning her face. "I simply can't stand unpaved streets. They're ghastly!" (Her mother had said that once.) Letting her eyes flutter, she gave a flip with her hand.

Louis made his move first. He dug the dime from his pocket and held it out to her. She opened the tiny patent purse which hung from her wrist on a brass chain. She smiled and waited. But Louis did not drop the dime in. He made her reach out and take it from his palm. Her cheeks flushed. But she continued to smile all the same. And when Geo fumbled so much that his dime slipped through his fingers, falling into the grass, and he had to go scampering froglike after it, she laughed, shielding her mouth delicately with the back of her hand.

Geo did not dare look her in the face when he handed her the money. Not even with the goggles. He wondered if she could tell it was stolen. Nobody seemed to. Anyhow, she had it and he was glad. The very act of giving it to her sort of erased things. Now nothing was left. No licorice. No bubble gum. No dime. He felt absolved. This gave him a fresh burst of courage, so he called her *bitch* (to himself) and sneered at her, raising his lip slightly.

"Little Benny doesn't have to pay," Julie declared.

"Why?" Louis demanded.

"Because if he did it would be incest."

"Infest?" Geo repeated mechanically, thinking of lice and chicken mites and starting to itch.

"In*cest!*" Julie repeated. "*Cest!*"

"Incest," Louis repeated. "What's that?"

"That's when you do something with your relations."

"Is that a sin?" Geo blurted. He did not want to sin again. The last one—the triple sin, compounded in a way that made it nearly as serious as Adultery—was barely over.

"No," Julie said. "But it's against the law or some such thing."

"Sometimes sin and the law is the same thing," Geo argued. Obviously not smoking and drinking. But Stealing and Murder. And he did not know about Adultery.

"Everybody just going to stand around and talk?" Little Benny asked, his feet stepping itchily. "Who gets first here?"

"First what?" Geo asked.

"First to do it to me, *stupe,*" Julie murmured.

Do what? Geo wondered vaguely, although he thought he knew. Or at least thought he ought to know.

"I speak!" Little Benny persisted.

"Wait a minute, you guitar picker," Louis interjected, shouldering Little Benny out of the way. "I want to see it first."

"It?" Geo swallowed hard. "See what? What's *it?*"

"Her thing."

That statement made Julie laugh. Sometimes Louis was so funny. With a great deal of ceremony, she stretched and tugged, wiggling her little fanny, and got her tight cotton panties pulled away from her body. She let them stoop and look at her.

This was the first time Geo had ever seen a girl's thing. He was flabbergasted. It looked funny. Like seeing nothing at all. Except that it was all puffy and soft. He shook his head. What good was a thing like that? It looked worthless, even accidental. She would pee all over herself. Geo was glad he was a boy. Glad he had what he had. A driving wave of superiority swept over him.

But just the same, that thing of hers—all naked like it was—did give him a good scare.

"How do you get hold of it?" he asked.

"Keep your hands to yourself!" Julie snapped.

"I mean *you*. To pee."

"You don't *hold* it, stupe!"

What? Did it just run wild?

Julie lay on her back, craning her head up the way a turtle did when it was marooned in an overturned shell. She felt all alone. She needed to swallow and could not. It was the waiting. She loved to watch them come to her. Eager, like Benny. Afraid, like Geo. They always did whatever she asked. Once (now, just thinking about it, she bit the inside of her cheek and got goose pimples all up her back) Little Benny had touched her there with his tongue.

Benny was crawling on. He had talked them into letting him be first. She made a little sound, imitating her mother: she had heard it during that last hour of her father's furlough, when they had been on the way to the bus depot. They had both pushed her into the back seat and told her to sleep. And then they did it one more time, one more time before he had gone off to be killed forever.

When Little Benny began puffing against her neck and started slowing down, she pushed him away. It was Geo's turn. Modestly holding up the bib top of his farmer overalls, he scooted between her spread white legs.

Geo heard her say something.

"Huh?"

"Take those silly things off."

"No."

"Take them off or you can't do it."

"Benny never took his pants all the way off."

"I mean those goggles."

"No."

And before she could protest further, he fell on her—as he had seen Little Benny do. He found himself moving automatically. It seemed he had always known what he ought to do. What he needed to do. Though he did not exactly know why.

"Touch my bunny," Julie instructed in a soft voice.

"Huh?"

"My bunny. Touch it."

He thought he knew what she meant. He thought he knew how she wanted to be touched. He strained, trying. (Maybe this was what that thing of hers was good for.) He felt himself blunting against those two folds of secret soft flesh. He moved rapidly now. It seemed he was trying to get to something. But he did not know what. Something. He stared over her shoulder into the grass and dirt.

"Kiss me," Julie cooed in his ear. "Oh, kiss me, Geo!"

Geo had never in his life kissed a girl. Julie said it again, her passionate voice tinged with impatience. He looked at her mouth. She was making it ready for him. He knew that much from Saturday movies. He started for it. Then he saw her eyes: even through his misted blue goggles they looked funny and hungry. And empty. So he missed. On purpose. He shook his head and pressed his face down over her shoulder. He rocked hard, thrusting blindly at her crease; and he stared through the blue lenses at the dirt. Trying to see that something he was trying to reach.

"Hurry!" Louis said, shuffling his feet, the tin cans clicking. "Hurry it up, Geo."

Hurry what up? Geo asked himself, still staring at the grains of soil. What?

"Hurry!" Little Benny laughed.

"Oh—that's enough!" Julie moaned.

Enough what? Geo thought. He felt her squirming, attempting to get him to stop. But he was not done. Not yet. But he did not know what more there could be. Something. There had to be something. Then Louis started pulling on his galluses.

"Lord!" Little Benny hooted. "Lord, don't he like it though?"

Geo got up. He hooked his galluses. His knees were dirty. He felt sinful. Worse than the night before, when he had accumulated a sin as serious as Adultery. He walked down to the creek, playing with his peter. He was confused. He liked what he had done, but he did not know what to call it. He thought of some of the dirty words he had seen chalked on the sidewalk in front of school and on parts of the foundation covered with shrubbery. He knew if he even said those words, like he had said hell once, his mother would wash his mouth out with green soap. But it had not felt like any of those words. He decided just to call it It. It.

Julie felt frightened when she saw Louis Light moving towards her. She felt it and did not know why. It was like seeing water come flowing over a low dam, or lotion pouring out of a bottle. Smooth, fluid. And for the first time in her life she felt she should struggle.

But Louis was too fast for her. He pinned her to the earth. The tin cans on his feet clicked together. She tried to outstare him. She could not. She looked away and shut her eyes.

She felt it every time. He thrust furiously at her. Not just touching (which felt so good). But pushing into her. He was not hurting her. Except in a way she liked. She wished she knew what he was thinking. She could tell with Benny and Geo. But she did not know with Louis. And that started the tears. She cried tears. Nothing more than that. No sobs. Just hot tears she could not stop. They streamed silently out on her flushed cheeks.

She did not know whether it was because she was seeing his face through the salty film of her tears or whether Louis Light was really smiling.

2

A Brief History of the Light Strain

࿔࿔࿔࿔࿔࿔࿔࿔࿔࿔࿔࿔

1944

1.

> Ump tump tump
> Tootle tee
> Little Brown Jug
> Don't I love thee!

Emma Light's wrinkled arm reached over the dark polished body of the Gibson and down between the blond sunbursts around the F-holes to pick and strum the steel strings. The short crabbed fingers of the other hand, her left one, stretched along the frets to form chords on the ivory-spotted neck. The old woman's hair was raked back in grayed furrows and pinned in place by a large shell comb with pierced rapier-shaped teeth. As Emma sang, her face, as tight and knotted as a small cabbage, wreathed with laughter. The heel of her Red Cross shoe raised and fell with every other beat.

Fascinated, but bashful, Geo watched Louis and then did exactly as he did. He took a sip of paper tea (a mild beverage steeped from fresh peppermint picked along the ditch behind the tent-house, whitened with milk and sweetened with sugar) and munched on a fat square of spice cake. He caught the moist crumbs in his cupped hand, then he licked his palm clean when he was done.

Even though she was singing to them and she had her whole heart in the song, Emma Light's soul was somewhere else. Because she had seen the violin. Bill had brought it out of the tent-house (where he had summered for the past three years, stubbornly refusing to sleep any nearer to her than he absolutely had to—though not getting far enough away that she could not cook for him and wait on him, hand and foot) and loaded it into the pickup with the rest of the camping gear he and the little boys were taking to the mountains.

She could never catch sight of that violin without remembering the first time she had ever laid eyes on Bill Light. Her family had been in the process of settling a homestead in the northeastern end of the valley—miles from the three main clusters of Mormons who, her father contended, thought they held title and deed to all of Utah. At dusk one evening, a strange young man all fit out in rough corduroy pants, a plaid wool shirt, hog-nosed work boots, and a brand new, bowl-top derby hat rode up to the house, dismounted, stepping out of a fustian cloud of summer dust, and without one word of who he was or why he had come took a stiff arrogant stance in the middle of what would in time become a yard, tucked the violin under his chin, and played "Underneath the Bright Silvery Light"; then, mounting hurriedly, although not without displaying a certain amount of stylish swagger, he set his spurs solidly and rode off into the still greenish haze of autumn twilight. The final few notes of the song hung in the air like wheat chaff.

The next time Bill Light came, a few months later, after a roundup and a harvest, his return a kind of signal that the first visit had not been as purely accidental as it had seemed, he drove a black buggy. It was brand new—with yellow-spoked wheels and yellow fringe around the top—and was drawn by a sleek, small-boned Hamiltonian stud as black as the thin lacquered shafts between which he eagerly bowed and danced. Bill Light had worn a dark suit that buttoned high, a snug vest that buttoned even higher, and a soft felt hat slanted at a serious angle. In spite of a faint stripe of closet dust over the shoulders of the suit and an uncanny imperfection in the knotting of his cravat (he must have invented his own way of tying it—he would, she knew, before he would ask anyone to show him the right way) he stood out with a kind of elegance. She knew, thinking back on it, it was complete in him then, that same ostentation that had been—she knew this absolute and certain— plague and ruin of the Light men since the very beginning.

Chortling, mostly because laughter was her nature, Emma Light stopped playing and laid the guitar in the purple plush interior of the black case.

"Won't you sing another one?" Louis asked.

"No, I'm give out. When Willie comes home, he'll tune this back up to regular guitar and we won't be doing any singing." She sighed, chewing secretly on the white piece of Feenamint she kept cached back in her jaw.

"When is my dad coming home?" Louis asked.

"As soon as that war's over with."

"When'll that be?"

"Nobody knows that yet, honey. Not even those high mucky-mucks in the government who'd like to have you think they know it all. We've got to whip the Germans and Japs first. Then the boys'll be coming." With an anonymous-looking piece of rag, Emma lifted the kettle off the middle of the Warm Morning stove to keep it from whistling. "What do you hear from your mama, Louis?"

Louis shrugged. "Grandma had a letter about a week ago. She's still down in California working in an airplane plant."

It was a damn pity, Emma Light thought, a damn pity indeed that they could not have stuck it out together and been decent folks. Not that she was sentimental. No. She was far from that. But at least Willie would have had something to come home to. Even a fight. For the good lord knew both Willie and that girl had been shameless hellers. On two occasions, a nosey woman living near where they had rented that little house had called to tell her she thought they were on the verge of killing each other. Well, let them, she had said. It was their right and privilege. She screwed up her face and took a couple of fierce chomps on her gum, remembering how she had slammed down the receiver.

At least Willie could see Louis. Which was something. But that was all. The court had awarded full custody of the boy to Leon and Louise Fulton. Lord knows why. So far, she had not found out Willie's opinion about any of it. He chose to ignore it. And he never replied to her questions about it or to her suggestions that he try and do something about Louis when he got back. Of course, Willie never talked like any of the others in his letters. Not like Doris Colman's boy Jess or Lena Meade's Brad, who had been Willie's best buddy throughout the part of high school she was reasonably sure Willie had attended. No. Willie never spoke of his feelings or what he planned. (He never had, though.) Willie wrote a lot about the weather. Maybe it had rained some. Or maybe there was snow. Sunshine. Wind. . . . France, it seemed, was not much different than here. In spite of all the stories you heard. It was always like Willie had just stayed home from the war that day to write down something that happened to strike his fancy. He said they slept out—mostly. In tents. Though he had mentioned farm houses and one small hotel somewhere. And they ate cold rations when a fire was not allowed. He just went on and on like this. So she knew, because he never mentioned it, that Willie was bothered about Louis.

The war had not changed Willie. In his most recent letter, he had mentioned a motorcycle. It had, she figured out from his description, some sort of little car hooked on it, a sidecar, he called it; and he and another soldier, a New York City Jew named Bernie Schwartz, rode around in it quite a bit. Whether for business or pleasure he did not say, but probably both. So she supposed that the Germans in France took time out from whatever war was going on at the time to watch them pass. Willie was like that with machines. (And this was not his first go at either motorcycles or spectacles.) He had an enviable way of handling them. He could always coax more of almost anything out of a machine than anybody else could. He just needed to fiddle a minute with the carburetor, holding his ear close to it, so he could get the right amount of suck and draw, and the whole thing would calm itself into a smoother, more powerful sound.

And like as not Willie and the Jew passed the scene of the war the very same way he had always flashed by the house. The car would be at full speed, the whole thing shuddering on the frame. She would glimpse his face turned to the window, that look of platelike arrogance flattened all over it. And then he would come creeping back, barely idling along in second gear and sometimes even low, give a hand signal that nobody but a fool ever used out in the country, and swing cautiously into the driveway. Yes, like as not, Willie even did that in the war, too.

"There's Grandpa!" Louis crowed, springing up from the table.

The concatenate rattle of the old pickup vibrated along the north side of the house. It came to a delayed stop in back. The horn began honking.

"Louis . . ." Emma Light said. Then she just shook her finger at him, as if to warn him about something. But she decided against it. Then, as she dropped her finger, she knew she should say it. It was her duty. So she did, "Just you remember this, Louis Light. You've got it in you. You've got the plague and the ruin. You Lights aren't the same—none of you. You've got trouble built in. You want too much."

She pondered that, arms folded, and chewed on her Feenamint. "Trouble is, you don't know what it is you do want. And none of the rest of us can help you. Because we don't know what's going on in those crazy damned heads of yours. So we can't do anything for you. . . . Go on now. Git!"

"Louis . . ." Geo whispered urgently as they banged out through the screen door. "I need to visit . . . the toilet."

Following Louis outside with her eyes, noting the way he pulled at the bill of his cap, Emma Light recognized vestiges of his father in him, although Willie had never been quite as narrow through the shoulders—which was obviously what living in town with the Fultons had done to the boy. The rest, though, was all there. It was complete and evident in every move that Louis made. Light all the way, like his father, grandfather, and probably his great-grandfather as well (although she could not say too much about the latter Light: he had merely been a tombstone to her, a man killed in a pistol fight over a horse and a woman—not his horse, or his woman either). It was in his eyes, too. Yes, especially in his eyes. They all, all the Light men, had

gray eyes that seemed to bore right through anything short of
steel to where they could see some glorified version of themselves. And it was evident, as well, in that mysterious silence that
he maintained to keep everyone else shut out of his life. As if it
were some kind of secret he had to guard. Or the entrance to a
private hell.

Emma lifted her finger and shook it again, this time at the
screen door. "Go on, you little shit. I learned a long time ago not
to trust any of you," she said, satisfied her words would have as
much effect on the screen as if she were speaking to his face. "I
should have known. But I had to learn the hard way."

She might have been watching Willie's back as he left for
school the year he was eleven, his dinner pail swinging inno-
cently on its wire bail. Just before Christmas that year the girls
brought home notices of a parents' afternoon—a new thing. Parents were supposed to come and sit in their children's seats and
find out something about how the school was run. And that day,
when she asked Mrs. Artell, the fifth grade teacher, which of the
seats was Willie's, Mrs. Artell had tilted her head with a look of
blank henlike thought and repeated, "Willie?"

"Yes, William Light, the second."

But no. There was no seat for William Light. Any William
Light. The first or the second. He had never as much as put in
one single appearance that entire fall. And it turned out (Willie
had finally made full confession of it at dinner that evening, after
quoting a long passage from Ovid's *Metamorphoses,* a book he
claimed they had been studying in his class) he had been slipping off to the foothills, where he had a trap line set along a couple of streams. By then, the skins of the muskrats had brought
him twelve dollars and forty-six cents, every last penny of which
he had niggardly stashed in a flat tobacco can under his bed. He
had finished reading thirty books, cover to cover, earning both
his sisters gold stars from the librarian, while back at school his
classmates had barely made it halfway through their readers.
(There had been some serious debate between teacher, principal, and herself about actually holding him back—so he could
make up the work.)

She remembered how furious it made her to see Bill shaking
his head and trying to contain a smile about the Prince Albert tin

and the money Willie had spilled onto the table. So she asked
him to do something about it.

"What?" Bill had asked. "Do what?"

"Punish him, of course."

"Punish? How come?"

"Because you're the father," she had to remind him. "Now you
give him the licking he deserves."

"Deserves? I don't know as I blame him none for going off like
that," Bill said, wiping at a scum of gravy on his lips and mum-
bling something about the school of life. "But if you want it
done, I'll whip him."

Yes. There it was. That was a Light for you. One and the same
all the way through to the core. Yes, the same and different to
boot.

2.   Sitting on the wooden hole (the little one, the square lid
was hinged down over the big hole), looking at the brown,
weather-parched pictures of women and cars cut out of *Life* and
The Saturday Evening Post that had been pasted on the walls to
cover cracks and knotholes, protection against wind and prying
eyes, and wadding a page of ladies' unmentionables, as his
mother had called them the one time he had asked, torn from the
gradually wasting Monkey Ward's catalog—trying to get it softened up enough to use—Geo was wishing his father had gone off
to the war, too. It was a touchy issue he had been hedging all
summer with Louis and Little Benny. It might even have
counted as much if he had had someone like Little Benny's
Hartt. Someone right in the family, a brother. (Which was impossible, since he was an only child—and a blessing at that.) But
all he had was his Uncle Jed, his mother's brother, which was
pretty good for her, but which did not seem like much to him.
What did it matter that his father was a little bit too old? He was
tough. Nobody could quarrel with that. And he would have
made a good fighter. Good enough. Though probably not any

kind of hero. Except that he was religious. But the Book of Mormon was full of religious men who were also mean fighters and sometimes heroes. Geo sighed and shook his head.

Louis had his problems, whether he would admit it or not. While waiting this morning, Geo had heard his Grandma Fulton calling the Lights a "tribe" and then saying she hoped he would have sense enough to see what they were and to grow up to some good. He thought he would ask Louis what it was about. But he already knew the look he would get. And maybe that was the answer—even before there was a question. And maybe that was what Louis's Grandma Light meant just now when she was yelling through the screen door and they were beating it out to the truck.

Geo was beginning to worry too much about his present condition to bother about Louis. With all the excitement, it seemed he had developed a slight touch of diarrhea. (Grandma Light's warm, milky paper tea had not helped calm it down any.) And he did not want that happening on the way to the mountains. Because he knew he would be too scared to ask Louis's Grandpa Light to stop the truck. He did not want to think about the rest of it. He shuddered, remembering how it had been just talking to the old man.

"You ever been fishing before, boy?"

"Yes—in the canal."

"Hmm. It'll be different this time," the old man snorted. "Trout up there ain't muddy. They ain't mushy either. They're solid. The meat's sweet and pink. Pink as a . . . pink. Got yourself a coat?"

Geo named off all the things he had brought. He listed them one after another. His voice quickened. The pitch rose in proportion to the pressure in his bowels. And here he was. He had had to run the final few steps, his pants already undone, galluses trailing, one hand holding the bib, the other fumbling at the door.

Now he kept remembering all the things his mother had warned him not to forget, checking down a scrawled notebook page (the laborious, uneven printed lettering that his second grade penmanship had left as the start of a style). Toothbrush. Socks. Prayers. He tried one for his diarrhea. Naturally, it would be answered. That was not the problem. His father had ex-

plained how prayer worked. God decided what was best for a
Mormon. You gave him your opinion and what you hoped to get
out of it. But it was up to God. So Geo crossed his fingers for a
Yes prayer.

He opened his eyes. The horn was honking, a brassy *beep-
beep*. He saw he had crumpled and pumped the pages featuring
the female body devices until he had worn the paper to a pulp in
his damp hand. And before he left the outhouse—confident now
because of the prayer, but still burning with uncertainty all the
same—he dipped a little lime out of the bucket on the tip of a
small shovel and tossed it like dry snow down into the darkness.

3.   At the first stop sign, Bill Light fished from his pocket a
plug of Day's Work and a small knife. He pared away the tan
outer leaf of tobacco, measured off enough to last a while, cut it,
and poked it back in his cheek; he got it seated along his jaw-
bone with his tongue and felt the saliva flow to it, corners soften-
ing, the rich flavor starting to spread in his mouth. He paused.
Then he held the plug out to Geo, who was sitting between him
and Louis.

"Like to fix yourself a chaw?" he asked, looking down into the
narrow face that had been scrubbed till it shone and still smelled
of soap.

"Nope." Geo shook his head stiffly.

Bill did not offer the plug to Louis. Something about the cool
manner—he would almost have called it insolence—the kid's
eyes fastened on the tobacco told him Louis would take it and
then chew until he was bright green in the face and puking all
over the place. Christ, yes, he would. He was Willie's boy, a
kid sired on that little hellion Gloria. Goddam! He gave his head
an imperceptible shake. If that was not the wildest combination
of humanity imaginable!

Geo was trying to think: the Mormon Sunday school rule had
a thing about tobacco. But he thought it was only about smoking.

He had never heard anything about eating tobacco. Maybe it was all right to eat it. He glanced up once more at Bill Light. The old man had a big grizzled face, the tobacco pooching his cheek out into a white knot; his slender nose, curving gently down to a point, had sparse short hairs growing from the pores; and under the thatch of his brows, his gray eyes were sharp and bright, the skin at the corners scored with deep reticulate creases. A thin flow of brown tobacco juice started out over the old man's smooth red lip. He reached and pawed it away on the back of his hand. Geo watched the same hand, panoplied with thick calluses and discolored skin, bones and joints stiffened and reshaped from arthritis and almost a quarter of a century of handling carpenter's tools, clutch the knob of the stick shift and send it through the gears.

Yes. Let the sonofabitch rattle, Bill Light thought. He mashed the accelerator to the floor and bent over the wheel. We'll get there sooner or later, by god.

They turned at the store and flew past the Maeser School, an old, square, orange-brick building of two stories with four equal triangles of roof, and the same thing repeated—from bricks to tin spinelike cornice—in miniature on top, housing the bell. Geo hated the sight of it. Louis, who would only be seeing it for the first time in September, punched him in the ribs surreptitiously, flashed his eyes toward the building, and in a sheepish half-whisper said, "There's your favorite house!"

For a few seconds, they scuffled, hissing schoolhouse insults and choking down their laughter.

Bill Light was pouring it on to get out of the valley. He took corners under full power, sliding on the gravel, feeling everything becoming dangerously light when the outside wheel crept out onto the sandy shoulder. It always happened. He got this far and he could not wait to get on to the mountains. But even here it was already better. The fields were a lush green, except where first- or second-crop alfalfa had been mowed and lay raked in long ropelike windrows like brown dry twists waiting for the baler. Tall oats in the breeze seemed tinged with silver. And plump heads of wheat, ripening, nodded heavily—rich and golden green.

Once through the mouth of Dry Fork Canyon, the old man

breathed easier. He thrust his shoulders back out of their weary hunch, relaxed against the seat, and no longer cared if the loose coil springs poked through the matted batting and worn upholstery. Here, in the narrow channel between two red-stone cliffs, he felt a release. It seemed the tight pumping urgency of his life had smoothed to a soothing flow. He slowed the truck to savor it.

"Three days," he muttered aloud, in case the kids happened to care to listen. "Three days up in them mountains, out in the wilderness, with the wind and the pines, and a man might, he just might get back to feeling like a man."

He sighed. This country was familiar to him. And it struck him, as they banged along the road, that there were some things that Louis ought to know about it. Maybe it would not hurt the other kid to know them, too. So when the right spot came, he drove off to the side of the road, the front wheel crashing into fender-deep brush, the dead growth snagging at the undercarriage, and stopped. Leaning, he peered up through the windshield to make sure what he wanted to see had not been vandalized or hauled off to some museum in New York City or Chicago to be put behind glass so city people and tourists from the country could shell out four bits to look at them and take colored snapshots.

"Look," he ordered. He pointed his finger. "See them poles sticking out. No—way the hell up there."

Louis rested his chin on the dash, craning his head. "Yes."

Geo crowded to the window. He saw them: two gray lodgepole logs coming out of the mouth of a cave.

"That's an Injun cave," Bill informed them. "They throwed out ropes, ropes made from vines and roots, and climbed up and down on them. People back in them days never had elevators. If they wanted something, they had to work to get it. Work even to get into their houses."

He chuckled to himself, remembering. "Them same poles was stuck out like that when I first came to this valley sixty-two years ago. I wasn't any bigger than either of you. I was horseback. Pa and Ma and all the other kids rode in the wagon. We pulled up in that draw yonder and had ourselves a look. Then a short piece farther and we come upon an Indian camp. Not them sky Injuns. These was new Injuns. I guess they had either forgot how to get up or else they'd become too damn lazy. They lived on the ground. The buck knowed a little English he'd picked up scouting for the soldiers over at Fort Duchesne. Said his name was Bent Tree in Wind. His squaw, she was called Little Rabbit. . . ."

Yes, he remembered it. He had watched with a boy's utter disbelief while that big squaw just kept right on squeezing out through the flap of that teepee. He had thought she would never stop. At least three hundred pounds of brown woman bound up in soiled doeskins and a cavalry tunic decorated with a few yards of dirty gold braid, the buttons coming a good foot from reaching the buttonholes on the other side of her flabby belly and unharnessed bosom. Her beaded headband held one drooping black-tipped feather, and her wide face was highlighted with generous smears of berry juice and some kind of root extractions, all so poorly aimed that she must have used the creek for a mirror. When his father had somehow finally made it clear that they were headed for Colorado, the old buck raised his hand in a solemn sign of Indian seriousness and advised—still brokenly—not to go. Colorado? No. Colorado was nothing but sagebrush. Miles of it. A paradise for lizards and snakes. Instead, he, Bent Tree in Wind, would offer them the valley floor, the fertile canyon in which they were standing. This canyon, mother to a river. He spoke at length, with much warmth and approbation, his command of language and vocabulary improving markedly as he recognized, with a carpetbagger's expert eye, the approach of a sale. During the oration, Little Rabbit rushed around and prepared a pipe. Not exactly an Indian's pipe. It was an old bent one, the yellowed meerschaum bowl fashioned into a Dutchman's face, grinning in fat contentment. She stuffed it with a little genuine tobacco from the fort and a filler of some faintly narcotic Indian equivalent and then hauled it back and forth between the two men, one smoking and thinking, while the other spit into the fire and spoke a mixture of business and sheer nonsense. They smoked and spat and dickered until they finally arrived at a price: one rifle with a few cartridges, two china plates, a cup, a heifer calf, and the brass bell of one wether (Bent Tree immediately strapped this bell on Little Rabbit, though god knows under what circumstances he would ever have lost her or why the hell he would ever have cared). To solidify the deal, the whole family stayed to a supper of roast dog. Bent Tree in Wind bragged it was a terrier—at least part, and maybe even full-blooded. Of course, the land had not been his to sell; or it had and it had not. Back in those days any Indian owned exactly anything and nothing and could, in fact, own and sell and own again the same thing over and over at will and random. So they had to go through similar procedures, minus the dog, with a government-approved land agent who was happy to sell it off out from under not only the Indians (who ought to have, in his practiced opinion, damn well kept their asses on the reservation, which was, at the very least, second- or third-class land, with maybe some fourth and a chunk thrown in here and there that was beyond official description and classification—until lately, when this latter had been labeled oil land) but out from under those goddam Mormons as well.

"That valley belonged to us Lights until nineteen and twenty-four," Bill said. He paused, then added quietly, "A bad year, that one. Bad all over."

Enough, he thought. Thrusting his face to the window, he discharged a copious stream of tobacco spit. It fell like a dotted line across the road. He noticed how Louis's little friend watched, how the spurt of the tobacco spit had brought him upright in the seat. He laughed. "I saw this road come, too. I watch them survey it and engineer it out of the hillsides. People were already talking about progress then. I always got a hollowed-out feeling when I heard the word. The kind of feeling you get when you know you're going to be sick. Progress. Blacktop. That's progress too. It's creeping all over the valley. A couple of years and it'll be up here. It's like people had some kind of fear the grass was going to cover up their tracks. But I've seen grass poke right up through blacktop. I've seen frost tear holes in it. Still, once a road's cut, the land's never the same." He paused, looking at the two kids staring up at him. Good god, who could tell what they thought about anything?

He turned the truck back into the washboard ruts of baked clay and cobbles. The clutch pedal hammered and banged on its bad return spring; the gearshift jiggled wildly. Dust boiled off the road into sage, willows, and chokecherry bushes, its choking smell swirling up in the cab like sulphur.

They crossed the narrow valley where the last of the ranches ended, turned northwest again, and started up through cottonwoods thinning in the creek bed into the first of the spruce and pine. The jagged teeth of Sawtooth Mountain seemed to have chewed a crude V in the wall of the canyon. They continued to climb. Higher, then, at a waterhole in a draw below a dense copse of aspen, the cacophonous clattering of the old truck flushed a bevy of blue grouse up from a cover of low junipers. They rose in a whir, soaring with incredible beauty, then suddenly stopped flying and dropped down among plumate stalks of lupine, leaving the air empty—crisp.

The driving here was harder. Deep in the old Chevy's engine Bill could hear the rods just beginning to rattle. Nothing serious yet, but they would have to be pulled, the babbit filed down. And he felt too damned old for all the things he knew he ought to do. He hoped Willie would get home from the war in time to rebuild it. That boy could fit the parts of a machine by touch. He could do it in the dark if he had to. He knew the feel of trouble by cupping his palm against the surface of the crankshaft; he knew the difference that a hundredth of an inch made in the way an engine responded. And he could gauge that much with his fingers. Yes, Bill Light told himself, he would try and hold out until Willie came home.

4.   There. It was right where he had known it should be. The canvas-covered bows, warped in the shape of a horseshoe, arched suddenly up out of the brush. Feed would hold here for another week, maybe ten days. Then the camp would have to be moved on to the northern slope. (Maybe he would mention this to the herder—as a means of establishing himself. And because he did know.) This had been his country. Once. Before the on-

slaught of that woman's stupidity, before 1924. Before then, this had been his country and he had had the sheep to run on it.

Leaving the road, they crashed out into the dense brush, bouncing towards the sheep wagon. When he brought the machine to an echoing stop, a lone piece of metal or a spring loose somewhere continued to swing and strike like a muffled bell. The dogs, three multicolored Australian shepherds with spooky crystalline eyes, were going crazy; they danced and yapped, leaping out of the sage and lupine in a pointless frenzy.

Bill Light took an empty pint fruit jar out of the glove compartment. "You kids wait here. I won't be but a minute."

The old man disappeared through the soot-blackened Dutch door on the front of the sheep wagon. One glassy-eyed dog darted in after him. Only to come flying out on the broad flashing toe of a heavy boot, land in a yelping heap among the turmoil of ringing clevis, doubletree, and wagon tongue, and then to go limping off through the sage, tail wilted with shame.

"Louis," Geo whispered, "what's in that bottle?"

"Nothing."

"No—I mean, what's it for?"

"Something."

Geo felt a furious pounding disgust inside. "You're just saying that because you don't know."

"Says who?"

Wasn't that obvious? "Louis, you're really a pain."

"That's the price you have to pay for being in the know."

"Whew!" Geo breathed through his teeth. "Boy, Louis, did you ever get gypped!"

There was something in the jar. Geo saw it when Louis's grandpa, stooping to keep from hitting the low frame, came through the door. It was a lump of something gray.

"I told you," Louis jeered.

Geo firmed his mouth, refusing to reply. What was the use?

As he stepped down out of the wagon, the smells of fresh lamb tied away from the flies in a seamless sack, of cooking lard and garlic, of macaroni and salted cod and the jar all still poignant to him, a wave of nostalgia swept over Bill Light. After all these years, it still seemed natural to be stepping across the doubletree and walking down the tongue. But in the old days, he would have waited for the herder to get into his shirt and they would have walked out together to check on the sheep, to speculate about the weight of the lambs. Yes, all that until 1924. In its undoing, that year was more like an entire age.

That spring, he had hardly recovered from his first bout with pneumonia in time to have a second, worse case, leaving him susceptible to every imaginable complication—some that even baffled the doctor. He had felt himself wasting away. He knew it was at her hand. She and that goddam doctor had refused to let anyone visit him. And the green foreman she had hired to do work he had never trusted any person except himself to do had done all he knew to do. His judgment could not have told him about bear country and a stampede that would take an entire herd of ewes and lambs over the side of a gorge—one third of the business gone in that single tragic surge. He could still see the bodies spread out among the boulders in the canyon bottom like seeded dandelions.

If only they had let that man see him for the space of time it would have taken to say half a dozen words, it might never have happened. Then, the bottom fell out of the autumn market. And the next winter a siege of embryonic disease took more—ewes with lamb. And that was the state of things as he found them after ten months of being laid up in bed. He swore and fumed and ranted until his weakened lungs wheezed like bad reeds.

"If I'd have let you," Emma said. "You'd have killed yourself." And that was one pleasure she had obviously saved for herself.

He had barely made it through one month before people got wind that he was out of bed and were at his throat—though some had not even waited that long. He had gone to hunt help. He could still see the vapid expression of nothing (or even less) on the banker's S-shaped face, which seemed to be constantly cut through by the bars on the teller's cage, while the man went through a practiced speech of hollow amenities and automatically shocked the papers concerning the long-overdue mortgage into a neat sheaf. To which he affixed a brass paperclip. . . . And Bill remembered still the sight of the last ewe trailing away from the counting corral, going around a mountain path, to be somebody else's life.

The herder slouched against the side of the door frame. His

Levi's barely clung to his lean thighs and he only wore a gray union suit above. Bill pushed the jar under the tarp that was stretched and tied over the bed of the pickup. And when his hand emerged, his fingers were forked around the necks of two brown beer bottles. He jerked off the caps on the door handle, passed one bottle up to the herder, and tilted the other one to his own lips. Bubbles in a quick string shone like pennies floating through the brown glass.

"Ahhh!" he growled, with pleasure. He tipped the bottle again.

Geo shuddered. All his life he had heard damnation heaped on the evils of smoking and drinking. He had never really been around any of it (only to tamper a little bit himself, though cedar bark was not the same thing, and Little Benny brought Camels down so rarely that it had never become a filthy habit, which was what seemed to be the main danger; and anyway it was still a couple of months before his baptism). And he had never ridden in a vehicle driven by anyone under the influence. He told himself not to worry. But he was convinced by the reckless way Louis's grandpa flung the bottle off into the brush that he was already drunk as a lord. Should he pray again? He looked at Louis. He licked the dryness out of his mouth so he could speak.

"Is he drunk?"

"He will be," Louis informed. "Just as soon as it hits him. It's a good thing we're driving."

"Why?"

"Because he sure never could make it walking."

Geo moaned and stiffened. He felt something else, too, something besides fear. He shoved it out of his mind. He refused to believe that his prayer had not worked, that God had seen fit to judge it a *No* prayer, that God would actually allow him this kind of embarrassment. The old man opened a fresh bottle of beer and got in, springing the seat down, banging the door shut. So Geo was trapped there again until they reached their destination.

Before starting the engine, Bill Light looked off down the draw towards the valley they had just climbed up out of. He shook his head. "Since that time, since we first settled down there, I've never left this country. The farthest I ever went was with an Injun, years later, when he took off to find his path to the sky."

"What kind of Indian was he?" Louis asked.

"He was the same Injun who sold us our land the first time we bought it, Bent Tree. He might've screwed us just a little there right at first. But he was our friend for life. He even lived on the land with us. All he ever wanted was enough room to pitch his teepee and pit a good fire."

"Then he was a ground Indian, right?" Louis said. "Did you ever know a sky Indian, Grandpa?"

"Well, he was a ground Injun and he wasn't one. When I knew Bent Tree up here, he was a sky Injun."

"How could he be that?"

"He found hisself a way up."

"I don't get it."

"Well, son, sometimes you can be one thing and think you're being something else. And the other way around, too. But with Bent Tree it never had anything to do with what he thought. It was always what he was. And when it came time to be something else, he became it. That's why we took the trip—to find his path to the sky."

"What was it?"

"I can't rightly say, Louis. Bent Tree found it. I didn't. He must've seen some sign that I missed. It wasn't my time. Folks all around here always referred to Bent Tree as a savage. But I thought different. I always thought I saw just a little bit of a god lurking in him—lurking just out of sight of where I could get a good look at it."

The old man tipped his body and started the truck. The pickup jolted back onto the road. They were going faster now. Geo braced his feet and clutched the edges of the seat. He memorized what he would do when they wrecked (feeling certain he would not be hurt): keep calm, stop all bleeding, pray. He prayed that he could save Louis Light's life.

Geo felt it stronger now. The black pressure rose stiffly in his bowels. He squeezed his legs tightly together and hunched down in the seat. So it would not be as bad.

They rattled through the woods, climbing to timber line and down again, winding towards old Baldy; majestic from the valley, up here the mountain peak was craggy and ugly, like a cancerous tit. Bill pointed the peak out to the boys and smiled to himself. They crossed North Fork bridge and left the road, now taking a timber trail, a mere healing scar in the grass.

(Oh, hurry, Geo cried silently. Hurry up and stop! He bit the inside of his cheek, trying to make it painful enough to take his attention away from the other thing, the thing he was even afraid to think about.)

New branches had grown on the pines since the days of the last logging and their twig ends screeched along the door panels of the old pickup. It crept through narrow openings, rumbled across patches of corduroy road that had rotted to a pulpy dust, juggled dangerously over rocks high enough to disembowel the engine, and moved steadily deeper into a forest of slender jack pines that appeared impossible to penetrate.

(Every jog and jaw brought fresh agony to Geo, as he cringed and tried to stifle his need.)

Finally, in compound low, "big hole," Bill Light called it, wheels spinning up the steep grade over slick grass and smooth glacial stones, they halted at the edge of a clearing where a pre-historic deposit of huge red boulders lay—crumbs of the destruction and violence of creation. With the engine shut off, the silent tranquility of the forest, disturbed only by a gurgling and hissing from the overheated radiator and the sound of something somewhere swinging and clanging, closed in about them.

Letting out a moan, Geo scrambled over Louis's lap, clawing for the door handle, and failing to find that fast enough, squirmed right out the window, headfirst and sprawling, to race with his need to the nearest thicket of jack pines.

5. Watching the ghostlike ebb and surge of the two shapes probing frantically for a sense of reality under the collapsed canvas, Bill Light was thinking: man no longer even knows the basic fundamentals. These two can't stretch a goddam tent over their heads without it falling in on them. He belched. Guzzling at a freshly opened bottle of beer, he walked around the campsite, his gumsole boots quiet in the spongy silence of the wasting pine nee-

dles. He hesitated now to be absolutely certain the boys were not making progress but merely becoming more claustrophobic and confused.

Yanking up the side of the tent, he ordered, "Come out of there, you two hyenas." He eyed them sternly as they scuttled out, blustery, mussed, ashamed. He handed his beer to Geo, who held it like it was a bomb. "Have a swig if you want. It's warm as horse piss. But it don't taste bad." He saw the little boy's teeth, like a row of white beads, fasten on his lip.

He firmed the ridgepole on the prongs of the two uprights, raised the frame under the canvas, and set the four corner guys— alone.

"Now then—see what kind of pure accident it takes for the two of you to finish pegging the damn thing down before it falls over again." He reached for the beer.

After the grub box had been unloaded and the heat-warped metal camp stove leveled on flat stones, Bill told the boys to take their fish poles and go catch some supper. "And from the looks of the sky and the water and just the way things feel in general, I'd say they'll be taking a black gnat."

He remained in camp to repeg the tent and move the stove so sparks from the smoke pipe would not shower down on the canvas roof, all the while shaking his head and grumbling that it was no damn use to try and fight the fact that women and fifteen-cent Saturday matinees were fast making babies out of the sons of men.

Without unsticking the hook from the cork handle of his fly rod, Louis set off briskly upstream. He was soon swallowed in the silence of the thick jack pines.

Geo watched him and decided to go downstream. Though he did not honestly see what difference it made. North Fork looked as fishless as the cattle trough at home. It was narrow—not more than two feet across in most places—with grassy banks that pillowed out over the edges of the water, widening slightly around the slowly swirling holes. There was not a single place where he could not see the pebbles in the bottom, like the colored dime-store chips in the fishbowl out at Little Benny's. But he cast into the dimpled current anyway, fishing toward the road, careful to keep his shadow off the stream.

He had a nibble. His heart leaped. The black gnat was snatched into the water. Something tugged solidly at his line. He jerked, setting the hook. He knew from the way the trout fought that it would be a whopper. His bamboo rod bent almost double. Something silver—or at least white—flashed, racing upstream and downstream, darting back and forth between the grassy banks. Reeling in only inches of line at a time, he played and played the fish, trying to keep it under control.

When he was finally able to land it, he felt the whole bottom of his stomach give way. Only the head and gills of the fish he had been fighting seemed to have remained on the hook. Only this was a whole fish. He straightened the little trout out of its flipping crescent and measured it along the marked part of his woven creel. Seven inches, mouth to tail. Six inches was legal. Though anything shorter than ten was usually considered a joke. Still, this one had fought like a bigger fish. So, after working the snelled hook free from the rind of its mouth, Geo kept it. Purely out of respect.

When it was almost dark, Geo started back up the creek towards camp. From the pines near the clearing, he heard Louis's Grandpa Light let out a resounding belch, a swear word, and a sigh. As Geo crept closer, he saw the old man was now drinking whiskey, sucking it from a flat pint bottle, chasing it down with quick swigs of warm beer. Geo stepped into the firelight and stopped dead before a pan in which lay eight short trout—cleaned and ready for the fire.

"Louis?"

"Louis, hell!" the old man snarled. "Those are mine."

"I got three," Geo said.

"Gutted?"

"Nope."

"You aim to eat them that way—guts and all?"

"Nope."

"Got your knife?"

"No—I never brought one."

"Take mine then. Go on back down to the creek and gut them fish."

The old man watched him from the camp and called out, "Make sure you get the fish and not your finger."

Barely more than a shadow, the kid stopped at the creek and reached gingerly down into his creel. A moment later and he was back, holding the bloody knife and a badly mutilated trout. His voice trembled when he spoke.

"I don't remember how." He stared into the fire.

"You mean you never knowed," Bill accused. "You mean your ma always did it for you."

Without a word, Geo turned back towards the creek. Bill Light followed him. If he did not show him now, the little devil would ruin the other two and they would end up eating sardines.

"First—cut out the asshole," he instructed, secretly grinning off into the dark when he saw Geo's shoulders cringe. He made two short slices with his knife, flicked away the bit of white flesh, then deftly slit the fish up the belly. "Get your finger in there and zip out the guts, Just like you was milking peas from a pod."

Back in camp, taking another snort of whiskey, the old man heard Geo's confident voice from the creek bottom.

"Clean your fish yet?"

"No."

"Got a knife?"

"No."

"Take this one." There was a pause. "Hell, Louis, can't you do nothing? Cut out the . . . asshole. . . ."

6. Stoked with pitch kindling, the sheet metal camp stove glowed pink in the middle and orange at the seams. It raged nervously on the flat stones that kept it propped level, sparks shooting out the smoke pipe, and the cast-iron frying pan rattled over the fire like a loose lid.

"Ha! Crisp!" the old man cried, forking a fresh batch of little trout out of the hot grease. "You can eat the whole fish down— bones and all."

Geo watched one fish disappear into the old man's mouth. Whole. Louis—naturally—followed the old man's example. But he seemed to have to look pretty hard into the fiery mouth of the stove to do it. The very thought of eating one that way made Geo gag. He tore the head off his first fish and spit out the tail when he came to that.

Louis snickered.

So, sitting stiff and straight as a post, Geo crunched down the next one in the Light manner, a blinding flash of nausea striking him as his teeth cut through one eye, the brittle skull, and went on into the brain. . . .

"Look here," Bill Light lifted the heavy top off a Dutch oven full of dough, rising. "Some sheepherder bread."

"Is this what you got in the jar?" Geo asked.

"I got the start."

"Start?"

"Yes," the old man said sternly. "The start of bread. Bread like no woman ever tried to make—or ruin. Women, they're the ones yeast was invented for. The end of decent bread. Chemistry and damnation."

Geo's mother used yeast. He knew that; she had told him it made the bread rise. Did this mean she was damned? And how could Louis's grandpa even start to talk about damned people, when here he was drinking and carrying on and making them all eat fish bones and fish heads.

Louis built up a fire in a circle of red stones. He banked it with heavy rotted logs. When moist white smoke began to seep from under the scabs of bark and out of the worm holes in the wood, fat black ants boiled onto the surface of the log and swarmed from the edges of flame on one side to the edges of flame on the other side. Louis, firelight sharpening his features, leaving the lines at the corners of his mouth deeply graven with shadow, picked up a stick and scraped the ants into the fire. He laughed with delight, flames mirrored on his teeth and in his eyes.

Geo shuddered. He watched the bodies of the ants char into curled black knots. He was transfixed. He knew that this was the way it would be at the onset of the Millennium, or whatever that thing was that his Sunday school teacher had said would come when the earth was supposed to be seared and cleansed by fire and thereby restored to grace (he did not understand how or when they expected to find anything good in all that black ash—

and for a moment he wondered if this were not just another cagey Mormon method of saying there was no more good left in this world). God, Geo remembered, had promised the whole thing, or maybe even threatened it, or promised it only to Mormons, who would be safely above the fire, viewing it from the clouds of their special heaven. No matter what, though, he was convinced it would look this way. People would shrink into knots of char. Just like these ants. Except probably bigger. Something more on the size of a baseball.

He shuddered again and felt his skin prickle. It was just scary as hell.

7.

Firelight caught the voluptuous dip and drag of the bow: one piece of horsehair kept swinging into the flames, burning shorter and shorter with each stroke. Geo knew Louis's Grandpa Light was really drunk now: he was playing his violin with a dark vengeance and staring hard into the fire, as if the flames in his gray eyes were trying to outburn the coals.

When he reached the part of "Underneath the Bright Silvery Light" where he had sneaked a look at her and had got fumble fingers (and had never been able to relearn that passage right) Bill snatched the violin away from his stubble bearded jaw and muttered, "Don't have nothing to do with them."

"What?" Louis asked. "With what, Grandpa?"

"Women!" Bill Light gesticulated wildly with the bow. The tip flashed dangerously near the flames. The single hanging horsehair flared up and curled close to the head. "But you will. You'll get caught up in the mystery. And you will." He took alternate drinks from the two bottles, no longer certain which was the initial drink, which was the chaser. But he retained the idea just the same. For the sake of appearance. "You'll do it. Both of you. Hell, that goes without saying. Men ain't got no better sense than to follow their nature. I never had it. You won't neither. Why should you? That's the design. This world is built and run on evil. Women ruin one man in order to grow others up to an age where they can be got at. And every man what comes along persists on the idea that he is the one destined to break the curse."

"What curse?" Louis questioned.

"The curse of the promise that it's not there. There, by god, or any other place either. No more goddam mystery to it than to the jaws of a bear trap."

What did the old man mean? Geo wanted to come right out and say that his mother was not evil. Then the thought of her made him lonely. He tried not thinking about her. He told himself tomorrow would be more fun. He thought of the water he had seen rising in the red rocks, bubbling clear and pure where a stream reappeared after being lost for almost a hundred yards. He thought of the little fish flickering between the grassy banks, darting upstream, taking his hook, fighting. Then he looked at Louis. Something stopped him, stopped his thinking about himself. What did Louis get lonely for? He never saw his mother. Was Louis Light just lonely all the time?

Bill Light kept talking about women. He was talking about one. But it amounted to the same thing. That one had been enough to bring about his ruin. Dammit. Goddammit. After he had made it to the phenomenal age of thirty without mishap—Indians not withstanding. What a goddam fool. First with the violin. And even after the violin, seeing what she did to him, what she did to his playing style, he had gone back. Knowing full well the threat that lay behind the white winking of the starched petticoat, the brief flash of an ankle. He had gone back in that yellow buggy. And got up like some kind of dandified count. She had giggled and cooed about the vehicle, about its black body, which shone like ebony, about the yellow fringe and the speed of the horse. She had scooted all over those leather cushioned seats like cold butter on a hot bun. But he could not touch her. He had had to marry her to get that. To get what he thought he could not live without. Then to have to accept the doom that automatically came with it. The summit. The downgrade. The utter damnation. Hidden clauses and fine print at the bottom of the page. Goddammit, wasn't this the history of man? Look at that little bitch who had married Willie. Ruin? Did they think for one minute that he was going to just overlook the place on the upholstery where it had happened and they had tried to scrub it off? Yes—if they did not get you one way, they got you another. Then Willie had gone off to the war. And she had left him. So it seemed. . . . He shook his head. But Louis had the name of Light. And that, by god, was one damnsight more than she ever gave him.

The boys were yawning, starting to slump on the edge of their log.

"You better hit the sack. I'm kicking your asses out at the crack of dawn to build me a fire." He considered the loss of time that would be, the sheer aggravation. But they had to know something about the world—before it crept up on them and they were lost under it. "Then we'll hike to the lakes. For some big ones."

He reached for the whiskey. A look of fright crossed the face of Louis's friend. He chuckled to himself. Whiskey hadn't ought to scare nobody.

Later, when he checked to make certain they were in bed all right he noticed they were both grabbing and scratching in their sleep. They had most likely spread their beds out on an ant hill. Boys were like that. No more damn sense . . . Men, too. Hadn't he driven back there in that yellow-wheeled buggy for christsakes, buying the sonofabitch first, checking the front of his pants and the tilt of his hat every other minute. Thinking that nothing could even begin to touch him for style and good looks. He groaned. Oh my god.

Seventy years old, he thought, bending to undo his bedroll. A little light-headed right now from the whiskey. But strong. How many more years would he be able to hold out against her? He swore under his breath, stringing together all the unholy combinations that came to mind. Finally, he simply stood there and shook his head. He undid the laces on his boots and dropped his pants. He rubbed his hands over the hard paunch of his belly. Slowly, then, he walked out to the edge of the ring of firelight. Standing there, a silhouette against the moonlight, he peed out into the crisp mountain dark.

3

The Pit, The Pollution

✦✻✦❀✦✻✦✦❀✦✻✦✦❀✦✻✦✦❀✦✻✦❀

1947

1. "You know," she said, breaking into the conversation she had for miles known was a mere cover-up. "I get the vague feeling you're trying to pick me up."

"Are you offended?"

"No—not particularly."

"What, then?"

They were whispering, leaning toward each other on the high-backed seats spread with changeable white linen covers. Gloria considered her own position, his, the tiresome jolting of the bus.

"I guess I'm just puzzled."

"About what?"

"You."

"Me? What could be puzzling about me?"

She did not make the snide remark that came automatically to mind. "I've always been under the impression that this sort of thing didn't appeal to your type."

"Type?" He frowned. "The academic type, you mean? Professors and critics."

"That's right."

"What *do* you think? That we're austere, condemned to celibacy, to mousing lives down among cobwebs and sour wine, sort of safely tucked away in the sterility of some dank, vine-covered cloister? Priests, for godsake, or—or *monks?*"

"Yes. I guess that's what I thought."

"Well, we have the normal drives."

His all-American smile vanished when she moved his hand and said: "Yes, that's the impression I get."

"Does it bother you?"

"The hand does. It's wrinkling my blouse."

She kept hold of the hand, which seemed (and had since somewhere in the Wasatch Mountains, when his eyes had gone black with lust and he had stopped talking entirely about himself and leaned to smear her mouth with a wet kiss—afterward apologizing that he had not been able to help himself, the bastard!) to have mind and purpose of its own. With her forefinger, she bored lightly at the hairless craterlike scar deforming one of the tendons on the back of his hand with a white knot.

"Wound?"

"Yes."

"From what?"

"A bullet." His eyes glowed with irony. "Yes. Believe it or not, I was even in the war."

She knew he had felt her tighten; she knew he was looking at her. But she tried not to show anything. Still, she knew she had. It was hard to hide all the bitterness and hatred that had accumulated over the two years she had been sending out letters in her attempt to locate Willie.

"Did you lose someone in the war?"

"My husband went."

The critic frowned silently. His body rocked gently with the motion of the jolting bus as it slowed and turned through the little town of Roosevelt, Utah. Populated primarily by Mormons and Indians, it had already settled into that pattern of laziness that would let it ease on through the midday swelter, though it was barely midmorning and looked as though it might be a cool day.

"Then you did lose him—" the critic tested.

"Lose? No. You might say I ditched him. . . . Yes, I guess I was really pretty lucky the war came along when it did."

She glanced down, watched the shaped and painted point of her fingernail probing the smooth scar in the fork of a blue vein, and thought that his hands did not fit the rest of his body. Or they did and they did not. There was something delicate about them, something that suggested they might have been refined from something rougher. Still, they were strong, tenuous. And that made them work with the face. It was round—pleasant, the shadow of his beard stubble emphasizing a slight sagging heaviness in his jaws. His green eyes reflected a placid watery calm; his brows were thick, but uniformly short, as if a barber might have kept them trimmed.

Now his hand was struggling, with an almost imperceptible persistence, to slip away from hers, to move, she knew, onto one of two tempting regions of her body. And to find itself there by sheer accident. Good god, what did he think he could accomplish? What—in seven miles? In broad daylight? She tightened her grip.

They were all sneaking bastards. Descended not from apes, but snakes—or worse. Egotistical sons of bitches, every last one to the man.

The last time Gloria looked at anything through the narrow slit of window between the stiff stay rod on the blind and the bottom of the frame, she saw the white facade of Welter's general store flash past, a place not far from the Ute Indian reservation. But her mind continued on from where her eyes left off. She knew she was near the place. She could feel it. The familiar turns in the road quickened the throbbing of her heart; it shook in her chest like a clock. She could see the flat gray wall of sandstone, the stain down its face. She could see that in her mind. She ducked her head and tried to quiet her deep breathing. And she watched, as though in some sinister dream, the critic's hand free itself from hers and his fingers curl, soft with lust, over her thigh.

"You're so silent," he whispered, his voice growing solicitous. "What is it?"

She took a deep breath. "My sister. She was killed back there."

Self-consciously, he disengaged his hand and attempted some feeble amenities.

"Please," she sighed. "You didn't know her, and it's been a long long time."

Jo—she had not said the name in such a long time that it sounded funny, sounded wrong—had been a pretty, dark, self-possessed girl. Gloria had never loved her. No, she had never loved her without hating her more. And that dated right from the instant her mother married Leon Fulton. Although one year older than Gloria, Jo had been smaller, fine-boned, lissome. Gloria, who had had her mother's more vigorous frame, had never been able to wear Jo's clothes, those hand-me-downs that little sisters secretly love. She remembered one silk frock she actually *ached* to have. It was blue and beautifully finished, with a sash low on the hips. It hung so smartly on Jo. Once, when she had been alone in the house, Gloria had sneaked in Jo's room and tried it on. Only to find that she stretched it in an unsightly way. Jo had caught her in front of the mirror and had said, "It makes you look like a . . . a whore."

Leon (never, as much as he had asked, as much as she had wanted to, had she been able to call him Father) had sometimes taken Jo in his arms and sat in the porch swing, swinging and holding her gently against him. The crickets could stop while Leon, in a voice mellow from memory, would tell her how pretty she was, how much like her mother.

What had Leon ever told her? What?

She had had to do everything Jo did. Dancing. Piano. Cooking classes in school. But always one year behind. Always in competition. And a million times, out of what she had finally come to admit was pure jealousy, she had wished Jo were dead.

Which made it really hard when it happened. It was like a perverse prayer that had been answered. And in spite of her mother's warning, she had sneaked down to the garage on lower Main Street and looked at the car. She could see right where Jo had gone through the windshield.

"I picked her hairs out of the cracked glass and kept them." She said it straight, matter-of-fact, for the full shock value.

"What?" The critic studied her face.

"Out of the glass. Jo went through the windshield. I picked the hairs out and kept them."

She had, she remembered clearly, climbed up onto the fender, the hot crumpled metal hurting her bare knees, worked the black hairs out of the glass, and bound them in a little bundle. Then, she had ridden her bicycle seven miles out on the highway to see the place. And she had. There had been a stain where Jo had hit and lain. She had not looked just now. She could not. But if she had, she knew she would have seen it. As clearly as the day it had happened.

"Why are you going back?" the critic asked.

"I left something." She laughed privately. Something—a child. Of course, there was more.

"And you're going back to get it?"

"No. No—I only want to look at it." No, she could not take little Louis. Not even if she wanted to.

The critic was sensitive enough and embarrassed enough to stop feeling her up. So she could at least relax for a moment. She felt the bus heave forward as it topped the hill at the edge of the valley and started down toward the town. "We're nearly there," she said quietly.

Reaching into the slatted rack above their heads, the ciritic brought down his brief case. He pulled out a stiff new book in a gray dust jacket, his picture on the back, a stylized pattern of roses and flames on the front. *The Thorn in the Flames* by Nathan Rand. It was, he explained, a book about the sonnets of William Shakespeare, the English poet.

On the flyleaf, he inscribed: *To my own dark lady, Nate.* He put down a telephone number in Denver.

"You think I'll call?"

He pursed his mouth. "I hope you will."

She bristled slightly. "Do I strike you as cheap?"

"Cheap? No. On the contrary. You strike me as being very lovely, a little bit lost perhaps, and beautiful—unbelievably beautiful." He smiled. "And I'm a critic."

"Not to mention that you've pawed around enough to prove to yourself that it's all real." That took care of his smile.

"If you insist—yes. I'm an empiricist."

Well, she had her own name for it.

The bus cruised into the town of Vernal, causing no perceptible change in anything—except an occasional turning head or merely lifting eyes (Leon Fulton did not glance away from the invoice slips he was checking) and an unpleasant swirl of dust mixing with the diesel smoke. With a sharp *ch-ch-king* of the stuttering air brakes, the bus roared into the alley off Main Street and eased itself out through a portico beside the depot-cafe.

Putting his book in her hand, Nathan Rand kissed her fingers lightly. Gloria waited for him to finish, said goodbye (thought: good riddance), and climbed down out of the bus.

Then, squinting in the hard morning sun, she suddenly wanted to hide. That was the first impulse to strike her. She did not want to show her face. If it had not been for the critic and the fact that she was too damn tired to fight him for another eight hours, she would have turned right around and climbed back on the bus.

She left her suitcase in the lobby, which was partitioned away from the cafe only by the closed ends of the booths, and went into the WOMEN.

First, she deposited the book in the waste can. *My own dark lady,* my ass! she mocked defiantly. They were all the same, every sonofabitch. Only some had a thicker coating of sugar and more patience. One would rip and snort. Another would coo and pet. But the ultimate destination was the same. Oh, he did not know how dark, how utterly dark, the bastard! Wetting a coarse paper towel, she rubbed lightly at her face and mouth. She fixed up as much as she could—a touch of powder, fresh lipstick (bringing it out not quite to the edges of her lips nor to the corners of her mouth), a few strokes of the brush. And she did not allow herself to look at any more of her face in the mirror than the immediate areas she was fixing.

At the door, she paused. She retraced her steps. Brushing aside the wet paper towels, she picked *The Thorn in the Flames* out of the waste can and slipped it into her handbag. Even she had heard of William Shakespeare.

2.   "This here quarter makes that statement," Little Benny Westlake replied, smugly hooking his thumbs in his Levi's pockets and doing a cocky knee bend.

"Where'd you get a quarter?" Geo asked, his entire face narrowing suspiciously.

"Hell, Hartt gave me a whole damn fistful of change when he got home from the war the other day."

"What war?"

"The Big War."

"That's been over for two years now," Louis challenged, leveling his eyes on the coin in Little Benny's palm.

"Yeah—poor Hartt. He had to suffer this last stint out in a Army hospital somewheres." Little Benny shook his head sadly and moved his fingers, flipping the quarter over, watching Louis's eyes dart away from it. "Pa thinks Hartt's some sort of family disgrace and won't even talk to him no more."

"What happened?" Geo asked. "Was he wounded?"

"That fact ain't exactly been pinpointed yet. Ma says it was some internal poisoning he picked up right at the tail end of the war. Pa hasn't exactly stopped shouting long enough to say. But whatever it was, it sure does set Pa off. Whew! Damn! At the height of one of his atomic spells he up and called it a social disease. So I reckon it's something Hartt caught at a French social. Them Frenchies likely all got it. That's my theory. Hell! It's hard to understand Pa's gripe. He hollers at Hartt and says he never had the decency to go out and get something blowed off, he had to go and rub something on it. . . ."

Louis was still eying the quarter. So Little Benny said, just to goad him on, "Besides, Louis, your old man ain't never showed up yet, neither, has he?"

"No. But Brad Meade told my grandma that my dad stopped off to work a while."

"Two years is a hell of a long while."

"I guess he's not through with what he's doing," Louis said.

"Where's he stopped?"

"I don't know. Nobody does except maybe Brad Meade, who won't tell."

"Maybe he's doing something secret," Geo suggested.

"Looks that way," Benny mused. "What do you think, Louis?"
Louis shrugged. "You mean a quarter I can't ride up that hill?"

"Nope." Little Benny firmed his lips negatively. "Riding up ain't nothing. You said that hill wasn't steep, Louis. I said it was. You can't prove steepness by just going up. Because you can poke-ass along and grab yourself a breather whenever you take the notion. And that only proves you ain't in shape. But there ain't no rest coming down. That's the real test." He pulled off his straw hat, exposing the poorly cropped puff of his white hair, and wiped his sleeve across his forehead. He closed one eye craftily. "You chicken, Louis?"

His face growing dark, Louis Light firmed his jaw, turned in the road, and started pumping his bike towards the ski hill.

No one really skied on the hill, of course. But all the kids within a couple of miles brought their sleds out and coasted down it. They all wished they had skis; and they probably seriously imagined that they were skiing when they were slipping along the icy run on their Red Devil or American Flier sleds. So they had given it the name—the way people paint technicolor into their own dreams. And they had worn the trail so firmly into the face of the hill that now it remained bare of brush both winter and summer.

"It's our hill," Geo reminded, catching up with Louis and Benny.

"Jeeezuus!" Little Benny groaned. "You only tell us that about fifty times a day."

"Well, it is."

"So what?"

"So—I just wanted you to know."

"How could we ever forget?"

Near the bottom of the ski hill the trail made a turn shaped like the hook at the top of a question mark, in order to miss a corn silage pit. The pit was fifty feet long, ten feet wide, and nine feet deep. But it did not look all that deep because there was at least one foot of the previous year's silage liquor ponded in the bottom, a sourish black muck as thick as molasses. That year, Jeff Seagram was building a concrete silo at home and did not plan on using the pit again. He had already dragged a dead cottonwood tree out and dumped it into the slime at one end. Eventually, he intended to fill up the whole thing—so it would not be such a hazard.

"What're you going to do to that tree?" Little Benny asked, screwing up his nose at the stench of the ripe juice. "Going to soften it up for cow feed? That's Mormons for you, Louis."

Louis did not reply. He kept on going up the hill with his bike. Geo was right behind him, pushing on the rear fender.

"Hey, Louis!" Little Benny howled, clomping wearily up the hill in his cowboy boots. "Hold up a damn minute. I'm pooped!"

"What's the matter," Louis called back. "This hill too steep for you?"

That shut Little Benny up.

Louis kept plodding doggedly towards the top. And by the time Little Benny finally did make it, puffing so hard he thought he would collapse, he heard Geo pleading in earnest with Louis, "You hadn't ought to do it, Louis. You might get us all in trouble."

Louis just looked past him at Little Benny.

"Okay—where is it?"

"Louis—" Little Benny started, his small face a knot of fear. "Anybody can tell by just looking that it's steeper than the walls of hell."

"Where's that quarter you've been bragging so damn much about?" Louis's eyes were the color of lead slugs.

Little Benny produced the coin from his pocket. He held it out in the palm of his hand. Louis reached and snatched it up. Then, as Geo and Little Benny were opening their mouths for one final futile protest, Louis's foot came off the ground and firmed itself on the pedal. The chain tightened between the sprockets.

3. The same old dump, Gloria thought, emerging from the depot and coming face-to-face with two enormous black steers squeezed between the manure-scabbed racks of a parked pickup

truck. Right on Main Street. A town full of Mormon dirt farmers. And Indians, she added, passing a squaw in white-framed sunglasses, a shawl stretched over her fat back, a papoose poking out of the bright pink folds and clinging to one of the squaw's thick lusterless braids. Then, Gloria watched her own shadow, long in the morning sun, sliding along the sidewalk in front of her.

TARZAN! The marquee poster at the Vogue Theatre showed Johnny Weissmuller, with Cheetah riding on his back and Jane tucked under one arm, swinging out over a river infested with hungry crocodiles.

Gloria caught the flash of her silk dickey in the window of the Vernal Drug. She had an impulse to go inside, to see if it were still the high school hangout she remembered: the few leatherette booths in back near where the patent medicine and veterinary supplies were shelved. She smiled to herself, thinking of the time when Willie had chased Brad Meade all over the store with a pair of nickel-plated cattle emasculators. Her smile left. Willie. (She almost spat the name.) He had always had money for the drug. Some kind of car, too. And the gasoline to get them out to the boondocks. And (she could not call it sugar or patience either with Willie) the brazen audacity to come right out and say what it was he wanted. The sonofabitch.

But she had got it all back. She had waited, getting him a little at a time, and finally really shocked him with that one little statement of her own. For once it had not been a matter of what he wanted to do but what he damn well *had* to do.

In the next window, a butcher shop, the white case lined with meat, long worms of flypaper spiraling down from the ceiling, she checked her beige linen suit. The lap of the skirt was badly wrinkled from sitting so long, and—of course—from the ardent advances of Nathan Rand, the intellectual prick.

Despite the corduroy of steel strips inset with spikes and cemented into the ledge under the low windows of Uintah State Bank, a collection of calloused loafers squatted there. They interrupted the train of their interminable meteorological speculations to mark her passing. Smiling, she kept herself close. Then she continued across the street to where their less pretentious, mute counterparts sat in front of J. C. Penney's to smoke and spit and idly blink in the fierce Utah sun. They, too, stopped to watch her approach. Someone sighed. A couple ground shoe leather.

Midway through the next block, Gloria brought herself to an abrupt halt. She backed up and read again the black letters neatly shaded with gold leaf: BRADFORD MEADE, ATTORNEY AT LAW.

"So," she mused aloud. "Local boy makes good."

She would pay Brad a call. Maybe he could tell her where Willie was holed up, Willie and all the alimony she had coming to her. But would he? It was understandable, naturally, that Brad would want to protect Willie. But he might, he just might tell her anyway. For men's loyalties, she had learned, were not insurmountable. And she wondered why she had not thought of Brad before.

She found herself at the door of Utah Freight and Storage sooner than she had calculated. She was still getting accustomed to being back, crumbling that cloddy first feeling of not wanting to be seen into the grit of no longer giving a damn.

She saw a secretary, her glasses slipping on her nose, her fingers descending in a stilted onrush upon a typewriter, nothing moving beyond her elbows, except probably her eyes, working in their sockets to unscramble the cryptic symbolism of the shorthand on her green pad.

Gloria pushed on through the door. The clerk was just wetting his mouth and starting to speak his practiced how do you do when she passed the end of the counter and entered Leon's office, the suddenly soft square of heavy carpeting and suddenly lowered, white acoustical ceiling absorbing the sound of her coming.

A model of an old-time freight wagon, detailed, exact from tongue to tailgate, as Leon had known them, sat on the desk. The corners of pink and yellow invoice slips curled around a paperweight made of a polished cog. Looking at Leon, his head bent over a stack of papers, hair only starting to thin at the crown, six additional years of gray mixed through it like a light penciling of frost, Gloria felt a melting tenderness.

As he looked up, looked up and saw her, saw the brunette hair falling softly to her shoulders, brown almond-shaped eyes, thin face with a slightly too-large mouth, knowing who she was and crying out her name in pleasant surprise, Leon Fulton had a retake. He saw Louise standing in his office, inquiring if her trunks and boxes had arrived, leaving him—a man who in those days had known not only the point of departure but the precise weight as well of every piece of freight that came through his office—completely blank. . . . For days after seeing her, he had brooded and walked the streets, passing the place where he knew she was living—a single one-room house she could hardly afford. And each morning for a month he had waited and watched for her to appear at the corner, take a few steps along Main Street, and disappear into the double doors of the General Merc. He had walked and watched and waited, keeping up an unceasing nervous vigil, not even certain at first why he was doing it. Then one day an inclination came. He had his suit brushed and pressed, while he waited in a closet, and his boots shined (a luxury he allowed himself twice a week—not the luxury of the money, the five cents then, fifteen cents now, but the luxury of looking down and watching the boy dig off the mud and daub on the polish with his smeared fingers). He had crossed the street to the store, rubbing his gold watch chain—a habit he still had—and nervously rehearsing what had turned out to be the prelude to a proposal.

"Well," Leon sighed, shouldering into his pinstripe suit jacket, simultaneously drawing his thin Hamilton watch out to the full length of its gold chain. "I suppose you're pretty anxious to get home and see Mother and Louis."

"Yes," she said. "I've hardly been able to contain myself since I got on the bus in San Diego."

"I imagine that's a long lonesome ride with a bunch of total strangers." Leon slipped his watch back into his pocket. The gold chain dropped in a neat loop over the hard barrel of his belly.

4. It seemed to take him forever. He was an insignificant speck, or—at the very most—a sustained flicker on the brown face of a changeless panorama stippled with mauve patches of

young thistles. The bike assumed a sweptback look as it rattled and hammered, back fender and loose reflector clanging like a soldered bell, over the ruts and rocks on the run and gradually gathered speed from rise to incline, rise to incline. Louis's shirt had come unbuttoned and was flapping behind him like a pair of wings.

Then, suddenly, the bike seemed to be going too fast. Geo tried with all his might to squint hard enough to make it slow down in his mind. And he began unconsciously to make a little squeal of protest with his mouth.

Louis's shirt whipped and flapped. The bike raced downward, vibrating fiercely, a tight spiral of dust seeming to cushion the tires from the earth. The turn came. It appeared that Louis was not even going to try to make it, was not, in fact, even giving it a thought. Or if he was he had also discovered that he was already in the air when it came time to twist the handlebars (which Geo was doing for him, thrusting his whole body around, squealing; but Louis, true to form, did not respond). It was like a scary movie. Geo was convinced that if he could only shut his eyes and plug his ears for a minute, peering first through his webbed fingers, everything would be miraculously changed for the good. Or at least it would not be as bad as it looked like it might be. Louis would slow down. The hill would not be as steep. Geo would awaken and find it was only a dream. But he could not get his eyes shut.

For one brief second, his hopes soared. It looked as if Louis Light would fly the full fifty feet over the gaping pit, land on his wheels, and keep right on going out to the road.

But Louis's wings seemed to melt at the joints and wilt against his back. Geo thought he saw him deliberately glance back over his shoulder to make sure he and Little Benny were still watching. And then, as though God had seen this display of arrogance and had reached down and taken a smart pop at him with something like an invisible fly swatter, Louis Light plunged out of sight, crashing down through the limbs of the dead cottonwood, into the pit, even the dust disappearing after him, a small funnel sucked down among the leafless limbs, leaving only silence.

Petrified in place, Geo tried to stop the sound he was making with his mouth. But it went right on sounding. He gritted his teeth. He closed his lips firmly over them. Still, the sound persisted. Now it seemed more like an echo. He turned. Little Benny Westlake was holding his eyes squinched shut, and from his thinly parted lips there issued a high, forlorn wail of pain and grief.

"Shut up, Benny!" Geo reached out and gave Little Benny a good shake. "Shut your mouth and come on."

They started running down the hill, legs flickering like spoked wheels.

"I'll bet you anything that bastard lost my quarter," Little Benny fretted, between breaths. He clutched his cowboy hat and his free arm jerked helplessly at his side with the relentless momentum of his short, running legs.

"I'll bet he never!" Geo shot back. He knew Louis better than that. So did Benny. "Besides—who says it's still your quarter?"

"What!"

They reached the pit. The branches of the supine cottonwood were waving vaguely, as if a soft breeze had just passed through them. Here and there, like strange stray leaves on the limbs and brittle twig ends, were scraps of ripped and shredded clothing. But there was no sign of Louis Light.

"Louis," Geo tested, his weak voice croaking.

"Hell," Little Benny whispered with wonder. "Maybe he drowned."

Slosh-ploop!

They turned their eyes towards the mouth of the pit. Louis stood looking out at them. His body was slopped with a camouflage of gummy silage liquor, black and streaked with green. He had ended up wearing only his torn shorts and one tennis shoe—still tied. Welts and lines of crimson blood were starting to show through the blackish muck. He took another step, trying not to limp, holding his shoulders stiffly squared, his back straight. But he had to lean on his bike. A few broken spokes clicked against the fork and fender braces.

Geo raced around to the incline, which was webbed with the cleated tracks of tractor tires. He was hurting for Louis, half wanting to limp and cry out himself, as though his body too were wounded and painted with pain. Then he stopped and stood in silent awe while Louis ascended the mouth of the pit, dripping the viscid silage juice and ignoring them with incredible style.

"Where is it?" Little Benny charged.

Louis's eyes, like carved slits in a black mask, sought Little Benny's. His voice was brittle as glass. "Where's what?"

Little Benny tried to sound nonplused. "That quarter."

Nothing about Louis changed. Not the mask of his face, not the thin cut of his mouth. Except one fist, which must have been frozen shut (and must also have been the cause of his missing that turn), that slowly raised, opened, and revealed a clean white palm with the silver disc of the coin safely inside. He did not offer to return it to Benny. After a long silent moment, he stooped and, with his free hand, wound the broken spokes around the nearest good ones. He swung his leg over the frame and began pedaling slowly homeward, the bent wheels making the bike roll along with a crooked, wobbling limp.

"Hell, Louis," Little Benny cried, catching up. "I never seen a ride the likes of that in all my born days. As Hartt'd say, you sure was motating. Ha ha ha," he cackled and gave his head a shake. "You can just keep that money. Lord, I think if I had another two bits on me I'd just fork it over to you as a bonus."

"I won," Louis said, holding his breath back in an obvious attempt at hiding some pain.

"What!" Benny screamed. "How do you explain your wreck?"

"It wasn't the hill that did it," Louis reasoned. "It was the stupid pit. That pit'd be dangerous on level ground. . . ."

Louis stopped talking. Geo looked on ahead. Louis's grandpa's Dodge was just rolling bluntly into the driveway. A strange woman in a beige suit got out of the passenger's side and started for the house. Louis's grandma ran from the front door and embraced the other woman. Louis got off his bike and touched at his shorts, blindly trying to put them in place.

"Who's that?" Geo whispered.

"My mother, I suppose."

"You never said she was coming."

"I didn't know."

When she saw Louis ride his bike into the yard, an anguished look passed over Gloria's face. He dismounted and came towards

her. She steeled herself. He halted and looked up into her face
with what seemed at first to be simply a bemused expression of
inspection and curiosity. She was almost sure he had done this
on purpose. He had smeared himself with something sticky and
was going to try and rub it on her. And he reeked. She caught
the smell again and took a step back, her spike high heels sinking
in the damp grass, sticking there. She raised her hand to cover
her mouth and nose.

"Mother," she said in a whisper, one foot pulling out of her
shoe as she tried to keep a careful distance from the kid.
"Mother, he stinks."

Louis turned. In the midmorning sun, his back shone brown
like a shell—except for the stripes which actually looked like
blood. He climbed the steps into the house alone, leaving the
three adults staring at the grass.

Geo wheeled his bike around. He felt all swollen and awful.
He turned his head to tell Little Benny that they had better go.
But he did not say anything. Because it looked like Little Benny
was going to break down and cry.

5.   It was the only thing he could think to do. And when he
finally did get around to doing it, the gesture was warmly appropriate and even genteel. Gloria had not, and never would have,
complied with the mere formality of allowing Miss Peacock to
announce her. No. He had felt something, felt her presence, and
looked up (from he now no longer remembered what) to find
her standing squarely in front of his desk. Thrusting himself out
of his chair, after what seemed an entire afternoon of protracted
silence, he blurted her name and offered his hand.

"Well?" she asked, aiming a derisive half-smile from the hand,
which she held hair side up, to his face. "Am I expected to kiss it
—or what?"

Gradually, Brad Meade recovered from his initial embarrassment. He thought Gloria was more beautiful than he had ever

seen her. She had lost the girlish fullness of her face, although she retained that deceptive, sweet look she had always had. He smiled to himself. Her mouth, too, was still the same. She was as self-conscious about it as she had always been. Only now she had become more artful, perfecting her makeup, painting the lipstick not quite out to the edges of her lips, not quite to the corners of her mouth. And she spoke with a careful control, never letting it open too far.

Gloria motioned vaguely around the room with her hands. "When?"

"Three months ago. I passed the bar and bought out Blaine Pit. He retired."

"Then you must have gone back to school as soon as you got your discharge."

"That's right. I was home about a month." He reached out and touched a polished agate paperweight, then a bayonet that he used as a letter opener. Both felt cold.

"And Willie?"

"Willie was discharged."

"That much the Army could tell me. He got out about the same time you did. What happened?"

"He hasn't come home yet."

"Well, I guess that's pretty obvious, isn't it? I mean even to a fairly stupid person."

Brad had the feeling that the usual subterfuge of rhetoric and language was somehow going to prove inadequate; and, glancing back at his desk, where his hands were nervously ensnaring each other in a red rubber band, he convinced himself that he had no idea why. He would try, of course. Certainly, he could handle himself. She was only a woman. After all.

"Willie stopped off someplace," he stated carefully. "He is planning to come home, though. Or at least he says he is. And I think he will. Sometime."

"When?"

"He hasn't said that."

"You have had letters—of course."

He almost nodded, then did not. Which was enough.

"But you refuse to tell me where he is." There was a hint of scorn in the crooked line of her mouth.

He focused on the window behind her. The sun hitting the dusty glass left the movie marquee across the street swimming in a haze.

I'm not sure myself just exactly where I am—yet, Willie had written.

"Willie asked me not to tell anyone. Not even his mother."

"His mother! My god, not even his mother!" Gloria mocked. "Well, naturally, I'd never think of asking you to violate your promise to Willie Light. I might, on the other hand, ask you to do what you think you ought to do—as a man dealing in what you probably call justice."

Brad, standing now, became aware that something was terribly wrong. He felt that his fly must be gaping, or his shirt must be on backwards. Except he knew it was not anything so inane, so simple. "Justice," he said, reaching up to duplicate the tone of her question, "isn't so weak and corrupt that it has to worry about being right, too—I hope."

She closed her mouth carefully. She reopened it. Then she spoke. "Do we have to stay here?"

No. I mean—should we? Yes. . . . But by then they were already going down the stairs to the street. If I keep driving and keep talking and keep thinking about only the next curve in the road and the shape and structure of the next sentence, I think I am going to be all right, Brad kept telling himself.

But it continued. Even after they were in the car and moving and he was attempting to analyze and then forget the look of bewilderment (and maybe disappointment) on Janet Peacock's face when he had told her he would be gone for the rest of the afternoon. Yes. Even then Gloria insisted on breaking and entering the private domain of his thoughts. Not with a question, but an accusation, "You're not driving me through town."

It was true. He had taken the back streets. He looked off into the hills to the north, hoping that the rhetoric in which he had so thoroughly schooled himself would stay with him now, in this time of crisis. They passed the power plant. "I'm in town most of the time." They passed the dairy. "So I find it pleasant to get out now and then." The car rose and settled onto the bridge spanning Ashley Creek. "I didn't think you'd mind."

For all the endurance and time-proven qualities which left it blistered and, perhaps, even slightly warped—though certainly nonetheless classical—the rhetoric did not hold up; because something else, something more classical, something possibly even preclassical, came along to strip the lawyer, the man, of his cloak and shield. They dropped away, the rhetoric, the professional bearing, the moment he allowed his eyes the crippling human luxury of falling instantaneously to her knees. He found them casually bare, shapely calves smooth, shining from the recent razor. And the paucity of language, the substitute, gave way to a plethora of lust, the real.

So, under it all, naked, he was merely a man—brash, clumsy, male. And he was not surprised in the least to see his own hand, partly identifiable to him by the ring with the Sigma Chi crest on the third finger, settling where preparation had been made for it. There. Yes. And then reaching farther. Automatically. As though for the next rung on a jiggly ladder.

Even her feigned indifference was overwhelming. For he had seen her—or thought he had (would, in fact, have sworn testimony to it) in that supreme moment when his male ego was swollen and throbbing with greatness—choke and swallow down her cry of pleasure. She filled him with doubt about everything in his life, left him willing—though much of this had died down with the first climax and the increasingly uncomfortable jabbing of the steering wheel in his kidneys, but threatened to rise up again, and would, he was certain, if he touched her—to drop all the things he possessed and all the things he was and all the things he wanted to be and just go away with her. Anywhere. Dammit. Gloria.

But he could not let it happen. This wisdom, rising not out of any sense of decency but out of a healthy fear of all the machinery of fate, spoke to him in strong tones. He wheeled the car around and drove back to town so fast he was afraid he might remind her of Willie (he cringed), remind her of *his* furious hurry to get past his destination so he could sneak up on it from the opposite direction, catching it unsuspecting under the settling dust of his first passing, and measure the effect. Consequently, he overshot the corner she designated and was barely able to bring the car to a stop in the middle of the same block. Keeping his hands clamped on the wheel, vaguely aware of the futility of this act—which he had conceived, he realized, in not too brilliant a display of hindsight—he watched her swing easily out of the seat and unhinge her body (which he had just possessed, he thought; but no—he revised that: which had just possessed him) beside the car.

Before shutting the door, she leaned down, pushed her head inside, her hair swinging softly against her cheeks, and said, "Nice to see you again, Brad."

On the way home, it returned. The rhetoric. He struggled into its plating and mail. Then, suddenly finding he was once more in voice, he upbraided himself passionately, profanely, for his cowardice in telling her, when she closed her legs threateningly on his hand, Willie's address in Council Tree, Iowa. And yet, right in the midst of his fury, he halted, calming, and savored for a single moment the sugary coating of his own hypocrisy. He congratulated himself profusely on his male supremacy, preening slightly in the seat, his shoulders well back against the upholstery, his elbow cocked out of the window, before turning into his driveway. To face his family. And deny his guilt. Secretly, of course.

For now, he told himself, he knew what it meant to have committed something undeniably beyond his control. And it was absolutely the first time in his life that he had ever felt any real sympathy for God. Yes, what a shuddering tremor must go through God's body each time he finds himself confronted with a single rib of man.

6.   Why not? she thought. Why not let the silly fool dish out his dough? She would gladly keep her own, and keep as well the five dollars Leon had given her so she could show Louis a good time. Five dollars was five dollars. God knows, she could always use it.

The calliope wheezed, pumping in a close circle, its music barely drowning out the rickety labor of the old engine; the pastel ponies rose and fell, whinnying children clutching brass poles, a few long-legged fathers looking foolish and cruel astride the little horses.

"Pea——nuts!" a man shouted in her face. "Cotton Candy!"

She snatched two clouds of the pink cotton candy, stuffed one in each little boy's fist, then told the hawker to go get his money from Ronnie, the gentleman standing in the ferris wheel line. Gentleman! Ha!

Gloria smiled bitterly to herself. When one of them found out that you had been married, had had a kid (even ten and a half years ago), and had somehow survived both mishaps with good looks and a body he could not keep his rough bastard's fingers from pawing, he no longer bothered to employ the conventional techniques of petting and coaxing. He knew what he wanted and right where to find it; and he was convinced—in spite of your protests—that ultimately you could not refuse, and he went about trying to prove that he had invented the whole idea and then perfected it and that all the others before him in the whole rotten history of horny man had simply been mere imitations of the Real Thing. Dirty sons of bitches to the man.

"Everybody wins . . ."

"Three throws a quarter . . ."

"See the boy with big toes growing out of his kneecaps . . ."

"Peanuts . . ."

She waited with Louis and his little friend while Ronnie whatever-his-last-name-was leaned and pushed a bill through the grate into the red-and-yellow ticket booth. Flashing back what he obviously considered his most sexy, seductive look, he grabbed the tickets and carelessly scooped up the change. It sounded funny to hear a man called a kid's name; but it fit this one. Ronnie. He had a red crust of moustache like a rusted wire brush worn close to the backing. His tight features formed a small neat pattern of circles, and his tobacco stained teeth were as uniform as kernels of field corn. He wore starched suntan pants and a matching shirt, with a white circle of teeshirt and a few curls of hair showing at the throat. But his fingernails seemed to have been pared with a jackknife.

She had flinched when he told her, "I'm a driller."

Laughing, he had explained (not without a meaningful wink

and a peal of laughter) that his work was primarily confined to
an oil rig in the Red Wash badlands east of Vernal. And, of
course, he was available for anything more interesting. Ha ha ha.

Each time he paid and got the boys settled down for a couple
of more rides on something, anything, he hustled her out to his
Ford, which was a maroon '47 convertible with custom-tailored
white upholstery, a plastic skull screwed on the shifting lever,
and a fifth of Jim Beam conveniently stashed beneath the front
seat. His plan, which was no mystery to her, was to get her ca-
joled into a state of drunken generosity. But she was, while faking long swallows, only sipping. He drank harder and harder out
of mounting disappointment and desperation, his eyes flooding
with tears each time he gulped and swallowed, and his tight little
moustache beginning to sneer over the top of the bottle.

As soon as the man locked them in the seat of the gondola and
moved out of the way, Geo looked for Louis's mother and Ronnie. They were gone. Again. They always did it. They had on the
tilt-a-whirl, the merry-go-round, on the octopus, the hammer.
Ronnie bought the tickets (Geo's own money was still in his
pocket, though he made an honest reach for it each time) and
then disappeared. Geo could not figure it out.

"Where'd they go?"

Louis shrugged. "Off to look at the sights. They're probably at
one of the booths pitching baseballs through a hole in the canvas
or something."

"Yeah. Well how come he don't win nothing then?"

Louis's mouth creased darkly, curling down at the corners. "He
doesn't look like much of a shot to me."

"Me neither," Geo agreed hastily. "I don't like him a bit."

"What don't you like?"

"I don't like a whole lot of things."

"Like?"

"Like all them snakes he's got tattooed around his wrists," Geo
declared, choosing one thing at random—though, in truth, he did
sort of like the snakes.

"They're all right," Louis said.

"It's just him," Geo declared firmly.

The ferris wheel rose slowly, making frequent stops for new passengers, and gradually took them over the top. It was from there that Geo got his first glimpse of them.

"Look, Louis. Look. There they are."

"Who?"

"Your mother and that Ronnie."

"Where?"

"There."

"That's not them."

"It is so," Geo argued. But they were already dropping out of sight. "That was his car. And they were in it. And he was smooching with her."

"You didn't see them," Louis maintained stiffly.

"I did."

Louis grabbed his shirt front and twisted his fist in the fabric, tightening it on Geo's throat. They were now climbing backwards up the other side.

"You didn't."

"Did."

"Didn't."

"Did."

Glaring fiercely, his teeth gritted, he twisted harder on the shirt front. Geo, horrified, felt it cut harder into his throat and tried to back away. He glimpsed the tops of the tents and saw how small the people looked. Suddenly, he was afraid of falling. Louis pushed his face close, forcing Geo against the metal frame of the gondola.

"Goddam you, Geo. If you don't shut your ugly mouth I'm going to throw you out."

Geo froze. The name of the Lord in vain. Geo started to ask Louis why he had said it. But he stopped. Louis was glaring at him, his eyes as hard as stones. Geo shut his mouth like a steel vise; he kept his thin face averted, his eyes wide open, glazed with bewilderment and fear. Louis let his breath out through his teeth and, turning, eased back against the other side of the seat.

Geo found it hard not to watch the spectacle that was taking place on the white seats of the maroon Ford down below. He could not exactly figure out what was the matter with Louis. It was plain as day who the two were, and that they were smoking and drinking and carrying on. When the gondola went over the top again he saw them smooching. The next time they were smooching and drinking. Then it looked like she was hitting him. But the ferris wheel dropped and the gondola went down too fast for him to see for certain. He raised up, straining against the locked bar. And they did not go up again. The ride was over.

Gloria waited in what few scanty shadows there were, trying to hold her blouse shut and not be too obvious about the fact that most of the buttons had been ripped off. Her hose were snagged to pieces (she had felt them go when he was clawing for her with his rough nails; and an uneven pressure on her left calf told her she had at least one long fat run). She could not believe it. Right there in the car, on the street, open and visible, with half the damn town of Vernal and most of the dirt farmers from the valley gooning their way through the carnival—not ten feet away.

Men! Blind bastards. Like a kid with a top. Every man had his own little filthy world and was looking for a place where he could get it spinning. As far as they were concerned, when they wanted a woman, every woman was nothing but a whore and a slut whose head could be turned with a few egotistical lies and a fistful of money. . . . Until they went hunting a wife. *She* had to be a virgin.

"Louis!" Gloria cried, when she saw him alight from the ferris wheel with his little friend. "Bring Geo and let's go home."

It was worse on a woman—that smell was. And Geo did not like it one bit. For one thing, she was not funny like Louis's Grandpa Light was. And there was something else the matter with Louis's mother. She kept her hand up in front all the time now, like maybe her chest hurt or something. She was kind of messed up too. Not quite as pretty now as when he had first seen her.

After they let him off, Geo stood in his driveway and thought about the things that had happened. Louis's family was one real puzzle. Here was his mother, home from California, drinking and carrying on with that Ronnie from the oil fields. And Louis's father had not even as much as come back from the war yet.

Geo shook his head and shoved his hands down in his pockets. What really bothered him was that Louis had used the name of the Lord in vain. That made him sad. He watched the car. He realized it was not heading home. It turned instead towards the highway out of town. He thought about that until he felt something. He still had his money. Then he wondered what had happened to that Ronnie.

She could have driven to the place blindfolded. It was not a matter of following the broken white line, which sometimes ran parallel to one or two yellow warning lines. It was merely watching to see that her turning of the steering wheel was concomitant with the turning of the oncoming road. Gauging everything over the curled horns of the ram on the hood of the Dodge, she could tell each spot where a curve had been straightened, each place where the road had been widened. She drove into the treacherous section of the highway known as the Twist, and she followed the tight switchbacks right down to the place where it had happened.

She passed it. She could have seen it. Even in the dark. In the fringes of the headlight beams she could have made out the stain on the gray sheet of sandstone.

But she did not look.

After a moment, she remembered little Louis. She turned to look at him. He was staring at her. She realized what it was: sometime during that last mile she had let go of her blouse. It gaped. The blunt stitched cups of her bra probed out—full, white, patterned in the light from the dash.

"For the love of Christ!" she sighed, her mouth sagging wearily. "Not you too. . . ."

Louis squirmed, crawled over the top of the seat, and tumbled down into the back.

7. "Hurry, Louis," Louise called.

If only he would not try her today. Today of all days. It was hard enough to have to stand back and watch Gloria leave home again. This time, Louise had seen something in the girl she had never before noticed: Gloria seemed to spend a lot of time reading. Even now, her packing completed, she sat in the next room with that book she had brought. It was the first time Louise had realized how really lonely Gloria must be. Once again she felt tears burn back in her eyes. She swallowed them down.

"Hurry, now, honey. We've got to be at the depot in time for your momma to buy her ticket."

Louis sat huddled in the oval tub, holding a green wash cloth up as a flimsy shield over his boyhood. His hair was plastered in a wet fringe on his forehead. And his narrow shoulders, still scabbed from his plunge into the sHage pit and still slightly iridescent with Merthiolate stains, were taut, drawn, birdlike.

"I don't want to go," he said in a low voice.

"What?"

"I don't want to go," he repeated, louder.

Reaching quickly, Louise closed the bathroom door. "That's enough of that kind of talk, mister. You know you want to go." She bent over the tub, keeping her voice low. She felt the soft steam from the hot bath warming her skin. "Come on, let's get you finished."

Louis, squirming from embarrassment, shrank against the sloping back of the tub. "I don't want to go."

"Louis," she coaxed. "This is the last time you'll be able to see your mother until she can save up enough money for another visit."

Like two halves of a shell, his lips cracked open: "I don't care if I ever see her again!"

"Louis!" she gasped, starting to cover his mouth with her hand. She stopped.

Louis had dropped his wash cloth. He thrust himself towards her, his hands fastened whitely on the sides of the tub, his face tight with anguish.

"I hate her!" he hissed.

"*Louis!*" Louise threatened a slap she knew she could not deliver. Her hand trembled in the air.

"*I hate her!*" he shouted triumphantly, his shrill voice multiplied in all the tiled corners and in the curves and hollows of the porcelain fixtures. He started flailing with his arms, furiously splashing water all over the walls and floor, hammering his elbows brutally against the sides of the tub, swelling up and stiffening with tears she knew would never flow.

"*I hate her! I hate her!*"

Louis, Gloria thought. Little Louis. She sat on the edge of the bed and stared at a page in Nathan Rand's book, a page she had been trying to read ever since her mother left the room. Blindly, her eyes traced the last line of one sonnet:

Lilies that fester smell far worse than weeds

Her fingers closed on the page, crumpling it; she ripped it out of the spine, the sharp folded corners like thorns in her palm.

Her suitcase was packed, folded shut, latched. As she glanced at it, she started to cry. And she tore out the next page.

Why should she cry? After three hundred and fifty miles on the bus to Denver, where she intended to phone the critic (to find out, naturally, that he was married, but that that did not really make any difference as long as—well, and he would stutter through the next couple of sentences) she would forget. She let another page fall in a crumpled ball on the floor.

Yes. She would forget. Maybe not everything. Maybe only enough that she could laugh about the rest of it. Enough that she could laugh, for instance, about Brad Meade. Brad. Ha ha! Willie should have got him that time with those cattle emasculators. But Willie did not have the guts. She would have done it. She would have clamped those nickel-plated jaws down on Brad. On Willie, too: but she had fixed him for a while once. Yes, she would have made a eunuch out of a gutless wonder.

But Gloria cried. In the bureau mirror, her features (weren't they still lovely, youthful, still fresh, sweet?) broke up in a kaleidoscopic wash of tears. She ripped another page from the book

and threw it at the image rippling in the mirror. She emitted a
stifled cry, then a high piteous wail, a mixture of grief and bewilderment, like a female puppy caught in the confusion of first
heat.

She sniffed. Why should she cry? She loved leaving. She felt a
deep, inexplicably deep, delicious ache. . . . Feeling the touch of
her mother's hand, Gloria sucked in her breath and tried to hold
down the heavy sobs that continued swelling sporadically in her
chest.

"Darling, he didn't mean it."

"He did. He did. I know. I deserve it."

"Sweetheart—please. Please, don't torture yourself."

And Gloria broke down and cried much harder against her
mother's solid bosom.

4

The Formative Years of Love

❋⊹✿⊹❋⊹✿⊹❋⊹✿⊹❋⊹✿⊹❋⊹✿⊹❋

1951

1.   After Geo's thirteenth birthday party, all the guests trooped out to Melody Mountain, a roller rink and dance pavilion built on one of the low hills at the outskirts of Vernal. The rink was slick concrete surrounded by a stockade of seven-foot-tall pine slabs, the rough insides of which were heavily doped with cheap calcimine paint; anyone skating into this fence or leaning against it for any reason was likely to come away with a palm full of splinters or a marking of telltale white. At one end of the enclosure was a refreshment booth where pop and candy were sold—Tootsie Rolls being a big favorite with the fast skaters and fat caramel Sugar Daddy suckers lasting the slow skaters most of an evening. Directly across the rink from the refreshment booth stood the stage, elevated and recessed in an enclosure shaped like a crude shell. The Westlakes, who had built Melody Mountain, played here on Friday and Saturday nights and all regular American holidays and many Mormon holidays as well. There was roller-skating from six to nine, and

dancing from nine to one. Naturally, a thin line of demarcation existed between the block of time for skating and the block of time for dancing; and that hazardous time from about ten minutes before nine to about ten minutes after nine was not without its mishaps and disasters for those few skaters who could not bring themselves to a stop and those few eager dancers who could not wait to begin.

The Westlakes (who liked what they did and had never heard of the labor union for musicians) performed right through it all, performed from the early evening right on into the late night. Little Benny played lead guitar, an electrified Spanish, which seemed to know no limits of style and perfection. Benny was accompanied on the piano by his mother, Belle Westlake, her fat red forearms trembling and shaking happily above the keyboard, her tromping foot widening the holes already worn in the centers of the brass pedals. Benny was backed up by his father, Golden Westlake, whose skinny knees poked out from under his steel guitar stand, the left one always bouncing a shade out of time with the right one. And Benny occasionally shared solo spotlight with his brother, Hartt Westlake, who cushioned his violin against a wild, red, full-faced beard and played as if drifting in a divine spell (most people maintained the world war had done it to Hartt).

To Geo's party, and consequently as a part of the crowd that continued on out to the Mountain, as it was called, came a new girl in the seventh grade at Maeser School—Sue Ellen Bolt. Sue Ellen wore a peach-colored frock. She was, at a ripe thirteen herself, very outstanding and wasted no time on modesty—false or otherwise. She had moved to Vernal from Louisiana (her father was a tool pusher for an oil company that was sinking some wells in the area). Geo had invited Sue Ellen more out of sheer impulse than for any other reason, although he told his mother that it was because she was new and had no friends yet. This was a gross lie, preposterous in every sense of the word, for in the course of her first two days at school, Sue Ellen had won over the heart of every boy in their class, as well as a good number of the eighth graders. And it was not only the boys. No, during any recess a continuous train of little girls trailed in and out of the swinging gray door to the girl's lavatory, all giggling into their blouse sleeves at some story she had told them. And whenever Geo saw her, he felt the same strange urge he had felt with Julie Volks—a long time ago. He wanted to bump into her.

After Sue Ellen had her skates screwed to the soles of her saddle shoes, the straps securely buckled across her ankles, she glided over and did a neat spinning turn in front of Geo and Louis Light. Her skirt flared up filmily and settled, without her trying to slap it down the way most girls did.

"I think I ought to have the honor of skating this first number with the host," she declared in her sultry Louisiana drawl. "I mean, if y'all don't object, Louis Light."

With a grin and courtly half-bow, Louis rolled back and gave Geo a shove into her. "There he is." He spun then and skated away, the bearinged wheels of his skates clicking lightly as he walked them in stylish rhythm around the first turn.

Sue Ellen Bolt took Geo's hands in her soft white palms (Geo was mortified by his own awkwardness and felt his face flush a bright crimson); then, arms crossed, hands tightened in a clammy clasp, they skated around and around the slick concrete rink. After a few rounds, they coasted to a stop in front of the orchestra shell to watch the Westlakes play.

Little Benny was perched on his Gretsch amplifier, earnestly picking at his guitar, fingers flying over the frets, the melody rolling out between his short dangling legs.

"My goodness, that Little Benny Westlake is divine!" Sue Ellen marveled. "Such a talent! Why, one time I went to the Grand Ole Opry up in Nashville, the famous one, and even there I didn't hear anything to equal his guitar playing."

She grabbed Geo's hands again and they skated out the rest of that number. Sue Ellen thanked him and went whirling away, to be caught and passed from boy to boy, changing each time a new tune came up. Jealously, Geo kept track of every move she made. And he could not help noticing that the one person who did not bother to take a turn with her was Louis.

It was during Hartt Westlake's solo on the violin that the accident occurred. Hartt, the tallest of the Westlakes (he had a good inch on Belle) stepped to the front of the stage and rendered "Rose of San Antonio." He held his violin's ebony chin rest against the woolly cushion of his big red beard and played beautifully, his eyes closed in solemn revery. Geo and Sue Ellen—he had swallowed fear until he was able to blurt out an invitation—were paired up again and moving with a certain spongy precision around the outside of the rink. A carload of dancers had just arrived, and one couple, in their careless haste and impatient abandon, whirled out onto the slick concrete floor. They went into a deep dip-and-drag and held it for one long moment. Geo and Sue Ellen, clothes flying, whipped past the refreshment booth. Geo saw the dancers too late—a half-naked shoulder, a red bow tie, a set of white teeth bared in a grin of pleasure. Sue Ellen never did see them. They collided. There was a maelstrom of arms and legs, with the occasional flicker of a coasting skate wheel, as the four of them went crashing into the calcimined fence, Geo on the bottom.

The Westlakes stopped playing. Or all except Hartt, who was not about to be interrupted. He doggedly continued his solo, standing at the edge of the stage under the shell, sawing at his fiddle, his bearded face widened with the rapturous smile.

Geo was suffering. He wanted out. He started clawing.

"Geo! Honey!" Sue Ellen Bolt was whispering.

"Sorry," he moaned. But he did not stop.

"Geo," she purred. "I hate to have to say this, but I believe you're being *fresh*."

Geo discovered, to his intense shame, that he was pumping on one of Sue Ellen's big breasts. He moaned and tried to shrink away.

Aiming over someone's shoulder and arm, Sue Ellen planted a wet sugary kiss squarely on his mouth. Geo felt that he was going to explode. Just then, the voice of Belle Westlake broke through the crowd and confusion, "Everybody still alive here?"

She pawed into the tangle of appendages, standing the dancers on their feet first. Then Sue Ellen. And finally Geo. She dragged him to his feet. He just stood there.

"You okay?" Belle inquired.

Geo nodded. His only pain was a hungering cramp in his right hand.

"Wind's knocked out of him," Golden observed.

Geo saw Sue Ellen casually fasten one button on the front of her peach-colored frock. A shudder passed through him like a sudden gust of fierce wind.

"Man," Louis whispered. "You sure fell for her!"

Cackling, he skated away.

Geo blinked and sat down.

As if in fantasy, Hartt Westlake continued his soulful improvisation on "Rose of San Antonio." When his idea began to peter out and it seemed he was feeling around for a new opening, Golden Westlake broke in with a shimmering run on his steel guitar. Hartt finished up and retired to the back of the stage to stroke his bushy red beard. Little Benny gathered up all the loose phraseology and shaped it neatly into a dying tremolo ending.

And the dancing began at Melody Mountain.

2.   "Yes, a medical doctor gave it to my sister," she said. "She lives back down in Baton Rouge. The book contained no news for her, so she just passed it on to me."

"What is it?" Geo crowded close and peered curiously at the powder-blue book. There was a black question mark printed on both pulpy covers, which were curled and smudged from repeated surreptitious readings and hurried concealments.

"Well, Geo," Sue Ellen said in an intimate voice that made him dizzy, "it's a private little marriage manual containing the most fascinating collection of charts and diagrams imaginable."

Louis Light reached and took it out of her hands. "It doesn't look much like the plan to any marriage ceremony to me," he muttered, unfolding an oversized chart, studying it.

"Well, it certainly isn't that veil and flowers part they always feature at the picture show," Sue Ellen stated critically. She did not give the chart more than a sidelong glance. She had spent countless hours poring over it. Instead, she ran her fingers back along her neck and fluffed her blond hair, as much a gesture of boredom as any attempt at added beauty.

Geo looked over Louis's shoulder and drew back abruptly in horror. Every admonition he had ever heard in church flashed through his mind. He thrust himself forward again. The drawings on the chart were of people in various positions of conjunction. "They're stark naked!" he managed to utter.

"Why, Geo," Sue Ellen scolded, smiling with wry superiority. "One really ought to broach the subject with a certain display of maturity. It just so happens that that little book is chock-full of the most useful factual information—without even the least hint at out-and-out smut. This is an educational text. Where is your mind?"

Geo did not tell. But he felt better instantly, knowing it was educational.

"Like what information?" Louis questioned pointedly.

"Almost anything you might want to know."

"For instance—"

"*For instance*—" Sue Ellen duplicated Louis's slightly corrosive intonation. "Times of safety. Which for me, incidentally, is right about now. I mean as near as I can calculate. Of course, you understand, a woman can never be one hundred percent sure."

Geo tried to puzzle that one through his mind.

"A woman?" Louis repeated, his voice hard with mockery and challenge.

"Why, Louis Light!" Sue Ellen cried, painfully dismayed. "Do y'all mean to say y'all can sit directly across this room from me and honestly contest that statement?"

She stood then, straightening to show her body to its best advantage. She was a soft, bosomy girl—flushed now with a mixture of pride and indignation. She wore a golden-yellow sundress—probably for the last time that season, since it was late September—one of the straps fallen casually on her arm, exposing a white nylon bra strap that cut a weighty crease in her shoulder—and pink wedge-soled house slippers trimmed with bits of smokelike fluff.

Louis stared at her. Geo's face had gone gaunt with bewilderment; he seemed prepared at any moment to shrivel into a helpless heap of char. Good, Sue Ellen Bolt beamed to herself.

"Don't they look like the most fun?" she said.

"What?" Louis spoke, still staring at her.

"I mean the pictures—all those positions."

"It looks like some kind of circus sideshow to me."

Geo wished he had thought of something like that to say. But all he could do was stare at the chart.

"Well," Sue Ellen came back smoothly. "A barrel of monkeys certainly would not be an exaggeration."

Though Geo had been her initial choice as a beau and common sense told her to stick by it, Sue Ellen was overwhelmed by Louis Light's electric powers of arousal. However, she refused to let him know of this weakness. She continued to bicker with him and to favor Geo. She explained—and lord knows why—that her daddy was out checking on some trouble at one of the oil wells and that her mother was off with another tool pusher's wife and would likely be gadding about for hours. . . . So, actually she was home alone in the trailer.

Before Geo could think his way through all of that and realize what was about to happen next, though he knew something was and that he ought to prepare himself, Louis volunteered to watch the road.

"Wait, Louis!" Geo cried. But Louis had already disappeared out into the September night, the metal door on the trailer closing behind him with a harsh click.

Sue Ellen called him honey-love, cooing softly in her quiet Louisiana voice. She reached out and touched him with her hot soggy hand. His saliva turned to cotton. She led him back into the narrow passageway and past the compact caverns of the long metal trailer. Her room was barely big enough for the narrow built-in bed, cramped closet, and crowded vanity. The close walls were plastered with photographs of Montgomery Clift and Rock Hudson that she had clipped out of slick magazines. Her cancan slip, hardened with starch and sugar, stood out like a stage cloud on the back of her door.

It seemed to Geo that Sue Ellen forgot all about those positions she had been so anxious to try. He thought maybe he should mention the chart and the educational benefits. But she kept licking her lips and moaning and preening with her shoulders and trying to pull him onto the narrow bed with her.

"Maybe—" he began shakily. He cleared his throat. "Maybe we ought to get that chart."

"No. We don't need it," she murmured, eyes half shut.

"I think I might."

"Don't worry." Her fingers were seeking his fly. "I know it by heart."

Something happened to Geo that he had never felt before. (Perhaps it was that something else he had been waiting for with Julie Volks.) His throat closed up and he grew light-headed. The room started to spin; it spun the other way. Then his hearing went dull and his ears popped, as though he had changed altitudes. He seemed to go brittle, to shatter. His heart raced. It stopped. It hung swollen and inert in his chest. Then it thundered on. He felt fire breaking out, something melting, something else exploding. Then he could not move. Each time he did, it hurt. Or it tickled.

"More!"

Geo had to hear the word a couple of times before he realized it was a command and not a question. Sue Ellen Bolt was impatiently, gluttonously, going at it herself. It hurt and tickled at the same time. Geo could not move. But he had to. Oh! It hurt—and tickled. Hurt. Tickled. Oh! Oh! Oh!

Opening his eyes weakly, Geo came face to face with Montgomery Clift's brow, wrinkled sensitively, hair tousled on his forehead. He saw that Sue Ellen was staring at the same picture, transfixed.

"Don't!" he cried.

"More!" she grunted hoarsely.

Geo turned his head: Rock Hudson smiled down at him from the other wall. "Oh, don't!" he pleaded.

"More! More! *More!*"

"Don't, dammit!" He ground his teeth.

Sue Ellen was the toughest girl Geo had ever seen. Her powerful southern arms were locked in a tight circle over his back. He thought she was going to squeeze him in two before he broke free and leaped away from her.

Then, panting, grabbing his clothes, not caring about the change that spilled on the floor, he sprang to the door. Sue Ellen was hanging halfway out of bed, clawing futilely for him.

"Don't move!" he gasped. "I'll get Louis." He spun and went stumbling and bumping down the corridor like a steel ball shot from a pinball machine.

"Hurry, Louis!" he urged, stuffing his rubbery legs into his pants. "Hurry and do something before she comes after me."

Louis went into the trailer and shut the door.

Outside, standing in the moonlight, watching the road, trying to catch his breath and cool down some, Geo heard a muffled shriek, then a prolonged squeal. It was a sowlike sound, one of the worst sounds he had ever heard in his life. Louis, he thought, don't kill her. Then he asked himself what difference it made. He hoped Louis would kill her. But he kept hearing the sound over and over and concluded finally that that was probably the way it was with women: Sue Ellen Bolt had been undone. And Geo was glad.

Nonetheless, dressed and back on her feet, she was just the same as always, her natural luxuriant self. Sue Ellen. She shuffled around the living room in her pink bedroom slippers, serving them ginger ale, salting her own so she could watch it fizz and feel the bubbles burst in her face. She lighted a filter cigarette and did an unctuous gliding turn onto the couch. She blew out a thin stream of smoke.

"I have to turn on the fan and eat literally whole packages of Sen-Sen because mother swears smoking will stunt my growth. But I don't know about that. It doesn't seem to have done a whole lot of harm to date. And I've been doing it for years—on the sly."

"Time to go," Louis said, emptying his ginger ale.

"Yeah." Geo followed suit, the pop burning up in his nose.

Sue Ellen saw them to the door and bade a cheery, "Good night, gentlemen. Y'all take care now. Hear?"

As soon as they were a safe distance along the road, Louis looked back over his shoulder and said, "Keep your fingers crossed."

"Why?"

"Just in case."

"What?"

"There's an accident."

"Accident?" Geo questioned, knowing there was something to the apprehension he felt.

"Those books, Geo. They're not always sure fire."

"They're not?" Geo said. "Then what?"

"Then she might be knocked up," Louis said. He paused, then added, "Knocked up tighter than a drum."

For a moment there were no sounds except the faltering of Geo's footsteps and a host of crickets competing somewhere in the trees. Geo, his narrow face drawn, came to a complete frozen halt and stared at Louis. He was confused.

"That means pregnant," Louis said. "And don't go acting like you don't know what *that* means."

"Pregnant." Geo tried to swallow. "Knocked up, huh." He tried to swallow again. His eyes smarted. "I got it."

"So one of us would have to marry her."

"Marry—" Geo stiffened. The other words were not so hard to get used to. But *marry*. "You sure?"

"Sure I'm sure. . . . And you know who she asked to skate with."

"It was my birthday!" Geo protested.

"Good night, gentlemen," Louis sang, mocking him. "Good night, gentlemen. . . ."

3.   "Say, Amos, you heerd 'bout Kingfish?"

Geo heard the program starting and scooped a fat square of chocolate cake up in his hand. But he bumped his elbow on the refrigerator door and dropped the cake. It hit the floor—icing down. He sighed and suppressed a curse. So far, his thirteenth year had been easily his worst. His whole body was out of whack. He tripped over anything. Even things only remotely in his way. He dropped everything. He was always hungry, always eating, always stuffing his face with food. Yet he did not get fat. He seemed capable only of growing arms and legs. "Dangling," Louis's Grandpa Light had described him the week before, "just arms and legs dangling from that one long gut." He stooped now and scraped the cake off the linoleum with the knife, leaving icing in a wide smear clear across one square tile.

"Sssssssst!"

He spun and looked at the dark blank of the screen door.

"Sssssssst!"

"Louis?"

"Sssssst!"

"That you, Louis?"

"Sssssst!"

"What's wrong? Come on in." He put his face to the screen.

"Can't tell you here. Come out."

Geo followed Louis's form, which he glimpsed only momentarily before it disappeared around the corner of the house. He wished he had stopped long enough to get another piece of cake. He could not eat this one. And he was still hungry. They hurried along the shadowed path etched lightly with pale moonlight, through the yellowing cottonwoods and box elders, past the mailbox, to the road.

"They took her to the hospital," Louis announced, his teeth gleaming in the light from the thin sliver of moon.

"Hospital?"

"Yes."

"Her?" Geo cocked his head. "Who?"

"Sue Ellen. Who do you think?"

Sue Ellen Bolt. Geo repeated her name through the drying phlegm in his throat and mouth. His narrow face slowly drained and assumed the blue-white color, shape, and texture of an ice cube. He wanted to ask why. But he could not push the word up into the dry cavern of his mouth.

"What's this?" Louis reached out and broke off a piece of the chocolate cake. He munched calmly. Finally he took the rest of the cake out of Geo's woodenly outstretched palm.

Geo brushed the moist leftover crumbs on his Levi's. "Don't eat that," he said slowly.

"I already did."

"I dropped it on the floor."

"Why didn't you tell me?" Louis demanded.

"I just did."

"You prick!" Louis burst, turning his head and spitting.

"Ditto."

Louis calmed. His voice assumed a ring of crystalline inno- cence, and he asked, "What're you going to do?"

"Well, I—" Geo began, then thundered: "*Me!*"

He measured Louis, watching his eyes blink once—not out of guilt or embarrassment or anything else that could have been construed as decent, but as a simple action to clear the lenses, the lids sliding down, lifting, revealing the same expression of unfathomable depth.

"Think she'll tell?" Louis asked.

"That we done it to her?"

"No—that's probably history by now. I mean which one it is."

There was a brief pause while Geo thought that one over.

"Which is what, Louis?"

"What! Don't be a dope. Which is the father."

Geo echoed the word, his monotone dulling it. "How could she know? I mean for sure? Both of us . . . It could be . . ." But he was remembering what he knew Louis was also remembering: Sue Ellen Bolt had danced twice on that birthday night with him and none of the time with Louis. And he was also remembering something that Louis did not even know: that one mushy kiss she had given him while they were pinned under that pile of dancers and he was doing that to her titty. It was a stain on his innocence as wide as the white patch of calcimine paint that had never washed out of the new blue shirt he had been wearing that night.

"It looks to me like she's got herself a choice," Louis said, delib- erately turning his head so the moonlight fell weakly on his features. "Hasn't she?"

"You made her sound that way, Louis."

"What way?"

"Like a sow taking on a boar hog."

"I don't think she cares about that—not now." There was not even the slightest shading of guilt in Louis's voice.

"What're we going to do?"

"I suppose we ought to call her up and get the story straight from the source and not wait around for the first big wave of gossip." Sometimes Geo thought Louis sounded just like a movie.

They could not call from Louis's house. The phone was in the living room, where his grandpa was snoozing behind the first section of the Salt Lake *Tribune* and his grandmother was reading a mystery novel. Geo's phone, however, was in the kitchen, and his folks were still staring at the front of the radio, trying to visualize the antics of the Negroes whose voices they were hearing through the fancy woodwork and cloth mesh of the grille.

"I'll keep them busy while you put in the call," Louis offered.

"Louis, I think you ought to do it. You know the procedure."

"What procedure? It's your phone." Then, in one chicken move, Louis walked on into the safety zone of the living room. Geo stood there, burning. Then, he heard Louis let out a too-loud laugh, an obvious beginning of the cover-up, and he automatically picked up the phone. Speaking quickly, he said the number to the operator. He pitched his voice deep and tried for an easy, mature, southern drawl.

A nurse said they had rules about calls to patients in Miss Bolt's state.

State! The word rang with mystery. They probably had her locked in or something. Geo reached and supported himself against the cabinet. "Well, y'all this here's her father." He spoke with stiff authority, holding his sweaty palm clawed around the mouthpiece. There was a moment's delay.

"Geo Seagram! You old sneaky! This is a surprise!"

"What'd you say?" he blurted.

"I said, you great big silly, this is certainly an unexpected and pleasant surprise."

"No—I mean what did you say to them?"

"To whom?"

"Them."

"Geo, what on earth are you referring to?"

"Did you tell them who it is?"

"Did I tell them who what is?"

"Yes. Did you?"

"Wow. I must say, y'all have me plunged in the most lightheaded state of confusion imaginable."

"Did you tell them who did it?" he demanded, his voice breaking.

"Wowee! I honestly don't know whether it's you, Geo, or the drugs they've been giving me . . ."

Drugs! Geo's body was suddenly gripped in icy panic. They were probably shooting her full of truth serum. Then he heard her say:

"Know what? I've been lying here thinking about y'all."

"What about Louis?"

"Louis? No . . . no, I guess I haven't really given him a thought." She moaned heavily into the phone. "I'm so glad y'all called. They're going to take it out in the morning."

Geo stiffened. "Out of where?"

"My little old sore tummy."

"What?"

"Why, don't y'all know? It's my appendix."

"Appendix?"

"Yes. That itty-bitty thing stuck to the side of my intestine to serve no conceivable good purpose except maybe to make a body suffer a lot of pain and go through a devil of a scare."

Geo heard her repeat his name in her lilting Louisiana voice, but he set the phone back in the cradle anyway. He stood there in a state of mild shock, a little surprised to find himself at home, in the kitchen; and the shadow that had clouded his narrow face began to lift.

Louis slipped out into the kitchen. "What're you grinning about?"

Geo assumed what he thought was the appropriate theatrical expression of high seriousness.

"I'm afraid," he anounced. "Louis, I'm afraid you're the one."

Louis Light did a funny thing: he smiled, too. Louis smiled not in the way he would at hearing a joke. But he smiled in a way that seemed to go much deeper.

Geo frowned. "What's so funny?"

"I've ruined one."

"Ruined? One what?"

"A girl, Geo. I think I really got her."

So they were both smiling. The one because he knew he was not. The other because he thought he was.

PART TWO

5

The Light Method:

Part One—An Introduction to the Formal

Characteristics (Theory, Technique, etc.)

⁂⁑⁂⁑⁂⁑⁂⁑⁂⁑⁂⁑⁂⁑⁂⁑⁂

1945

1.   It should not have been worse than the ship. But it was.
Not the musty soldier closeness of the clicking cars jolting on the
rails. He was accustomed to that. To that and to the utter anonym-
ity of everything except his rank. It was the blur of the actual
continent, which he remembered as being reasonably solid, this
land not quite under him but pouring at him, threatening to
swallow him—the whole thing mollified to the point of being
bearable by the dull sameness of the worn coach. Now, his mute
features were so textured that what should have come off as that
blank look he had cultivated and had always flashed at a passing
destination were worn to the threadbare appearance of wearied
apprehension and—yes—even fear.

"Hey, Captain, what's the idea clutching all your gear like you
was going to lose it?" grinned a friendly corporal from across the
aisle. "We're at least a hundred miles out of Chicago by now."

"I'm thinking," Willie muttered absently.

"You sure go to a hell of a lot of bother," the corporal winked.

"I'm thinking, soldier, and you'd better watch that lip."

"Yes, sir."

Yes, Willie was thinking. About his possessions (in order to avoid thinking about his destination, his destiny), thinking so hard, in fact, that he felt a ring of fire under his stiff collar and the sweat from his armpits flowing down his ribs like melting wax from a candle. There was a sword—his own, unused—and a Jap's head carved from a coconut, and the Light Album, as he called his collection of photographs. This last item, consisting of page after page of glossy, eight-by-ten memories of the war, was most significant. Mentally, he leafed through them. A picture of a young Harvard philosopher named Stone, Robert Stone, dying. A pilot (he had climbed a tree with a rifle and his camera while a flight of Zeroes dropped down and strafed the camp; as he shot, mostly photographs, he had heard the chattering of bullets picking leaves all around him) giving a buck-toothed yellow grin of glee between the curved mullions of the cockpit. A line of GIs at the door of a grass hut, holding candy bars and C rations; and inside a pair of gigantic wrinkled knees poking up on either side of a blur of white buttocks and a couple of OD-clothed legs. In another, nearly a hundred shattered bodies lay on a beach, nationality and rank and any evidence of final thought or wish obscure against the Mediterranean sunset. Two fat French peasants were petrified in the urgent clutch of their final copulation. And the last picture in the Light Album showed a bodiless head in a sterile bomb crater: it might have been a dirt- and grass-stained golf ball in a sand trap. It seemed to say nothing about itself. But it did have a lot to say about war. If anyone cared to listen.

Just prior to the landing of his troopship, Willie Light had gone to the rail and pitched his camera into the sea. He watched it fall, the strap like a ribbon, and saw the splash. There were, he knew, some painful things awaiting him that he could not capture on film.

Suddenly, he could no longer stand the same duplicate of the same hill and the everlasting same drying color of the late summer countryside, which poured past him like lumpy khaki paint. So he stopped a porter who was sidling along the crowded aisle.

"Porter, can you tell me the name of the next town?"

"Council Tree, Iowa, suh."

"I want off."

"But Cap'm, yo pass taken you all the way to Salt Lake City. And we ain't even startin' to get close to that yet."

"I'll write a new pass."

"T'won't be genuine." The porter shook his head. "Besides— why'd you ever want off here? This country ain't fit for human beings. Ain't nothin' but maybe a few stalks a cawn and wind enough to make 'em rustle."

But no. There was not even the wind. Unless perhaps the slow swirling wake of the train pulling out of Council Tree, shifting some anonymous trash, paper and leaves, for a few feet along the siding could be counted as one. An empty baggage truck, standing awkwardly on its high, spoked wheels, was nosed against the paint-thirsting, ship-lap siding of the square, once-yellow depot.

COUNCIL TREE   POP. 704

A woman, wearing (and these were the only two summer fabrics he could call to mind, since he knew it was not cotton and would not be wool) a silk or organdy dress, the hem swishing around her ankles, hurried expectantly onto the platform. Seeing him standing there, she seemed completely taken back.

"Oh!"

Willie nodded and reached politely for his overseas cap. His black hair stood bunched in a travel-weary hackle on the crown of his head. His nose was straight, narrow, a white shadow of cartilage showing down the bridge. His eyes were a glassy gray color, the skin at their corners wrinkled years beyond his age by a hyperoptic squint.

The woman touched her flattened palm to her lips, then let it drop lightly to her breast. "Well. You aren't who I was expecting at all—are you?"

"Well—I don't know," Willie said, dumbfounded. "No. I don't hardly see how I could be. I don't think."

"No. Certainly I would know him. Certainly I would know my own brother." She laughed a tinkling laugh and then paused to draw an almost apologetic breath. "His name was—no, I mean *is* Robbie Rydell, a private. But you're more, aren't you. You're more than that." She gave his uniform a fleeting scrutiny, which obviously left her knowing no more.

"Yes." A smile flickered through his initial expression of bewilderment. "Yes, I'm a captain. Captain Willie Light."

"Captain Willie Light," she repeated, lyrically. "I'm so delighted to know you, Captain. I am Vera Rhodes." She inclined her head slightly and he noticed, for the first time, the small swatch of white netting and blue velvet cornflowers that constituted her summer hat, a reminder to him of how far fashion could take nature and need. "Light? I don't recall ever hearing that name around here. Are you from Council Tree?"

"Oh, no. I just stopped off. For a rest. Yes, a little time to think."

"Of course." She seemed to understand it better than he did. "Of course you would."

"Mrs. Rhodes, could you direct me to a rooming house?"

"A rooming house?" she repeated vaguely. "Yes. There is such a place. I would hardly recommend it, though. The stories I've heard! No—I really couldn't. What? Are you hunting a room?"

"Yes." He wanted to shake himself. It was not real. It seemed they were totally unable to reach each other, that in the air between Mrs. Rhodes and himself the words broke apart, becoming isolated syllables and even single letters, their relative meaning and value somehow lost.

"You could use Robbie's room," she offered. "However, if he . . . no, I mean *when* he comes back, then you would—ah—"

"Yes. I understand."

"Good."

And Willie Light found himself following the swishing silk or organdy dress and the little scrap of expensive millinery perched on a high stylish wave of brunette hair—and still somehow escaping comedy—around the depot to a long-snouted white Buick coupe parked at the curb.

One wall was solid with books, an imposing imbrication of leather and buckram bindings embossed with impressive-looking black and gold lettering. The desk looked as though it had been abandoned no longer ago than the previous day (he decided that Mrs. Rhodes dusted it daily, replacing each pencil, sheet of paper, and book in precisely the same spot she had found it). He dropped his gear beside the bed and clawed off his overseas cap.

"Now then," Mrs. Rhodes sighed happily. "Is this all right? Do you think you can be comfortable here?"

"Yes. How much is the rent?"

"Rent? Rent! Oh, yes. I hadn't thought about rent. We can discuss it with my husband when he comes home. He owns a lumber company. The M. T. Rhodes Company. His name's Martin."

2. "Republican or Democrat?" Martin Rhodes inquired, thrusting out his meaty right hand.

"I haven't given it much thought," Willie admitted. "The last two or three years I've been worrying too much about whether I'd be alive—or dead—to think too much about politics." He saw Vera flinch and stare out through the white curtains that hung like a film over the living room windows—thinking, no doubt, of Robbie Rydell.

"Same answer, son. Same answer."

What? Willie asked himself. What was? To what?

"Republican, myself. Uphold a rigid platform of change, progress, and peace. All geared to a definite plan of action." Martin Rhodes paused to consider, with raised eyebrows and a thoughtful hook to his mouth, the significance of what he had just said. He was rotund, with red, veiny cheeks and a prominent chin, undershot by a second and third, like a gradual terracing, down to his tie. He explained that he had been a few years too old for the service. But he had done his part. At home. "Oh, you'll come around, Light. Right now, about this room. We need to set a rent. Hmm. Well, how's a few bucks a week? That sound okay?"

Willie hesitated. The thought crossed his mind that during the time he had been out of the States, yanked from one theater of the war to the other, what Martin Rhodes had just said might have acquired some definite value and meaning. "How much's that?"

"Oh—I don't know. We'll have to see. It all depends, I suppose, on Vera."

"And Robbie," Vera interjected quietly.

"Yes, Robbie." Martin cleared his throat, the wrinkles above his tie shaking gelatinously.

"One thing," Willie said. He watched Martin's eyebrows go up again. "You ever think about changing the plugs in that Buick?"

"What's that?"

"It'd run smoother. Probably improve your gas mileage. Might just need cleaning, reset the gap."

"What? You think they're dirty?"

"Well—that and the timing's off. Just a hair."

"Do you do that?" Martin asked.

"I've done it."

"I guess I have noticed something sort of slow about it. But it's thirty-five miles to the closest garage a man can trust."

Willie nodded. "Why don't I have a look at it in the morning. I'll see what I can do to straighten it out."

Alone. Finally. Willie felt that whatever it was that had plagued him on the train was at least slowing down some, slowing down and losing much of its menace and immediacy. He went to the window. The lawn in back was halved by a path; a row of roses bloomed along a fence of white pickets; beyond the yard was a peaceful wooded gully, a green knoll, an endless sky. It was all very quiet and calm and clear.

He noticed a book open on the desk, *The Writings of Thoreau* . . . *Walden*. A passage at the bottom of the right-hand page had been carefully underscored with fine red pencil along a ruler edge: "I went to the woods because I wished to live deliberately, to front only the essential facts of life, and see if I could learn what it had to teach, and not, when I come to die, discover I had not lived. . . ." Willie winced and repeated the final few phrases aloud.

Two days later, Willie Light had read all of *Walden*. (He had had an interruption from Martin Rhodes who marveled about the difference in the Buick coupe. Personally, Willie had never cared for a Buick; he hated the way the transmission whined; but he was satisfied that it ran at least a hundred percent smoother. There was another interruption from the neighbor next door who was willing to pay for a tune-up on his Chevy. Another man watched him work—another customer.) Time and again, parts of *Walden* reminded Willie of that winter he had spent all of his school hours in the shack on the homestead trapping muskrats and an occasional beaver, stretching and salting the hides, stashing the money from their sale in a Prince Albert tin, then sitting for long hours by the round stove, alone, reading the books his sisters checked out from the school library for him (they got gold stars; he had the stories, the myths, the philosophies). This Thoreau, he concluded, was a pretty damn sensible fellow about a lot of things, even if sometimes he did seem too smart to make them clear; a lot of the things that were Greek to Thoreau—and probably understandable—were merely "Greek" to Willie. Then, too, Thoreau was not always right. But Willie did not care about the bad places, when he read things like: "The true harvest of my daily life is somewhat as tangible and discernible as the tints of morning or evening. It is a little stardust caught, a segment of rainbow which I have touched."

He brooded over certain chapters and passages—even as he dropped his ear to the carburetor intake on the neighbor's Chevy and started twisting the screwdriver a fraction of a turn to the left—until the following Monday morning. Then he decided he would go to work.

"So you did a lot of building over there in the war, huh?"

"That's right."

The contractor, a man named Gebhardt (Martin Rhodes had recommended him, had recommended Willie, too), braced his scuffed half-Wellington on the bumper of his pickup and looked across the fender at Willie. Gebhardt was bald, thick-necked, with short arms, fat callused hands, and shelly, battered nails. "I reckon you built stout."

"Built for about a thousand years," Willie declared, shaking his head, remembering.

"That right?" Gebhardt's pouchy eyes narrowed.

"Yep. The thing'd usually make it through the first bomb run, maybe a whole day. Sometimes a week—if the enemy happened to be pretty busy somewhere else. If anything happened to last longer than a week we painted it."

"Painted, too. I'll be . . ."

"Yes. We'd paint the things we didn't care about anymore. Paint'd hardly have time to dry on the damn bridge or whatever it was before they'd spot it and hurry over to try and blow it up."

"Opposite psychology, huh?"

"Something."

"Well," Gebhardt's forehead wrinkled, his brows bristling thickly. "Yes. Yes, that's smart. Listen, Light, I've got two jobs going right now. Another one starting up in a week. Things are looking pretty damn good. I'm spread between here and Rocky Fjord and I could use me a foreman. I need a smart man with punch and drive." He brought his fist down on the hood of the pickup. "How about it?"

Willie turned his left palm up, doubling his fingers in a line, and slanted a look down at the nails, as though after actually coming right out and asking for the job he might refuse to take it. On some obscure minor principle.

He sighed. "I guess," his voice trailed off for a moment. "Yes, I guess I could use the job."

3.   "I thought you'd be downtown."

"Good heavens, no! I'm nervous as a cat," Vera said, switching her slight shoulders and tilting her head. "Martin's at City Hall. He promised to call as soon as he knows anything definite. Willie, I'll bet you're just freezing, riding that bike of yours out there in the cold. Come in the kitchen and have a cup of coffee."

"All right, if it's made."

"I think there's probably just about enough left."

Willie knew the pot would barely have finished percolating,

the glass bubble on top still cloudy, clearing. He knew this as well as he had known she would not be downtown; and why. But he was accustomed to Vera's games. It was the same when he mentioned that an obviously fresh dress looked nice. She would shoot a blushing look down at it and say, oh, it was just some old thing she had put on to do the housework in—but thank you. He no longer had to look at Vera to know the expression on her face. How often he had looked out from under a car and talked only to her slippers and known precisely the look that would be pulling at her small features. She stood on one foot, changing, but seeming to favor the left. He knew, too, that everything she had said in the months he had been here in Council Tree was leading slowly up to something else.

Business had built up in almost every way. There was a Pontiac in the garage for a tune. A DeSoto waiting outside for paint. He had cornered the mechanical work for the whole town—people were beginning to bring their vehicles in from the country. He worked a solid seven days and most evenings. Five days for Gebhardt and at least another five for himself. At least ten days a week.

Tonight, though, he was finding it difficult to go out to the garage. Something was getting to him. Riding home on the bike, detouring past the Greyhound depot for a box of parts from Des Moines, feeling the biting air on his face, catching the promise of a frost in its smell, he was reminded of hunting. And that left him in a state of confusion—since he had felt at the end of the war that he could never again pick up a firearm. Never fire a shot and watch the blood flow.

"It'll seem sort of funny to have a mayor in the house."

"Now, Willie," Vera cautioned. "We can't count our chickens . . ."

Well, someone was counting something. Sure as hell. Two days ago he had come across a catalog opened to a page of hardwood gavels. One, of walnut stock, with a fourteen-carat plate for name and office, was circled and the order form filled out.

Vera brought an envelope from the sill above the sink. "A letter for you."

While she poured the coffee, fresh, red-brown, Willie read Bernie Schwartz's letter, thoughtfully rubbing his forefinger along one side of his narrow straight nose. Early in his second month as foreman for Gebhardt, when he had discovered that his pay checks were accumulating far more rapidly than he could spend them and that his sideline business was growing to noticeable proportions, and since he was working all the time and seemed to have no other immediate wants or needs, Willie had remembered something Bernie had yelled to him from the motorcycle sidecar one morning as they were bouncing and slithering across the rain-soaked French countryside:

"Before this frigging war came along, Light, I was making it. We were both working, my wife and I, living in a little apartment across the river in Queens, a cheapie, but nice enough, and I was sinking every goddam penny I could get my hands on into the market. Was I building a portfolio! Then out busts this lousy goddam war and wham: Greetings, Schwartz! Shit!" He had paused to wipe the last spatter of mud off his face with an already thickly caked sleeve. "But I'll be back. And I'll be moving up. You watch, Light. I'm going to have my pinkie pressed right on the pulse of that great big mother of a nation. Just remember, if you ever want to put some dough to work, Light, you just let me know. . . ."

Willie had reminded him about the *sir* and the *captain* he kept leaving off and they rode through heavy machine-gun fire to the crest of the next hill.

So he had sent Bernie a money order for the amount he had saved from his Army pay, which was almost all of it, except for the part the government automatically kept out for Gloria and Louis, plus his poker winnings, which were more considerable than the pay, and the three hundred and ninety dollars he had saved here.

The first letter back from Bernie had been in his own cryptic hand, the words cocked at such an angle of awkwardness on the lusterless Woolworth bond that they actually seemed on the point of sliding off the right-hand margin. A few weeks later, Bernie had a letterhead and the message was typed—poorly, with evidence of pain, a couple of erasure holes showing clear through the paper. Then after that the typing suddenly became perfect (*BS/emb* in the lower left-hand corner). The next letterhead, appearing within the space of a few weeks, read

Schwartz Inc. and the paper snapped with the crispness of rag bond. Today, Willie noticed there had been still another change: *Schwartz and Geller, Inc.* Bernie was writing a special letter to introduce Sol Geller, the new partner; writing, he said, because Willie was one of the young firm's best clients. Willie shook his head at that line. He had seen no evidence of anything yet. As far as he knew, Bernie might have been stuffing his money in a hole.

"So—I'm probably losing Martin, too," Vera lamented. It was the first thing she had said after sitting down, as though the monologue that had been going on inside her head had, at that moment, finally reached the surface and become conversation. She looked up from her cup, her entire face a shadow of gloom.

"Only a part of the time," Willie assured her, attempting to alter the somber tone of things.

"Part time?"

"There can't be that much for the mayor of a town under one thousand to do, can there?"

Vera sighed yes and fell silent for a short time, finishing the final paragraph or so inside.

"You know, Willie," she began, after a pause. "I'm a little older than you . . ."

"Umm." He let his mouth linger over the warm coffee, feeling the steam beading the whiskers on his upper lip.

"Have you ever thought of that?"

"Crossed my mind maybe."

"That all?"

"Umm."

"Willie, what're you going to do with yourself?"

"What are you driving at, Vera?" But he knew, and he knew she would not say. Because she never had, never in all the numerous times she had tried to.

"I mean *ever*."

"Ever?"

"You didn't stop permanently in Council Tree, did you?"

"No. I just stopped to let the new wear off."

"It's been four months."

"And eight days—no, nine days." He looked at his watch. "Yes, nine almost to the hour."

"And it's taken that long?"

"It's not over."

"Won't you ever go back to your family?"

"What family? That dissolved before I was hardly out of town. I guess it went just before I left."

"What about your son? What'll become of him?"

"Louis? He'll make out. Boys have a way of doing all right when they're left by themselves." Then as if in defense of himself, he added, "Doing better, in fact."

Willie had to smile now, remembering his ma's letters in France. She kept him posted on Louis. The boy was fine, she said. And he always felt a grip of something get hold of the whole letter, pulling her style into a cramp, jamming the letters close, when she assured him that the boy was not becoming a Fulton any more than America was ever going to belong to Hitler or those Japs. He was a Light, poor thing, and would be right on to the grave.

"But doesn't he need love?" Vera was saying. "Robbie did. I gave it to him." These last words seemed to have been sucked out of her mouth before she could articulate them properly. They left her gaping.

"Vera, I don't think I know what that is." He watched her face smooth back to its normal plainness. "What is love?"

"Love?" she repeated. "Well, Robbie explained it once. Robbie had a way of putting things. He said love is like rain on flowers. It can tear us apart and nourish us at the same time. Flowers in the rain." Vera seemed suddenly upset. Her voice quaked. It seemed she was wildly reaching out for the present. "Can't you— can't you do something about your family?"

"Nope. A friend of mine, who's studying to be a lawyer, said I'd better give up on that family. And I don't believe I want to get myself another one right now."

"But, Willie, maybe it would go better this time."

"Well, maybe. Anyway, I'd sure be there to watch what it did do—one way or the other." He shook his head. "No. I've been thinking more along the lines of organizing a religion or starting a new war. I want to be sure of my chances. . . ." Then he looked her in the eyes. "But what you started to say, Vera, was that you're some years older than myself. . . . Didn't you say that?"

"Why, yes. Yes, I guess I did."

"All right, then. Let me say this, you don't look it. Even if I chose to think along those lines. And if when you climb the stairs to"—he almost said "my"—"Robbie's room, like I'm thinking you'd like to do and have been aching to do for some time, if you'll just kindly switch out the light, we'll try and forget who we are in the dark. And nothing will ever have to go beyond that." Try and forget, he was thinking, so maybe we can remember.

"Why—Mr. Light!"

He went directly to the room and picked up Ralph Waldo Emerson's "Self-Reliance," which he had begun reading the previous evening after installing a U-joint in a Ford. He read "Life only avails, not the having lived," when he heard the first creak of the stairs and felt an icy thrill which he could not easily understand.

"Life only avails, not the having . . ."

Another stair cried out.

"Life only avails . . ."

Creak.

"Life only . . ."

"Life . . ."

A satinlike white hand slipped around the door frame. Slender fingers found the switch, hesitated, and pushed it down. *Click!* Then, in the early winter dark, Willie heard the hiss of a falling wrap and saw the white flesh of a naked body stealing into the room. It came not slowly, but with the speed and certainty of someone who knew, either from habit or memory, the exact number of steps to the bed.

"Mr. Light? Willie? It's I."

6

The Light Method:
Part Two—Application and Results

❀✲❀✲❀✲❀✲❀✲❀✲❀✲❀✲❀✲❀✲❀

1947

1. There was a word for it: growth. Everything was growing. Expanding. The whole country seemed to be bulging and
cramping all out of proportion. There was something frightening
about it. Willie could almost feel the pains as everything strained
to become more.

Martin Rhodes was moving with it. The M. T. Rhodes Company was already established in Rocky Fjord. Martin had bought
property for two more stores and yards in towns within a fifty-
mile radius; he and Gebhardt were already pouring over the
plans for building the first of these. Rumor had it—Martin only
smiled when Willie mentioned he had been hearing it—that a
movement was afoot to recruit the mayor for the GOP half of the
ticket for the state senate seat from that district. Martin had a
new Buick, Dynaflow, though it still whined. His laughter was
mellowing.

Willie, himself, had not exactly been idle. He was now handling the major part of Gebhardt's building projects, while Geb-

hardt concentrated most of his efforts on bidding for bigger things—roads, a pipeline that stretched halfway across Illinois, a new hospital in the county seat (Martin, of course, was being useful here). Willie's salary had been increased as Gebhardt recognized his abilities and the danger of letting him even consider breaking out on his own. And there were incentive payments. In addition, Willie continued to tinker nightly in the garage behind the house. He dragged drop cords and trays of snap-on tools under the automobiles and talked frequently to Vera's restless slippers. Except on the nights when the town council met, the G.O.P. gathered, or Martin went to Rocky Fjord to have dinner with the Lions International. There was by now hardly a vehicle in Council Tree that had not been somehow improved by the sagacious judgment of Willie's ear and the perfection of his touch.

Money grew. At least Willie's money did. The initial four thousand, seven hundred and ninety dollars he had sent off to Bernie had been invested, collected dividends, split, doubled, and just generally fattened and bloated under the encouragement of the Jew's plump fingers. And Willie, having nothing yet to spend it on, since he maintained a bicycle and drove the company pickup with a two way radio that Gebhardt provided for him on the job, kept sending more and more money, hardly aware of why he was doing it, never having either thought or cared about having a purpose.

"Trust me," Bernie would whine over the phone, in a letter.

"Of course," Willie would reply. "Of course."   '

2.   Willie would have known her a mile away. She moved with the same smooth undulant precision she had always had, as though she were trodding a perpetual red carpet which continuously, plushly unrolled before her, according to the dictates of her capricious will. He froze, becoming a rigid oneness with the frame of the bicycle he rode to and from work (claiming to him-

self that he could not afford a car yet, a car or clothes or anything
else of extravagance, claiming these things in the same attitude
of matter-of-factness he used in signing over three of the four
weekly checks he received from Gebhardt each month plus
everything he took in from his automobile business to Schwartz,
Geller, and Levi, Inc.). He made a stiff, unnatural turn off the
sidewalk, parked the bike against a Dutch elm, stood on the seat,
and fled up into the tree's winter-bare branches with as much absolute purpose and nonchalance as he could possibly muster on
such short notice. He chose a place affording the greatest amount
of cover, which was—at best—meager, and peered back up the
block.

Gloria approached the mayor's house, consulted the scrap of
paper in her hand (like a butterfly she was gradually torturing to
death) then followed the unspooling of the regal carpet right up
to the door.

Goddammit, he thought. He struck his fist lightly against the
tree. Goddammit, he could not blame Brad. He could not blame
him at all. She had probably pushed him into it. Willie shook his
head. He remembered how it was. Knees first. A solid pressure.
Nothing but melting innocence showing in her eyes—if maybe
there was something like hunger on her parted lips. . . . He
caught himself clasping the branches too tightly, bark crackling,
flaking off in his hands.

Even the cold precariousness of the tree could not stop the
memory of the night he first got Gloria. I? He stuttered in amaze-
ment. I got her! Ha! After all those months of being slapped silly
for coyly touching at a breast or trying to move the fingers of one
hand between her legs, he had looked up one night to see her
standing beside the car, stripping. Her fingers picked down a row
of buttons; she let her blouse fall on the seat. She stepped out of
her skirt. Reaching behind her back, she unsnapped her bra and
swung it over the top of the open door. She hooked her thumbs
and forefingers delicately in the elastic of her panties. She
paused. Something rustled in the night. She slipped them off.

Then she stood there.

Completely naked.

Willie watched. Helpless. Teeth feeling like so many wooden

pegs driven in spaced rows in his gums. Until his right knee started to twitch. . . .

The sharp sound of her knuckles rapping on the door sent an echo through him. Once again he began to feel the wind around the leafless branches of the old elm.

All afternoon he had been thinking of Kierkegaard, recalling parts of the journals he had found among Robbie's books. And he caught himself thinking of Kierkegaard now, thinking . . .

She should have guessed. But when she had seen the mink collar, her first thought had been of another collection. Red Cross. Polio. Something with a longer name. Scientific. Commercial Latin. It gave all those ladies who had gained so much experience peddling victory bonds something to do. And their first stop was always the mayor's house: they meant to get back every cent of that measly salary. . . . Except Vera Rhodes did not recognize this young woman. Only now, seeing the rest of her, the deceptive beauty, the thin veneer of innocence—over god knows what—did she realize what it might be. And, in fact, was.

"Yes?"

"Mrs. Rhodes?"

"That's right."

"May I come in?"

She seemed to force herself in, pressing Vera back into the cozy warmth of her own house.

"I'm Gloria Light."

"How do you do."

Vera tried to refrain from looking at the old pendulating clock on the mantel and to keep from thinking about the pot of coffee that had barely stopped bubbling. Nor did she offer to take the young woman's coat. Because it was almost time for Willie to come home.

"I've obviously come hunting Willie."

"Obviously?"

"I'm his wife."

"Wife?" Vera repeated—pleased with the subtle quality of her performance.

"Oh?" Gloria raised her brows. "Hasn't Willie ever mentioned me?"

"Well—not that I can remember."

"Then it might interest you to know that he has a son as well."

"Oh, yes. Willie spoke frequently about the boy."

"With a son, wouldn't he have to have a wife? Or something female? Doesn't that stand to reason?"

"It certainly does seem to, doesn't it? But I never really gave it a thought. Willie was such an unusual person."

"Was?"

"Yes," Vera chimed. "You see—Willie's no longer here. He left."

"When?"

"About a week ago."

She watched the young woman's pretty face fall slightly, catch itself with incredible resilience, and resume the powdery neutrality of its smile. And for a moment she felt sorry for her.

"Naturally, he left no forwarding address."

"None."

"And left without paying his rent, I suppose."

"You'd have to speak with my husband about that. Were you thinking of taking care of it for him?" she asked. She observed the first stages of an explosion, which was once again muffled and absorbed before it could break out.

"Mrs. Rhodes, do you go along with the concept set forth in the Bible that woman was created as a helpmate for man?"

"Why—why, yes, Mrs. Light. I think I do."

"Well, I don't," Gloria stated bluntly. "God was disappointed by the mess he made of man. So he turned around and improved the design. And man's been trying to ruin us ever since. Out of jealous hatred. But God fixed that. He gave us something else: the capacity for children. That's our greatest weapon."

"Weapon? I don't think I follow you, Mrs. Light."

"Yes, I mean weapon. They can't win, Mrs. Rhodes. They really can't win."

"But that's not what the book says."

"Of course it isn't. You know why?"

"No—I'm afraid I don't."

"That book was written by men."

For another brief moment, Vera Rhodes liked Gloria Light. She liked her, in fact, right up to the moment she saw her turn at the end of the sidewalk and start in the direction from which she knew Willie would any minute be returning from work on his bike.

Wasn't this typical of the sonofabitch! Sixth sense and all. Lying, sneaking, cheapskate bastard! She could have caught him if she had left Denver sooner. But Nate had carried on so. He was in the middle of a second book, a critical history, and he needed her. And she had stayed. Sometimes she was a fool, an utter fool about men. A fool when she damn well knew better. The critic had been keeping her for months (she had saved enough out of the allowance he gave her to make this trip, perhaps, too, to continue on to Chicago for a vacation. God knows, she needed it). Of course she could always go back. But it was tiresome to read in the Denver *Post* every few days that Mrs. Nathan Rand (Nate had married money) was doing something else for such and such a cause. Tiresome, too, to look upon the same lights from the same vantage point of the same high expensive windows night after night. But the most tiresome thing was Nate himself. The strain of middle age (though, she had noticed, not old age) seemed to fall early on the recondite and professional types. After the first couple of months he had actually begun to groan—barely audible in the beginning—while making love to her. And he insisted upon doing it daily (with the exception of the times when it was out of the question). It was a torture he seemed unable to live without. She tightened her fists. Men!

When Willie Light encountered Kierkegaard, he knew—although he was not sure how he knew or why he should know—that he had found a man not writing for the public but for the public of himself. And at that moment, isolated up among the lifeless winter branches of the Dutch elm, he thought he knew what Kierkegaard's life had been like and why he had written as he had. His eyes jaded, the narrow bridge of his nose white from the cold, he watched the mayor's house, wondering what the hell they were up to. Because you never could tell with women.

Then Gloria seemed to flow quickly out onto the porch. He felt a start inside. But his body was too cold to carry off anything other than his wooden squat. Gloria turned, coming towards him. He tried to shrink and wrap himself against a limb. He was afraid of her. He admitted it. He would never forget their wedding night. No, he corrected, *her* wedding night. He had crawled into bed and moved towards her already pregnant though not yet swollen body. And just as he had eased her leg over his hip and pushed into her, sighing against her body, she had reached down and caught hold of his testicles. He could feel her fingers now, the sharp nails biting. His loins shriveled. She had squeezed and pulled until he had howled like a dog. All night long he had vomited—worse than the worst sick wine-drunk he had ever been on. She had driven them back from Elko to Utah. And for two weeks he had been swollen and impotent, barely able to move. She had walked naked around the little house they were renting, and each night in bed she had pressed herself against him. . . .

He noted the repeated fluttering of Vera's diaphanous white living-room curtain, parting, swinging shut—nervous, discreet. "At the present time," he started, remembering it from Kierkegaard, seeing the ring of mink around Gloria's throat, glimpsing the few inches of lovely ivory skin, knowing it would cover her whole ivory body, then gnashing his teeth, denying voice to that thing inside him that wanted to speak up and claim her, trying desperately to keep himself from leaping out of the tree, he continued: "At the present time my existence is like that of a piece on a chessboard, of which the opponent says: that piece cannot move—like a deserted spectator, for my time is not yet come."

Gloria regarded the bicycle dispassionately and continued walking, an opulent softness to the motion of her body under the fur-trimmed coat, the whole thing set off, heightened, by the harsh clicking of her high spike heels.

3. Sometime during the next spring it dawned on Willie Light that his time had come. What it was or why it had come he could not say. But it had. He informed Schwartz, Geller, Levi, and Stein, Inc. of his change of address, ordered a brand-new Lincoln Continental (four-door, spare tire enclosed behind the squarish slope of the trunk) had a suit cut to his measurements, taken by Vera and mailed to Bernie's tailor in New York City, and generally got things whipped into shape.

On the morning of the final day, Vera Rhodes's face was blotched, her eyes reddened, the inflamed lids drooping with the weight of her grief. She could not keep the tears from falling into her oatmeal. The mayor, understandably embarrassed, left early for the lumberyard in Rocky Fjord.

"Now then," Willie soothed, when they were alone. "You shouldn't cry and carry on like this, Vera."

"Well, Willie Light," she sniffed, turning to a dry spot on her embroidered handkerchief. "Do you realize that through all these years we have become close. We have—in fact—" She paused a long time. "We have become actual lovers. We have and you'd better not deny it."

Willie did not. "Vera, you really hadn't ought to let yourself go on so."

"I guess if I had any sense at all, I'd leave the mayor and come with you." She frowned slightly. "But you don't need me the way he does." She hesitated, her confidence failing, her voice giving way to a tight, squeaking sob. "And anyway, you wouldn't even take me, would you, Willie?"

"Don't hold me to any formal declarations, Vera. I have enjoyed staying in your house and"—he was fumbling now for words to soothe and rescind—"partaking of your generous hospitality. And I wish the best of everything for you, Vera."

"Do you, Willie?"

He tried to see into her tear-clouded eyes. "Yes, I do. Now stop that crying. It's not at all what I've come to expect from you."

"I'll go up, Willie . . ." She sobbed and bit her lip. He could see the telltale signs of age ripening on her face and knew that it was not really for him that she was crying. Nor was this the first time she had made this same speech. "I'll go up every day, Willie. I'll pull the drapes and lie in the dark."

"Will you? Will you now, Vera?" He leaned over and kissed her dry mouth, which felt somewhat like the shell of a peanut; then he kissed each of her moist eyes, tasting of salt. He was touched as he looked on her bowed head, noting how small her ears were, how fine the hair was. He was genuinely touched. "Please give my best to the mayor."

He adjusted the side mirror so his line of sight was directed back over the sleek white body of the Continental before it came to focus on the highway behind. The rear-view above the dash caught the beige leather-covered tops of the seats and the oval rear window. Of course, the only really conceivable reason he needed to look back was to see how much of what he had blown off or scared off the road. Soundlessly, powerfully, the big car carried him over the bud-laden Iowa countryside. He noted the corduroy texture of rich soil under plow and the white knots of pigs above their troughs.

In the security of that ineffable wide silence, which dwarfed even the sounds of the deluxe radio, Willie gloated privately about the size of the account he had with Schwartz, Geller, Levi, and Stein, Inc. Bernie had put his pinkie where he had promised and his promise had payed off in a magical fattening of dollar bills that somehow became tens. There was a total of well over one hundred thousand dollars; and Bernie's last letter had indicated that one large block of oil stock was rising so rapidly that it threatened to double within the quarter. So Willie knew he was closer right now to being a millionaire than anyone had ever been in the whole history of the Light family. He touched his tie (by Sulka) with a gesture of careless opulence and gave the Lincoln another half inch of gas pedal.

He crossed all of Iowa without mishap. Once in Nebraska, however, a funny thing began to happen. It seemed he could not keep the car on the main highway. It was not any trouble with the running gear. He checked that out. It was just that when a side road presented itself he had all he could do not to make a turn.

And finally, worn out from fighting whatever inexpugnable force it was, he swung onto one of the roads and ended up in Cornflower, Nebraska.

4.   Bill Light watched her come around the side of the house, an envelope clutched in her fist. He had stopped out here in the sun to think through a problem. His stub of flat carpenter pencil paused above a piece of cardboard. He swung his head at an oblique angle to the path and tongued a soupy stream of brown juice towards a gray tomcat, which side-stepped the insult with agile delicacy and went on purring and flipping its tail in the sun.

"Another letter," Emma Light announced, twisting up her nose in a stiff grimace. "Another one scented up to high heaven. Lord, the reek of these pink ones is getting so bad I'm going to have to store them outside till he gets here."

"What? Another woman?"

"No—the same one. Vera Rhodes. At least them four New York Jews show the good sense to send white envelopes with no smell."

"Four? I thought it was five Jews," Bill said, thinking.

"No. It's four: Schwartz, Geller, Levi, and Stein. Four."

"What about Inc.? Ain't that Jewish, too?"

She snapped the envelope at him.

"That woman's sure as hell putting out a lot of bait," he observed.

"Maybe Willie's found one he can finally settle down with."

"Nope," Bill Light put down his pencil and thrust one hand under the bib of his overalls in a Napoleonic gesture of stateliness, sat up straight in his canvas chair, and spoke with firm defiance, "The woman ain't been built yet who can wield a pin to pop that boy's balloon."

"Ha!" The envelope cracked in her hand.

"You watch."

"Ha!"

Bill Light stood, spat again, hitting the tom this time, and stomped out to the tent-house to think the whole thing over.

5.   "Take me with you, Willie," Amelia Butler pleaded, the unceasing Nebraska wind lifting the starched white chevron of her waitress apron stiffly away from her flat, friendly thighs, jingling a few coins—the morning's tips—in her pocket.

But the freshly washed and polished white Lincoln was already in motion, leaving the Cornflower Hotel and Grill, where Willie had rented a six dollar a week room, in a swirl of tan street dust. Aside from his association with Amelia Butler, Willie had spent his time perusing market reports, free oil company maps, and *The Canterbury Tales,* a secondhand copy of which he had found in the local Salvation Army outlet store for ten cents. Partly because of this book, because of its promise of a destination, he had begun definite preparations for the continuation of his trip. A few days before, he had started taking short test drives out of town, vaguely in the direction of the main highway—to see if he could get up nerve enough to give it another try.

Now he was ready. The white Lincoln was full of ethyl. He had topped off the carburetors, cleaned the plugs, regapped the points. And although he had known it would be useless, he had given the running gear a thorough going-over, crawling the full length of the frame, checking each cog, each nut, testing each fitting, each pin, hoping to discover that the conspiracy had been in the mechanism of the car. Futile efforts.

He sped out of Cornflower, passing the city limits sign at a flat seventy miles an hour. And reached for high gear.

6.   Leon Fulton knew in advance. Just exactly what he did know and how far in advance of what thing or time he did not know for sure. But he did know. And he had a damn good idea it would all come to something. Sometime. And that was more than he had known about the matter for years.

The information—if it could be called that—reached him inadvertently one warm morning in June when he paused on Main Street to pass the time of day with Jesse Gordon, clerk at the post office.

"Willie Light around?" Jesse inquired, frowning schoolishly down over the tops of his steel spectacles.

"Willie? Well, if he is I haven't heard about it."

"I've been getting mail for him at the office. Been sending it out to his folks' place. It doesn't come back. Letters from the east. Long business-looking envelopes. Smarts. Warts. Some name like that."

"Schwartz?"

"Yeah."

"Jewish . . ." Leon mused.

"Mm. Expect him to be tangled up with them people, wouldn't you?"

Leon squinted. "That all?"

"No. Some others too. Different, though. Smaller. And pink." Jesse rubbed his chin. "And they've got an aura of something personal about them."

"What's that?"

"They smell."

"Smell?"

"Like roses—as near as I can tell."

"East?" he repeated. Gloria would not be writing Willie, would she? And she sure as hell would not perfume the letters. "How far east?"

"The long ones come from New York City. The short ones are from the midwest somewhere."

Leon tilted back on his heels, lowering his head thoughtfully, his gray hair as unmoving as comb-furrows in plastic. His fingers followed the loop of gold chain across his solid paunch to the pocket slit in his vest. "How long've these letters been coming, Jesse?"

"A couple of months," the postal clerk said, shaking his head. "You know, I never thought we'd hear from that boy again. When he didn't come right home after the war, I just figured that he'd settled somewhere else."

"Or been locked up," Leon suggested, watching the other man.

"That too," Jesse allowed, with a smile.

"You haven't seen anything but the letters, though, have you?"

"Nope. And that makes me wonder."

7.   Another one said it in Denver.
"Willie—"

And another one in Wyoming (because when he could not get the white Lincoln Continental out of Denver on Highway 40, the direct route over Berthoud Pass and the Rockies to Vernal, he decided to circle in on Highway 30, through Evanston and Salt Lake City, and sort of sneak up on it or on himself or on whatever it was that seemed to be keeping him away). And that one, the one in Wyoming, had beautiful wind-pink cheeks and a lilting voice with a sparkle like creek water. She also had a touch of VD. Willie did not, however, scorn this defect altogether, because it made it easier for him to go on—especially after convincing himself that he was running from her and what she represented and not toward that blank, or perhaps it was (after all) still merely a place or at least the idea of a place and (in truth) only shrouded with blankness.

He received medication and a mildly comical though nonetheless suspect lecture on how to go about checking a woman for it beforehand from a corpulent country doctor who handled the needle with the arbitrary aim and firm skill of a veterinarian and who smelled himself not a little like a horse. Whiskey and BO.

8. "They're probably from another woman he ruined, the sneaking sonofabitch!" With a sharp crack, she shut the mystery novel she had been reading. Her voice was crusted with irony. "An' now she's wondering where her sweet Willie went."

"Now, Louise, if I'd thought you'd get yourself all worked up into a fit, I never would have said a word. I just think it's damned odd that those letters are coming and being claimed and nobody's seen hide nor hair of Willie."

"Well, Willie's not here. I'd have felt it," she said. "Unless the war changed his whole despicable personality. And I doubt that even the world war was that big. No," she let her book drop on the floor. "Willie's not around. We'd have heard him."

"I guess that's true. You might not see that boy. But you could always hear him. He could floorboard a car deeper than anyone I ever saw or heard tell of." Leon was speaking from memory— with what seemed to amount to respect, or awe.

"What!" she demanded furiously. "Are you going to stand there and praise him for all the hell and gray hairs he raised?"

"No. No praise," he muttered, unable to quite contain all of his smile. He was thinking. Not praise. No, damnation. Faint damnation. And—yes—wonder.

9. Gradually, he almost made it. He reached the next town of any size, a place thirty miles to the west called Roosevelt, which divided its meager population into two parts—white and Indian. Everybody not strictly white was Indian (at the onset of the war, one Chinaman with a laundry had fled because he looked too much like a Jap for safety; and even most of the old-timers had never set eyes on a live Negro) except half-breeds, who were as contemptuous to the one pure race as they were to the other pure race, and were sometimes even quite a problem among themselves.

Willie parked his car on Main Street and walked into a hotel to rent a room, for a dollar. Two town thinkers spent the better part of an hour ignoring the sybaritic length and sheen of the white car. One whittled. The other spat. Finally, the spitter emptied his mouth, let his eyes travel from bumper to bumper, then said, "Now what the hell's that thing?"

Before even considering the Lincoln, the whittler methodically wiped the blade on the top of his shoe and folded it down into the handle of the knife. "Rich man's toy," he muttered after a moment. "All them easterners got something."

The next morning, Willie packed, checked out, and drove the twenty-odd miles over the polychromatic badlands and up the Twist, coming out on the overlook at the edge of the Ashley Valley. He stopped (he could do nothing else). He could see the town, Vernal, sort of shining dully in the middle of the tree-clouded stretch of flatland that tilted off toward Green River. He went no farther that day: Monday.

For the following five days he repeated this trip, barreling the heavy car up the treacherous Twist, coming to the inevitable halt at the rim of the valley. Each day he shook his head at the hotel clerk's offer of weekly rates and tried not to read what was obviously in the man's mind as he watched him shell out another dollar for another night.

On the seventh day he decided it was time. He nosed the white Lincoln down over the rim of the valley and sped towards those endless wastes of blank life he had been dreading since the war had left him helplessly on his own—three years, one month, and five days before.

Nothing was changed. He had the Lincoln Continental, the hand-tailored suit, and a comfortable niche in the Chase Manhattan Bank for his burgeoning collection of stock certificates, bonds, and securities. But, basically, nothing was changed.

He did not make Main Street on his first try. He circled through the residential district, going down Third South to Fifth East, turning to Third North, turning again to Fifth West—big tires howling.

When finally he did swing onto Main, he noted its deathlike Mormon desertion: nothing open, a few parked cars (owned, no doubt, by gentiles or profligate jack-Mormons). Back at Fifth

West, also known as the Maeser Road, he headed north, hitting high gear, and felt the automatic hinging of his foot as it mashed the accelerator into the tight pile of the beige carpeting.

The shadow of the needle was just moving smoothly down across the ninety when he shot past the house. He turned his face with a solid thrust out the window, like a pilot noting the position of a target or another plane. A star still hung in the living room window, sun-bleached on its scroll of silk.

He passed two section roads before he could slow down enough to turn around.

10. "Willie's come," Bill Light declared, focusing his voice towards the rusted opaque square of screen on the back door.

"I thought maybe it was—" she answered, the rest of her statement dying out between her mouth and the mirror.

Already Bill could hear the spit and crackle of the hairbrush drawing the electricity out of her fine gray thatch.

"I never seen him," she admitted, after a moment's pause. "But I heard it pass and felt the jar. Just the same as always."

"He'll be whipping in here any minute now, I reckon," he said, keeping excitement and everything else out of his voice except information.

She did not reply. There was the click of a lipstick tube, then the whine of a metal lid coming off the glass threads of a squat jar. Bill snorted and swore to himself.

The old gray tomcat stood up curiously, halting in mid-arch. The white car came endlessly around the driveway, moving with such ease and precision that there was hardly any dust.

Heaving himself out of the awning chair, leaving the frayed canvas bottom swinging, Bill Light sauntered out to where the car sat, cooling on its running gear.

"How was the war, son?"

"Not bad."

"I was under the impression it ended some time ago."

"It did."

Bill leaned a little to look inside at Willie. "What happened—yours still going?"

They looked at each other, neither one flinching. Bill reached out and knocked his knuckles against the side of the front fender, noting the quality of the metal and finish.

"Passed these things out when you was done, I suppose—as a bonus."

Willie swung out, suited, silk tie knotted. The door shut behind him, stopping solidly in place, without as much as an echo, as though it were magnetized.

"Take a spin if you like, Pa," Willie invited. "Key's in it."

The old man's eyes wrinkled. He spat. The long lubricious stream seemed to catch up with itself in the air, somersault, then splat and hold near the front tire.

"How you been, Ma?" Willie noticed she was busily tucking a wood-backed brush out of sight down between the cushions of the couch with her right hand while her left hand mussed a little at her hair—so he would not know she had gone to the trouble to fix it.

"Waiting," she replied bluntly. He glimpsed the white bit of Feenamint as she chocked it back in her jaw. "Waiting and wondering what kind of nonsense you were up to. You've been away a long time, Willie."

"Eight Light years," he said, flashing a grin that was gone the next instant.

"Where?"

"I stopped to think."

"Took you long enough."

"You know I never was too awful fast."

She puffed her breath out and shook her head. "Most of the boys come right on home after the war and got their families taken care of."

"I guess," he said hesitatingly. "I guess mine's what you might call an automatic family: it just took care of itself in my absence."

There was a long silence during which a green housefly

crawled in through a hole in the window screen and then buzzed against the tight crisscross of wires, trying to get out again. Willie saw that the star on the silk scroll had been taken out of the window.

"How's the boy—Louis?"

"Fine. He is all right except for something he's obviously inherited from the Light side of the family. Now and again, when I see him coming, I catch myself reaching out to find that willow switch I used to keep around for you." She saw Willie smile to himself and thought that she would just erase some of that smugness. "Why? You thinking about going up there to pay him a visit?"

The smile perished. She saw the tie move when he swallowed. "Sometime."

She sniffed. "Next year?"

"I suppose he's bound to be dropping around, isn't he?"

"Yes, maybe. . . . Should I tell you if I see him coming—so you can hightail it?"

Outside, the Lincoln roared and lurched. It came under control and stole quietly, dustlessly, around the driveway to the road. Willie's smile returned.

Emma Light chose to ignore the passing of the white car—not foregoing, however, the opportunity of muttering something half audible about men and their goddam playthings. Then she reached past the curtain, into the open window, where the letters lay in a perfumed sheaf against the screen.

"Mail's been coming for you." She tried to keep any sign of expectation out of her voice.

Willie took the letters. He separated out the pink ones and let them drop on the coffee table. "Stink, don't they."

"Who?" she asked, her leathery features drawing up with concern.

"A woman."

"Yes. I assumed it was. What woman?"

"One who never learned to quit." He held one white envelope up to the window light to get it ready for tearing. Then he looked at her. "Maybe none of you have."

She refused to move.

"This one liked poetry. Mostly the bad kind, though. The kind that lets you go on hoping. Shelley was the best of them. It was downhill after him. Walter de la Mare. . . . Lord, she loved to say that guy's name. She used to whisper it. She said it was a poem itself. If it is, it's sure the best one he ever wrote."

"What kind of hoping?" she asked. "Hoping for what?"

He looked at her. "That's it: just hoping. That was her trouble. She went on past where most of us normal people stop. Empty hoping."

"Well that is nonsense." She should have known when she smelled the woman's letters.

"Yes. One more way to limp on through life."

11.   "He's your pa, ain't he?"

"Yes."

Geo had to pedal faster to catch up. "Why don't you stop and see him then?"

"I only wanted to check."

"What? You mean we came all of three miles just to ride past that house and have a look?"

Geo did not hear Louis's answer, if Louis had even bothered to make one. He pedaled still faster to keep up.

"What's so wrong with seeing him?"

"Nothing."

"So—why don't we just circle back and get it over with?"

"Because I'm not ready for that. I just wanted to make sure. That's all."

"Why didn't you ask then? I could have told you fast enough."

"Told me what?"

"That he was there."

"How'd you ever know?"

"Hell, Louis, haven't I seen that white car zip past our house and go skidding too fast around the hill at least twice a week? And there ain't anybody in town that doesn't know who owns it. Hell, even Little Benny could've told you." Geo was up off the seat now, pedaling for all he was worth. It occurred to him that he had said *hell* twice and that was wrong; but he was pretty upset. "I'll bet it's him. And I don't even know what he looks like."

"Neither do I."

"*What!*" Geo slacked off in surprise, then resumed his speed, trying to keep abreast of Louis, who was bent seriously over his handlebars, his dark hair licking at his forehead.

"Haven't you seen him in pictures or anything?"

"No. The only pictures he ever sent to Grandma Light were of somebody else. And they were usually dead."

"What a family!" Geo puffed. "What a nutty family."

"We just don't happen to be close-knit like all you clammy damn Mormons!" Louis snapped. Then his voice seemed to go soft. "Besides, Geo, what would I say if I did see him?"

"You could introduce yourself."

Then Geo sensed it. He sensed it long before he could work up nerve enough to sneak a look back. He just had that feeling of something. He swung his head around. The white Lincoln had nosed out of the driveway and crept up silently behind them.

Willie knew it was the one who refused to look around at the car, the one who refused to swerve to the side of the road, the one who refused even to acknowledge the other kid's warning. Gripping the steering wheel, he wondered if he should not just run the little bastard off into the barpit. Damned if he was not as hellbent and tenacious as Gloria had always been. Stubborn little devil.

Willie eased the left wheel off the pavement and started up alongside the boy. Then, creeping over slowly, he forced him off onto the grassy shoulder and saw him overturn in the ditch. He touched the button, his right hand just a little bit shaky, and watched the window vanish down into the passenger's door. And he got ready to say he did not know what.

But something came to him. Right after he said his name. He watched Louis gather himself out of the ditch and quoted him the chessboard situation from Kierkegaard. Maybe that would get him on to Dostoevsky.

7

The Light Method:
Part Three—The Faults of Perfection

✽✾✽✾✽✾✽✾✽✾✽✾✽

1953

1.   "Had it rolled in your bed, didn't you?"

"Yes. But something must've happened. Maybe they got bumped on the way up here. You know—knocked out of line."

"Mmm. Or maybe a mouse tripped on them before you took the gun out of the rack at home," the old man suggested, with a snort. He reached and took the rifle out of Louis's hands, feeling the boy's fingers clinging briefly, guiltily to the stock before releasing it.

"Or maybe the wind moved the target," Louis ventured.

"If they was any blowing. I don't recall feeling any wind in the last half hour or so. Course now, one of your bullets might've accidentally come close enough to stir some up."

Bill Light sank down to the ground, sitting Indian style, legs folding easily under him. "We'll just forget about that paper target you set up. See that pine? About ten feet up's a knot with a gob of yellow pitch oozing out of it." Bill squinted at Louis until he winced. "Wind hadn't ought to move that there too damn far."

Raising the 30-30, pressing the stock to his whiskered jowl, his scuffed hands seeming to sink into the wood and actually become one with the finish and grain, Bill Light took careful aim. He loosened, turned away, spat. The stream broke in a brown pattern on the face of a white rock ten feet to his left. Again, he embraced the rifle, his forefinger closing slowly on the trigger. The report rang in the Pothole Canyons, echoing into one, filling it, flowing into another, until the camp was entirely surrounded by the sound of the shot.

A chip had flown out of the center of the knot.

"Well." Bill Light made his voice sternly matter-of-fact as he lowered the 30-30. "Everything seems up to snuff . . . here. Your trouble must be somewheres else. What'd you say?"

Louis did not say. His red hunting cap was billed down over his forehead, blotching the upper part of his face with harsh shadow. The corners of his mouth were deeply creased from anger or disgust—the old man could not tell which; but he knew for sure it was not shame.

Louis reached out for the rifle.

"Goddam," he was whispering. "Goddam!"

He squatted down and folded his legs in front of him, assuming, almost in parody, the same position the old man was in. Then, with one tense springlike movement, he threw a shell into the magazine and glued himself against the stock.

"Nope," Bill Light said, reaching out and picking up a cluster of pine needles. "What I figured."

Louis paused. "What?"

"It ain't the rifle at all."

"What then?"

"It's no damn wonder you can't seem to shoot for shit. You ain't the boss yet," the old man criticized gruffly. He broke the bundle of needles in two. "Don't let that thing mold you to fit it— grab onto it and mold it to fit you."

His eyes glowing coldly from their mask of shadow, Louis regarded him for a moment—unmoving. Then he lifted the rifle and snatched the butt hard to his shoulder, finally almost in possession.

Bill Light waited.

Louis glared through the V-ed rear sights and drew his bead

down on the target. The bullet picked a chip out of the knot. It hung in a string of pitch, stretching a few inches down the trunk before breaking free and falling to the ground.

"You'll get on to it," the old man said, moving a wad of tobacco to a comfortable place in his jaw. "It just takes time."

Louis spun and glared, speechless.

Bill glared back, letting his gray eyes go as cold as the steel in the gun. "You'll catch on."

"I hit it, didn't I?"

"Looks like you might've knocked a little hunk out of the lower right edge. That's how I read it."

"I still *hit* it!" Louis insisted.

"An average shooter might contend he had. But not a good one. Nope. A good shooter'd size up what you just done and call it something halfway between a hit and a miss. Good—but not good enough. The rind. But not the bacon." Bill Light paused, pressed his hands on the ground, and pushed himself to his feet. "It's up to you, though. But let me give you a hint. You shoot all at once. Average shooters usually do. You notice how I took my time? I got my bead. Then I looked away. After a little reflection —not enough, mind, for a second thought—I went back and shot quick. From memory."

"Not to say that he caught the target unsuspecting," Willie said. He emerged from the tent with the season's first pot of Big Red, deer-camp coffee.

"That," Brad Meade said. "That and the wind."

"Cup of Big Red to settle the nerves?" Willie offered.

"No!" Louis cried, waving his father and the steaming pot away. "Goddam, no!"

And he levered another shell into the magazine.

2.   It was right after lunch. They were all leaning back, savoring the crisp warmth of the wood fire in the tent and watching Louis do dishes, when they heard something coming up

through the trees. Willie lifted one foot and pushed the tent flap aside. A new Pontiac, metallic blue, with a chrome-trimmed traveling compartment suction-cupped to the top, was bellying along the bad road towards the camp, scraping and banging its low undercarriage on roots and boulders. It stopped. A man in red and tan garb climbed out and started unloading gear from the compartment. A woman snapped a round compact shut and got out to watch the man. She was dressed in a man's clothing, and she might even have passed as a man, except for the whiskerless mold of her face and the broom-straw swatch of bleached hair that stuck out from under her cap.

"Shellhorn," Brad announced from the cot. "The bastard who moved in to manage Safeway's."

"Woman with him, too. Chain-store sonofabitch!" Bill Light growled. He pushed himself off his cot and ducked out through the doorway.

Brad started to follow, but Willie put his hand on his chest, stopping him. "I guess this's one time when you better just settle for jury duty. If I remember right, he'll want to be lawmaker and judge to boot."

"Oh. Right."

So they watched.

Bill Light stalked out towards the chain-store manager's Pontiac, mashing down any knots of brush that happened to be in his path.

Willie wagged his head and beamed with admiration. "God, he'd walk down a tree if one got in his road."

"Say there *hello!*" Shellhorn called out, a salesman's voice, practiced, falsely resonant. "I hope you don't mind our intruding. But we thought this looked like a wonderful spot."

"It's that." There was no attempt at mere information in the old man's voice, only cold blinded fury. "And it's notoriously ours. We been coming here for damn near fifty years. Since before they was any ration. Before it got to be a paper kill with permits and tags." He stood there, his legs spread belligerently, his head rolled forward, bull-like, on his wide shoulders. Willie felt himself starting to imitate that same stance, as though it were somehow normal for the whole damn family.

The chain-store man, oblivious of any competition, his horn-rimmed glasses blinking the cloud-filmed ball of the orange sun, went on, "Then I suppose you can give a few pointers on—"

"And that particular spot where you're fixing to pitch camp," Bill Light continued, refusing to even acknowledge that the other man had spoken, "has always been our brush ground. Squat Acres, we call it."

The chain-store man moved now—as though on shaky ground. He cleared his throat. The woman caught her breath a second time now. She began casting mincing glances about her feet.

Taking one step closer, dampening his threats with an engaging whiskered smile, the old man went on, "Course now, this here forest still belongs to Uncle Sam. And you're sure as hell welcome to stake yourselves out a good chunk of it. This'n—if it takes your fancy. And as long as they's some daylight and we're all wide-awake, I don't reckon nothing's going to go wrong. But after dark, with a little sleep clogging his head, and a man in need's liable to act according to memory and fifty year of habit."

He stopped speaking abruptly and turned away, his body erect and swollen with age-tempered pride. Then, swinging only his head, he added, "There's always plenty of coffee in camp at daylight—if you'd care to come around."

When they bothered to look again, the log cleats on the bridge down in the draw had just rattled, and there was a faint trace of dust settling on the road over the hill.

3.   They could not hear the heavy wet snow falling. But they could not help noticing that its silent weight, which had all the feeling of sound, bowed down the two sloping roof sections of the canvas tent and that its whiteness added to the illumination of the two white wicks in the green Coleman lantern hanging from the ridgepole. There was a constant hiss and splutter around the hole in the asbestos triangle that let the black stovepipe, freckled with rust, stick out through the roof.

"How would we have known to do it?" Brad questioned generally, taking a second to sample the whiskey in his cup while he waited for an answer.

But the only human sound to come was Louis whispering, "Hot son-of-a . . ." from the low stove where he bent over the dishpan and seined out the supper knives and forks; he dunked each piece in a pot of steaming rinse water and blotted vaguely at it with an already thoroughly saturated dish towel.

So, watching Louis fish for the last tin plate, Brad went on, "It has something to do with essence, a man-ness that we need to keep feeding in order to believe in ourselves."

The silence again.

Finally, the old man spoke. But it was to Louis, "I sure as Christ hope you do better on the mountain than you do in the dishpan."

"You mean the killing or the need to kill?" Willie asked Brad, without once moving his eyes from the boy's back.

"The need, of course. That first. Then its accomplishment and fulfillment." Brad leaned towards the stove, spreading his hands to test the heat. "It's an archetype."

"Oh?"

"It must be. Because in it we find something upright and honorable. We kill with impunity and unquestionable innocence. Convinced that it's there to do."

Bill Light poured another slug of whiskey in his tin cup, held the square bottle up to the light, closed one eye to check the ullage, then offered to refill the other cups.

"It never used to be that," he muttered. Then he stopped. His whiskered chin hanging, his mouth open, he nodded and counted the cups. There were three: Louis, looking with absolute crystal-line expectation at the mouth of the bottle, had his outstretched, waiting.

"What was it, Pa?" Willie asked, whiskey and lantern light blazing in his eyes. "What was it way back there at the beginning?"

Squinting, Bill Light slopped a couple of fingers of liquor into the boy's cup and continued, "Used to be something else. Used to be grub. In them days we was hungry."

"Yes," Brad decided, almost blankly, almost entirely to himself, only aloud. "Maybe it's just that man has never gotten over the need to prove his mastery of the stark inevitability of his ultimate survival and dominance. Which puts the emphasis on the nutritive, the material rather than the spiritual."

"Nope. It was hunger. A belly full of meat." The old man frowned, his forehead bulging with wrinkles. "None of us tried to think why we done it. We was one-level people in them days."

Brad took a sip of the whiskey, feeling its comfortable glow going smoothly down to his stomach. "I guess we're talking about the difference between illusion and belief."

"Which one am I talking about?" The old man's frown gave way to a grizzled smile of challenge.

"Belief—I guess. Yes." Brad glanced at him. "Yes. You know, this isn't too very different from Plato's cave."

"Plato?"

"Are you familiar with his dialogues?"

"I heard the name," Bill admitted. "He run off to some cave?"

"He used one in the *Republic*."

"What'd he use it for? A hideout?"

Brad was never sure about the old man. Was he serious? "He discussed the shadows on the wall—shadows a lot like the shadows on the wall of this tent."

"Shadows, huh?"

"That's right," Brad said.

"Did they have women over there where this Plato was at?"

"Yes."

"Regular kind? Female and terrible and all?"

"I presume so." The gold face of Brad's bicuspid seemed to go liquid as the firelight from the open draft door caught his smile.

"Okay. There you are!" the old man cried, draining his cup. "Ah!" he sighed. "It's no goddam wonder he hid out in a cave. Men always get to thinking something's wrong after they've been around women too long. Does it to you. Reduces you to the shadow of your old freedom. Shadows and anything else that's likely to have to slink off and hunt a little bit of decent obliteration. A minute's peace."

"Hold on, Bill. Plato wasn't talking about becoming a shadow. He was simply using shadows to illustrate a point."

"He might can fool himself. But he sure as hell ain't fooling me."

"Goddammit," Brad burst. "You twist everything. You've just got a fixation about the curse of women."

"Yes," Bill Light admitted. "And, by god, I've had it long enough to know it ain't neither one of belief or illusion. . . . More whiskey?"

All four cups reached toward the bottle.

4.   "Come on, boy. Haul yourself out of that sack before I mess up here and tromp on your fingers."

A wooden match flared up in the prehensile warp of the old man's palms, the yellow flame picking out the hawklike perfection of his features, his gray suit of union underwear, his unlaced boots. The kindling caught. The little stove strained at its joints, popping and cracking as the fire spread through the splinters and shavings and started up into the bigger wood.

Louis sprang from his bed and grabbed his pants.

Willie appeared out of the dark morning with a high armload of wood. Brad Meade followed, wearily grinning his gold tooth.

Louis finished dressing and hurriedly unzipped the butt-end of his scabbard so he could get out his 30-30.

"Ain't no need," the old man said. He broke an egg, dropping it confidently towards the black iron pan about a foot below.

"What?"

The old man watched the egg hit and hold. "Ain't no need for that gun. We won't be going out this morning."

"We won't be going out—" Louis looked from face to face. "Why?"

"We won't." The old man broke two eggs this time, one in each hand, prying the shells open deftly with his fingers and thumbs; the insides fell simultaneously into the amber bacon grease, yolks miraculously whole, gelid clear parts quickly cooking white in the hot fat. We never do. You might get your gun out if you wish. But we won't do no first-day shooting. Unless it happens to be a mercy kill."

"What's that?"

Bill Light straightened away from the cast-iron pan. "That's when a befuddled buck comes down through the camp here to be shot and bled out decent, rather than wait for that pack of city slickers up there to skin him with bullets or run him until he dies of sheer exhaustion."

"God, but it must be hard for a deer," Willie mused. "It must be damn awful hard for something as proud and beautiful as a deer to have to wait around for a bullet that's close enough to jump in front of."

"You mean we're all just going to sit here?" Louis blurted. A wing of dark hair fell on his forehead. He brushed it away. "Just *sit* here?"

Bill Light knocked another pair of eggs together in the air and let the insides splash—whole—into an unused area of hot grease in the skillet. "How do you wish your eggs?"

"Sit here? Why?"

"Look." Willie threw back the tent flap, giving them a view of the mountainside, white with last night's snow.

Louis swore in his quiet boyish voice. He pushed the hair back up under his cap again and stared out of the tent flap.

It was as if the mountain had blossomed in the night. Against the fresh whiteness of the snow were gaudy splotches of red, sometimes whole clusters of them, like early geraniums. Hunters were beginning drives through brush-filled draws and protective copses of quaking aspen. Somewhere a deer must have been flushed out, for a sudden barrage of shots broke loose. A frenzy of shouting followed.

"One hundred pounds of hamburger," Willie muttered.

"Sounds a whole lot like the war," Brad commented.

Bill Light distributed the plates. He probed the yolk of an egg with the corner of a slice of frying-pan toast until he got it to ooze. "Same difference," he growled, shoving a crinkle of bacon in his fierce mouth before shutting it.

More shots sounded in the canyon to the right of the camp.

"Reminds me of a motorcycle trip Schwartz and I took down to the Riviera one time," Willie grinned.

"How's that?" Brad asked.

"Seemed like we were the only things moving and everybody

else was pot-shotting us. I was fishtailing all over hell and Bernie was firing blindly, emptying clip after clip into the hillsides."

"Yes," Brad said, smiling. "That was the main trouble with the war where I was. There wasn't enough sport in it."

"Which is why it happened in the first place," Bill Light said, then farted, clearing the tent.

5. There were four.

The first had just broken his way down into the bottom of the ravine, aware now only of himself and his kill. "Knothole in a goddam tree!" he was muttering, his mouth deeply creased from disgust, his hands shaking.

The second was watching the first slash the throat of a beautiful four-point buck which only the moment before had been shot through the heart, had leaped majestically into the air, and had clattered back to the earth—dead. "Could have been scared by the sound of the shot and broken its neck in the fall," he tested, wondering how it would sound when he said it back in camp.

The third was higher still, watching the other two. His grizzled face was wrinkled in a tobacco-stained grin below the two black tubes of the German binoculars that had finally been brought to him from the war. He followed the movement of the boy's hands as he straddled the paunch, slit the animal up the middle, and started to gut it—while a wide red patch of blood from its throat continued to spread and freeze into the snow. The grin vanished. Below the blue tinted lenses, his mouth unhinged. "God," he swore aloud. "Good god!" Then he thought, Look at how he's hacking up the asshole and trying to cut around the pecker. He saw the boy, the knife on top of a bush behind him, hesitate, his mouth hooking down with distaste, then go to work scooping out the guts. Even from that distance, he could feel their warmth, their smooth texture, as he watched them slide out into the snow.

There was a fourth. He sat across the ravine, shaking his head and commenting quietly to the cold pile of buttocks-numbing stones on which he sat and to the bush that concealed him from the three Light men.

"A family tree: three generations of furious silence."

Louis had lost his knife. Brad saw the old man lower his big binoculars and raise his rifle. Good Christ! was it a crime to lose something? Should he shoot the old man first? he asked himself, tightening his own grip on his rifle. But then he noticed that Willie, too, had brought the butt of his 30-06 up against his shoulder. Brad, confused, lowered his rifle, realizing that he could not get both of them.

It was—naturally—the old man who shot first, bringing his head around sharply and sending a stream of brown juice across the snow, in order not to have simply the aim itself but the all-important true essence in the memory of the aim. (Sometimes he wondered how he had ever gotten mixed up with these people and their thinking.) The bullet grazed the handle of the knife where Louis had laid it in the brush.

Louis, groping his pockets, did not bother even to look up. He reached back with his blood-scummed hand, grabbed the knife, as though he had never really mislaid it at all, and completed his task.

By noon, the buck was in a tree, its wide spread of horns curving up into (but not hidden by) the boughs. It hung right in camp, directly, not to say ostentatiously, in full view from the open flap of the tent. Louis had a fire raging in the stove, a tail of pitchy white smoke diffusing into the snowy pines.

Brad laid his rifle on his bed then turned to observe Louis. The boy sliced the heart of the buck, dropping the slices in a plate of flour and salt, and then transferred them to a pan of bubbling grease. Young as he was—fifteen—Louis even now handled the knife with a culinary precision that women had never been born with and could never seem to learn, a rhythmical stroking, the sharp blade going gently down through the meat.

"Nice buck," Brad congratulated.

"Not bad," Louis said and went on cutting, his face twitching under the strain of pride.

Willie appeared out of the trees. He walked into camp, passing not two feet from the hanging carcass, his eye never once straying to it or giving the slightest indication that he was purposely ignoring it. He put away his 30-06 and pealed off his red jacket.

"See anything?"

"One," Brad said. "Somebody else'd shot it though."

"Shot, huh?" Willie shook his head. "I saw one. But it had a broken neck."

Louis stiffened, his lips moved, then he continued with his preparation of the lunch.

The old man lumbered in, his silent rolling gait putting him upon them before they knew it.

"Just like an Indian," Brad remarked thoughtfully.

Louis nodded.

"You ever seen an Indian come in from hunting?" Willie asked pointedly.

Brad cocked his head. "No. I guess what I meant was Indianness." You could not even indulge your fantasics.

Setting his rifle against one of the pines between which the deer was hanging, the old man seemed about to give it some kind of appraisal. But he did not look at it either. He sought his plug and prepared a chaw, wiping his knife blade absently on the buck's stiffened leg when he was finished.

Louis fried all of the heart. Brad wondered how they could miss that. No one else had shot anything. They all ate in silence and stacked their enamel plates on the edge of the stove, where a pan of dishwater, put on to heat, was jiggling nervously on the fire-warped top.

Brad started to roll up his sleeves in preparation to help Louis with the dishes. But both Willie and the old man fixed him with harsh negative looks. He rebuttoned his cuffs and fought down a smile.

After the dishes were washed and dried and stowed in the grub box, Willie lighted a cigar. He handed one to Louis.

"Couldn't you find yourself a tree that was a little bit closer in to camp?"

Louis tore the cellophane from his cigar. "Nobody's using that tree," he retorted, allowing his eyes to proudly measure the length of the buck.

"Nobody using the goddam tent poles either," Willie said. Then he added derisively, "Maybe you ought to take it to bed with you so nobody'll swipe it."

Louis grinned and lighted a match.

"I don't think you got much cause to worry about any thievery," Bill Light broke in. "Hell, if I'd done that job of butchering up the asshole I think I'd be damn happy if someone did steal it. I'd at least have the shame to turn it the other way or hang something up to hide it. And if I thought I'd keep it in spite of all the mistakes on it, I'd sure prop it open with a stick. So it'd cool proper."

The match burned Louis's fingers. He dropped it and stuffed his fingers in his mouth with the cigar.

6.   By evening, when Brad returned to the camp, the buck was out in the trees, away from the tent, propped open. And a little dexterous touch-up work was evident between its hind legs.

"Three generations of furious silence and negative ostentation," Brad declared—to himself, to no one, to the trees and the earth in general.

Walking around the buck, he headed for the smoke.

PART THREE

8

Parables of the Land and the Sky:

Some Variations on Learning to Fail

✦✲✦✦✧✲✦✲✦✧✲✦✲✦✲✦✧✲✦✧✲✦✲✦✲✦✧

1955

1.   Late in September, a caravan of gypsies trailed over the hills from the west and laid evening camp along the Upper Canal, choosing a spot less than a mile from the Seagram farm. While he was doing his chores the next morning, Geo discovered that one pole on the chicken roost, a space where ten hens usually slept, was empty—a crust of mites, tweedy layers of dried dung, a froth of down. Then, too, the level of gasoline in the tractor, pickup, and automobile had dropped in the night, as though the full moon had brought a change in their tides.

Geo stopped for Louis and they drove to town to report the theft. There was a tent pitched just outside the city limits. A huge canvas sign in front announced:

PALMISTRY

MADAME ZELPHA

WORLD FAMOUS

50¢

"You suppose that's for one palm?" Louis asked.

"I'd say it was for both—at once," Geo suggested bitterly. "So they can get at your pockets faster."

One more tent was being staked down when they passed the place on their way home from the sheriff's office. Two strong brown backs glistened in the sun as they bent with the weight of their hammers. A curious crowd of people in town for Saturday were slowing along the barpit and watching from their cars.

It was Louis's idea to return that evening. (Geo told himself that he knew better than to listen.) By then, two more tents had mushroomed on the weed patch.

"Maybe you can buy those chickens back," Louis ventured—a brainstorm of his usual caliber.

"No—I don't think so." Geo shook his head firmly. "The sheriff said the gypsies were still picking meat out of their teeth when he talked to them."

"God—maybe you're lucky it wasn't a cow."

"That's what the sheriff said."

"What's that bastard good for?"

"The sheriff? That's exactly the same thing my old man asked when he came to the house today. The sheriff said he could do his job all right, as long as he was working with local people— because most of us at least show the decency to look guilty when he's out trying to pin something on us and make an honest arrest. But when he comes across a bunch of folks with no more moral fiber than to believe in a handful of marked cards and the stars, there's not a hell of a lot of hope for anything as scientific as truth and justice and the law."

In one of the open-front tents, a man with a dark lean physiognomy and two drooping ferules of moustache was running a betting wheel. Louis slapped down a quarter. A reed clattering against a circle of short dowel posts gradually brought the painted wheel to a stop. Louis had won something. The gypsy handed him a cheap molded-glass dish. Louis stared disdainfully at it.

"You don't like it?"

"I thought I'd won."

"Perhaps you'd like to trade that for something else?" suggested the gypsy, his waxed moustache moving stiffly.

"What? A chicken?"

Cringing, Geo punched Louis with his elbow.

"Chicken?" The gypsy regarded Louis for what to Geo seemed like at least an hour, fire blazing somewhere back in his eyes, nothing else showing on his face. "One of these." He beckoned them to one side. In the secrecy of his palm he held a box of small foil-wrapped packages containing Trojans.

Louis automatically handed back the glass dish.

"What'll you do with that?" Geo demanded, watching Louis slip the rubbers into the compartment of his wallet where ID cards should have been kept.

"Just a little security," Louis replied, an answer to nothing Geo could think he had asked. "I'll save myself a lot of needless worry."

"Worry?"

"Yes. Remember Sue Ellen Bolt?"

"Yeah." A smile started on Geo's face. Two years before, Sue Ellen had finally missed her calculations about herself. But she had spent a little time calculating on a few other people. Then he remembered something that had bothered him for a long long time. "How come you were so happy that time, Louis. How come you were so happy when I told you you were the one with her?"

"Stupidity," Louis replied. "Stupidity and inexperience. I thought that was the reasonable way to ruin them. But I was wrong, Geo. That's only the way to ruin yourself. With girls it isn't being pregnant that hurts—because they can catch you with that, which is what they want in the long run anyhow. The thing that hurts them is the idea that you got in and out without being caught."

"Me," Geo declared resolutely, showing both palms. "I'm just laying off."

"That's easy enough to say when you're not touching any," Louis said. Already his eyes were fastened on the palmistry tent and his voice was beginning to drift.

"So now I suppose you're planning to make a whole career out of going around defiling virgins," Geo said from the corner of his mouth, his statement ending up being a question.

"Virgins?" Louis halted.

"Yes. Haven't you ever heard the word?"

"It seems like a word I read—but a long time ago. Probably out of context. I've never seen one, though. Not one I could be sure of. Have you?"

"Yes," Geo admitted.

"When?"

"I see them all the time."

"Where?"

"Oh—in church."

"Mormon girls?"

"Yes. You can tell, Louis. They're the ones who nod their heads whenever we have a lesson about chastity in Sunday school."

"Christ, Geo, they *are* the ones."

Geo screwed up his face, trying to figure his way through Louis's reasoning. "Isn't that what I said?"

"What?"

"That they're the ones—the virgins."

Louis shook his head. "No, Geo. They're the ones who aren't. They're no damn different than the other girls. They've got the exact same trouble as Catholic girls and Baptist girls and Congregational girls. You can't really tell about any of them. They're all fake-outs. They walk around and put on like they're drifted snow—all white and pure. But the minute you apply the right kind of heat that snow melts fast enough. And under it, all you find is that what you thought would be a cool flowery path is a hot cement sidewalk. And another snowplow—and maybe even a dozen—beat you there. A long time ago."

"That's pessimistic."

"Bull. Think about the most sophisticated girl you've ever known. What about Sue Ellen? Was she a virgin? Christ, no! She was a bona-fide whore at age thirteen—probably younger. Married when she finally took her choice of the dozen guys who ganged her at the sophomore outing." Louis pursed his lips and then made a declaration, "If I ever do run into a virgin, I'm going to try my damnedest to refuse it. It'll be like a museum piece—that rare. Maybe not only refuse it, but dedicate myself to preserving it."

"That's crazy."

"Everything's crazy, Geo."

"How so?"

"People always miss the point."

"Which is—"

"That there is no point—not where people are concerned."

They were stopped before the palmistry tent. A string of lights sagged over the entrance like teeth in a grim mouth. Louis said, "I think I'll go in and blow four bits on the future."

"I sure hope it's worth it," Geo remarked, trying to smile, but still thinking of Louis's new purpose in life. "I'll wait."

Louis entered. As the curtain lifted and fell, Geo got a glimpse of Madame Zelpha. She looked authentic, right from the faded zodiacal figures stenciled on the canvas walls down to her crystal ball (a shadowy line ran under the cloth). Her face had the wrinkled, desiccated appearance of pressed flowers, though it was not quite flat; but it might have aged inside a tight nylon stocking. Two short gray tufts sprouted from her nostrils. And despite the close harvest heat, she wore a mountain of clothing in an unbelievable combination of colors and fabrics, dirt-spotted and faded. She looked more past than future, Geo thought.

He waited until he saw Louis sit down, then he hurried back and slapped a quarter on the board in front of the gypsy with the wheel. "Give me one of those things too."

"You too?" the gypsy grinned.

"No—it's—it's for a friend."

"She'll like it."

"No—he," Geo stammered, his narrow face flushed.

"He? You won't need one then. Not for a he. And I don't advise the whole thing."

"No—you don't understand. I want to buy one."

"You have to win it. Your friend did."

"Okay—spin it."

It cost Geo one dollar and fifty cents for the Trojan. But it was worth every bit of it. And he would need one. He would need one if even Mormon girls were that way. Yes, for his own protection, he would need one. And a buck and a half was nothing to the misery he went through over Sue Ellen.

As he approached the tent, Geo heard Louis ask, "What about chickens? Are there about ten Leghorn hens in the immediate past of my friend Geo? Or even a drumstick? Half a cold breast? Maybe a few feathers to be boiled for a pillow?"

No, Louis, Geo was whispering. Louis, you frigging fool! He poked his head through the opening into the tent. Madame Zelpha's hands were frozen around her crystal ball, thinly fleshed fingers grayly transparent, the craggy features of her wizened face gone spooky in the cupped light. She rose, buoyed up by a fury that left her skinny jaw hanging and her lifeless store-teeth glowing sulphur-yellow in the hard pink plastic of their gums.

"Get out!" she said. Then she shouted it—a strident, nervous scream, eerie as the screech of a shot rabbit.

The gypsy from the wheel brushed past Geo and burst into the tent, long moustache streaming. He thrust his hand inside his shirt. A knife flashed, leaping from his shirt like a lean polished tooth.

"Get out!" the woman screamed again.

Louis made a fast exit, running for all he was worth toward the car.

Geo tried to think what he should do. Finally, in the confusion he saw another flash of light on the curved blade of the knife. That told him something. He spun and raced out into the night after Louis.

"Dammit, Louis," he demanded, trying to get his breath as they drove toward town. "Why'd you have to go and ask that?"

"What?"

"About the chickens?"

"I thought it was a good exit line. I didn't want to have to pay her. It wasn't worth four bits."

"I told you so."

"No—not the future. I mean the easy way she put it."

"What'd she say?"

"She said something would happen this year that would completely change the course of my life. Hell, I already knew that."

"How?"

"I'll be eighteen. I'll be out of high school. I'll be free. I can start on my own."

Geo sank down in his seat, thinking he would sure hate to see any freedom after Louis got through with it. "I know something myself, Louis. I can't pinpoint it to any one year. But I think I've known it since the first day I met you."

"What's that, Geo?"

"Sometime you're going to get me into bad trouble."

"Me?" Louis asked incredulously. "Why me, Geo?"

"It's like those chickens."

"Weren't they your chickens?"

"Yes."

"Well?"

"Look, Louis," Geo said, feeling himself about to plunge into a vortex of confusion. "I don't even want to talk about it any more."

2.   Miss Tottle stood there. Like bronze. Thin and statuesque in his doorway. He sighed inwardly and repeated his question.

"Can't you just tell me, Mildred?"

She repeated her reply, "No. You'd better see it." Her leathery lips barely opened; nonetheless he caught the acidulous odor of her denture breath. It seemed to literally pry him out of his chair.

Mildred Tottle was already in motion, as though she had never really stopped, moving ahead of him down the hallway. Except when he passed a classroom door and a gentle hum would rise, the only sound was that of his nailed leather heels echoing between the steel locker-lined walls. He struck them hard, feeling the metallic jar in his joints, and set his jaw, his teeth meshed solidly, molar into molar, like cogs.

Martin Lukus, principal of Uintah High School, read the blackboard with disbelief, possibly because the spelling was all correct, possibly not. He wondered if he might not have said the same thing himself at that age, though he certainly had never been poetically inclined. Briefly, he was baffled. It was funny how none of the theories he had memorized in all those years of education classes ever quite seemed to fit any particular problem. They did, however, work pretty well in faculty meetings; and nothing was more impressive on a PTA night than two or three of

these abstract theories loosely strung together and summarily ap-
plied to some general problem. He read the poem again.

> This is the story of Miss Tottle
> Who tried to pee in a bottle.
> She fell flat on her ass
> And was cut by the glass
> Which left her walk a waddle.

Miss Tottle announced that she had brought in the principal to
take charge of this little problem, since she did not feel, under
the circumstances, that she could handle it with a clear head.
Listening to her, Geo was not convinced of this. She actually
seemed frozen in her own fury. On the other hand, when old
Pukus turned from the board, he did not look any too cool himself. His face was blazing red.

It was a puzzle, sure as hell. Who had done it? As many times
as Geo had looked across the seats to the row Louis sat in, he
had never once caught his eye. But that up there was not Louis's
handwriting, unless he had faked it. You never could tell about
Louis. That song up there might be an example of his real handwriting and what he did every day was faked. You just never
could tell.

Somewhere—someone hissed something to someone.

"*No whispering!*" Martin Lukus glowered. "I want the complete, undivided attention of every individual in this class." His
right hand checked to make sure his jacket was buttoned; his
whole body settled into a grand pose—solid, authoritative. "Students, what has happened here in this room today is evidence of
an element of smut and indecency among you." Martin Lukus
paused for effect and a second of silent personal praise. Marvel-
ous! Now if he could only figure out a way to work communism
into it, he would have a pretty important problem on his hands.
Smut was one thing, a moral slur that could bring one mind and
those of possibly a few friends into a mire; but communism was
political and that implied peril to the masses. He continued, "I
personally promise you that I am prepared to take any measures
to discover where it exists and who is the responsible party. This
act, you ought to understand, is not a little unlike the infiltration

of communism—which creeps in like a band of worms to undermine with corruption (!) the bounteous fruits of democracy and righteous living." There, he thought, a bit corny perhaps, but he could revise it and take it to a special PTA meeting (he would call it as soon as he got back to the office, call his wife also and have his best black suit sent to the cleaners). He would show its correlation with the recent still shaky situation along the 38th Parallel and make himself valuable enough as a guardian of peace and freedom in the eyes of the board of education members to merit another moderate raise in salary.

Martin Lukus sent the students all to the auditorium. He ordered the boys to return, one by one, as they were called. Rapidly, he reviewed the premise while he prepared his interrogation. The room was on the northwest corner of the building; its windows looked out on the black roof of the coal storage, the incinerator, a parking lot full of customized, chromeless, lowered and louvered and otherwise sinister-looking automobiles (no longer the jalopies sporting the foxtails, reflectorized mudflaps, and nonsensical ornaments of Martin Lukus's own high school years, when youth was innocent and at least literal about its folly), and beyond to the football field where boys in sweat shirts swarmed at each other or pumped along in lonely circles around the cinder track, avoiding the leftover snow crusted against the inside lane. The desks were all empty. Miss Tottle stood in the back of the room, thin and seeming slightly hunched, like one of those birds of prey. She stared at the blackboard, her glasses magnifying and washing out everything about her eyes except their intensity.

She had left her college Shakespeare, roll book, red pencil, and red rubber fingertip—perforated—ordered neatly along the front of the desk. She had done it, Lukus decided, during the first frozen silence before she came to his office. He picked up the fingertip, thrust it firmly over his pinkie, and called for the first boy. He would find the little bastard, the communist, he promised himself in an extravagant flare-up of jingoish fire.

The first boy to come in was Dal Turner. His Levi's clung beltless and low to his lean thighs, his short-sleeve sport shirt was cuffed to the armpits, and his grease-smeared hair was swept back in a classic DA.

"Did you write this?" Martin Lukus demanded.

"No."

"Reproduce it beside the other on the board," he ordered.

Dal Turner wrote; he had not done it.

Each boy came in; each boy denied it; each boy wrote and was dismissed. Mark Bennett, Bill Tulver, David Jones. Until Little Benny Westlake. He had to use the chair from Miss Tottle's desk to get up to where the first line began. Still, there was a slight— even more than slight—similarity in styles; something, too, in the flourishes. This might be the one. What could be more clear evidence of a revolutionary and communist than some kid who spent all his time on stage, playing guitar in all the weekend honky-tonks in the county. Lukus pressed him.

"What?" Benny turned. The principal was trying to frame him. He knew it.

"You misspelled bottle."

"It don't look right to me."

Lukus clapped one hand to his head. "Dismissed!"

Geo could hardly hold the chalk. He fumbled it twice, having to pick it up and use a smaller broken piece each time, before he finally got the verses written down. He had left one s out of ass.

"Write that word over," Lukus instructed.

"Huh?"

"You didn't complete a word in the second to the last line."

"Which one?"

"Look at it!"

Geo knew they were going to try and pin it on him. He saw the word. Ass. He tried to laugh. But no sound came from his mouth. So he started to correct it. The chalk squeaked and sent a chill through him. He spun.

"I never done it." The breath seemed sucked out of him.

"Did."

"I never!"

"Spell that word."

"A . . . s . . . s. Ass."

"Dismissed."

Louis Light did not even bother to look to the back of the room where Miss Tottle stood. Martin Lukus stiffened. He recognized a troublemaker when he saw one. If he had noticed this boy in the class at first, he would have known who had done it. He had more than a sneaking suspicion that this was their culprit (in fact, he found himself almost hoping it was).

"Louis." He addressed him in an exaggerated tone of quietness, shifting his tactics now. "What do you think of that thing on the board?"

"That poem?"

"Yes." Ah! There was something promising about his calling it a poem. It seemed to Martin Lukus that he had just now had a brief, though illuminating, glimpse into the ballooning ego of an aspiring young poet who might even consider scribblings on blackboards and lavatory walls and stall doors immortal, rather than immoral. "Yes. What about it?"

"It sure doesn't come up to Shakespeare."

"Shakespeare?"

"Miss Tottle's been teaching us Shakespeare."

Shooting a badly disguised look of outrage back at her, Martin Lukus thought that maybe she was only getting what she deserved. "Do you think the dirty parts in Shakespeare could have been the root of this outpouring?" (Martin Lukus foresaw the day when literature and the slur it left on the lives of youth, encouraging imagination and other sick forms of unreality, would be completely eliminated from the high school curriculum.)

"I guess those are the parts in Hamlet that we passed over."

"Oh? And how do you know about them?"

"I read them."

"Why?" Martin Lukus squinted and bore down. "Why?"

Louis shrugged. "The words were there."

"Words!"

"Words words words."

Miss Tottle snorted to contain a laugh.

"Young man, you be specific!"

"You mean by dirty parts the places where Hamlet says that about lying in a maid's lap? Is that what you mean?"

"Yes! What do you think about that?" Martin Lukus knew now that he was getting somewhere. His face burned a bright brick red.

"Hamlet says it's sweet."

"What do *you* think?"

"I don't know, sir. I haven't had a lot of experience."

Martin Lukus ruffled and spluttered. "All right, Louis. That's enough of your impertinence. Write what's on the board."

Louis chose a long piece of chalk from the rail. He paused and stepped back.

Martin Lukus eyed him suspiciously. "Why are you loitering?"

"I'm just trying to figure out why anyone would have written it."

"It's obvious, isn't it? It's the influence of communism," Martin Lukus said, unable to contain it any longer. Not just pink. No. Red as red. The whole nation was going to pot.

"That isn't communism," Louis argued. "I'd say it was some kind of hidden lust."

"Lust is communism!" Martin Lukus shouted, clenching his fists. He puffed full of air, held it, then let it out slowly. He said, "That's all."

3.   "You ever read *The Yellow River* by I. P. Freely?" Geo asked, grinning.

"No," Louis replied. "But I just finished *The Case of the Hole in the Mattress* by Mr. Completely."

"Mystery fan myself." Geo smirked.

Little Benny Westlake, who was quietly, thoughtfully, strumming his guitar, cut in with a cautioning hiss, "Not so goddam loud!"

"Do you know *Spots on the Wall* by the old Russian master I. Ben Yakenoff?"

"Shhh! Damn!" Little Benny giggled.

"What about westerns?" Louis asked. "Do you know the standard classic *The Bloody Canyon* by the Kotex Kid?"

"Nope," Geo stated righteously. "I stick to hunting stories for the bulk of my gore. Like *Antlers in the Treetops* by the Eskimo genius Whogoosed Themoose."

"You guys ought to be on that program tonight," Little Benny chortled. "You'd have the audience in stitches."

"You know they love your playing, Benny," Louis said. "Hell, you're the big main attraction."

"Yeah," Geo agreed. "Half the town'll be there on your account alone."

Little Benny was seated on the piano stool. The Westlake's living room was close, the walls papered with a few thousand repeats of the same flower; the furniture consisted of a bulky rose-colored overstuffed set and three faded floral chairs; musical instruments stood in every corner, sheet music bulged out of magazine racks and stood in stacks on tables, and porcelain figurines—from genuine Hummels to carnival Kewpies—graced almost all the other available flat surfaces.

"Aren't you ready yet, Benny?"

At the sound of Julie's voice Benny felt a little quiver of genuine grief go through him.

They all turned now to look. Julie Volks stood in the doorway to the kitchen. Two years before, Julie and her mother had moved to Salt Lake City (and Benny had been afraid she was gone forever). Then a couple of months ago, when it seemed everything was starting to smooth out for them, Edith Volks, a sad woman since 1944 when the war had taken her husband, had gone to her bedroom one night, taken a handful of assorted pills, and never wakened again. So Julie had come back to live with her Aunt Belle and Uncle Golden.

"You'd better hurry, Benny," she said. "Aunt Belle just went to the outhouse."

"Always takes her a while," Little Benny smiled. "Ma likes some quiet time to think a bit—if she didn't, she'd stay inside and use these facilities."

Julie shot him a forced look of disgust and returned to the kitchen.

"She knows?" Louis asked.

"Yeah. But she won't tell."

"She just going to live here all the time now?" Geo marveled.

"Yep." Little Benny twisted his mouth in an unconscious parody of a run he was performing on his guitar.

"Pretty nice setup," Louis snickered. "But you've always had it pretty damn good, Benny. She stayed up here a lot of the time before they moved out to Salt Lake."

Little Benny toyed with a boogie figure on the bass strings.

"Except you'd have to climb up on a chair to even kiss her," Geo reminded.

Little Benny, his round white head bowed, chorded softly, trying not to show the bilious pain that the truth in Geo's statement brought up in him. He paused, then clicked off the amplifier.

"But maybe your brother takes care of that end of things," Louis suggested. "He's a big bugger."

"Hartt?"

"You got any other brothers?"

"Hartt don't live in the house. He keeps to his tent." Little Benny laid his guitar in its case and closed the lid.

"Even in the wintertime?" Geo questioned.

"The whole year long. Hartt ain't what you'd call just right," Little Benny admitted. "You know that."

"Yeah." Geo shook his head. "He's got one messy attic."

"Now Hartt's worse off than ever. He's always had that bushy red chin-beard and that tent. But now he's taken up the habit of books. He reads when he damn well don't have to. Big books that come to him mail order. Reads them all the way through. Course that's Hartt's own affair. The old man doesn't care piss nor string beans what he does." Benny trailed off into his own thoughts. After all these years Pa and Ma still went the rounds every now and again about Hartt's social disease and the resultant family disgrace—which Pa had kept alive and bleeding out of his own stubborn hard-headedness. . . . He looked down at his wrist watch. "It's about time we lit out for school."

"One thing I don't get," Louis said, after Little Benny had loaded his guitar and amplifier in the back seat. "Why do we have to smuggle you out from under your folks' noses? I mean how come you don't want them at the concert? How come you didn't tell them?"

"I've been working on some new music," Little Benny confessed cryptically, feeling a sudden deluge of excitement well up and flood out to the limits of his body.

"They like music," Geo stated blankly. "I mean, hell, they do—don't they?"

"Not all music," Little Benny said. "Probably not this stuff. . . . You ever heard of Bartok?"

"Who's it by?" Geo tested. "This another book joke?"

"No. He's a composer. A Hungarian composer."

"They don't write hillbilly music, do they—those Huns?"

"No. This here's something else," Little Benny explained. "See —all my life I've been hearing and playing music that makes you stomp your feet and just feel pretty damn good. You play it till your fingers are numb and aching and you've got a river of sweat running down the crack of your ass. But this Bartok's something else. He's another breed of cat. His music doesn't make you bob all over. It sort of reaches in and grabs hold of your soul and gives it a good shake."

"I never felt anything like that in music," Geo said. "In music or anything else." He regarded Benny with a suspicious squint.

"Well, maybe you will when you hear this thing tonight."

"Then maybe I better not hear it. I don't think I want you or any other musician messing with my soul."

"But why don't you want your folks to know, Benny?" Louis persisted. He turned into the parking lot behind the high school gym.

"They wouldn't feel it." To make that statement hurt Little Benny Westlake right to the core. But he knew it was true. And he could no longer hide from the truth. "My folk've never been anything besides foot stompers. I mean, hellfire, they're plenty good at what they do, damn good at that foot-stomping stuff, and I love it. You know that. But it ends there. Even those composers who're stuck off in the safety zone of tradition, like Mozart, make the old man curl his toes and holler for somebody to shut off the goddam radio."

They were sitting in the parking lot now, the engine no longer running, the headlights reaching out across the dry winter grass, illuminating the vague outline of chalk boundaries on the football field, and cutting into the stands, which stood like a battery of empty shelves.

"Sometimes when I think about how much I like it myself I get worried in a creepy kind of way," Little Benny confessed softly.

"What way?" Louis asked.

"Hartt," Little Benny stated, as though he were purposely ignoring Louis's question. "One time when I was playing this record of string quartets I keep hid away—except for when Ma and Pa are out of the house—I looked up and there was Hartt, standing in the room with me. It was the first time I can remember seeing him in that house since he come home from the war and Pa booted his ass out to his tent. I started to pick the needle up off the record and Hartt reached out and took hold of my arm and lifted me clean off the ground. Damn near tore my arm loose from the socket before he dropped me on the couch. I never hear those few scratched grooves without remembering the way he looked. He stood there like a stone and stared off into space until it was all over with. He knew what it was. Hartt knew. It got hold of him too. You could see it in the way the black poured into his eyes." Little Benny let out a deep sigh, emptying his chest.

"Maybe your Bartok'll do something to me, Benny," Louis said, in a voice that made both Benny and Geo look at him. "I think I've probably had that same feeling already. But it's never come from sound. It's always been silence. Like when I'm alone at night and I start to wonder how I'm ever going to turn out. Sometimes I have to keep myself from looking up at the stars— because they do that to me."

"Man!" Geo gasped. "You two are morbid. Let me out of here before something tries to grab me too."

He had seen crowds all his life. The fact was, Little Benny had probably put in twice as much time onstage as he had in audiences. But, tonight, Little Benny Westlake was scared.

He had prepared three numbers (though, god knows, he could go on all night if he wanted) because people always whistled their lips dry and stomped so hard it seemed the floor would cave in until he played an encore or walked off the stage and let them get tired of trying to flatter him back. For his first selection, he played "Moonfingers," a funky boogie of his own composition. His encore was "Stella by Starlight," a jazz piece that allowed him to be inventive, shifting tempo, working out the idea of Stella, of starlight, and returning to the phrase that brought the two together. Again, applause rose and thundered throughout the high school auditorium. Whistlers screeched. From somewhere there was a muffled *Bravo!*

Little Benny leaned his polished Gretsch guitar against the front of his amplifier and walked out to the MC's mike. He could not get it telescoped down to his height, so he tipped it down and side-stepped to where he could speak into its grilled face—after the laughter died down.

"Thank you for your kindness. This last number is a solo line for guitar that I've translated from a thing called 'Sonata for Violin Unaccompanied' by Bela Bartok."

He stood there briefly, barely able to make out the faces—like so many bubbles on an ice-cream soda—over the harsh glare of the footlights. He walked the mike back up and retreated to his guitar. More than anything right now he wished Julie had just consented to come and hear it. But she had not. Silently, he dedicated it to her all the same. And this secret thought sent blood washing in a cold wave through his body.

Little Benny played, forgetting everything except what the music was doing to him. It seemed to throb against the inside of his body, struggling to get out, trying to break through the pores of his skin. It rang in his heart like the pealing of a million bells, echoing down through the corridors of his love-swollen soul.

When he finished playing, he was sorry. Sorry and sad and empty. His right hand reached automatically down to the controls, shutting off the guitar, the click of the toggle switch making a sound in the auditorium like a crack opening across a river of ice.

He listened. Complete silence, an ominous lack of sound that could only have been created by seven hundred people.

He looked up. Nothing was visible above the lights. He asked himself if any of them had heard it. Any of them.

"Likely as not they never." He whispered to himself.

He gave a short bow. And then the applause began—like a growing shadow.

4. "Indian." Bill Light looked up, a spark glowing in his eyes. "The Injun, you mean."

"Yes." He knows, Willie told himself, watching the old man as he moved back into the memory. "Once you pulled up and went off with that Indian."

"Bent Tree?"

"Yes."

"Bent Tree in Wind," the old man mused. One rough thumb lifted at his left gallus, sliding forward until it was hooked over the bib.

"What happened to him?" Willie asked. "I never saw him or heard of him again." He remembered wondering about it; he remembered, too, that you never asked questions when you were a kid. Or maybe you did in other families. But you did not ask the old man. But tonight, before the opening day, with the warm easiness of the whiskey, the closeness of the tent and the fire, and with the spirit of the hunt, he felt they could talk. In fact, he felt they needed to talk. "And you never talked about him after that."

The old man clasped his knees and rocked back, straightening away from the stove. "Bent Tree. . . ." He shook his head stiffly; his eyes closed then opened a little. "Damn few men could ever stand tall with that Injun. He wasn't fancy—Bent Tree wasn't that. He'd always sell his best feathers—and every damn thing else, too. And when he couldn't steal them back—since he believed they belonged to him no matter what fool he could talk into buying them—he did with what he could get. But he was solid. Down inside, he was solid as steel. And he had a history."

The old man's eyes softened—with time, with distance. His brow creased. "We each had our hurts." He sighed, "That ranch had just dissolved out from under me. Bent Tree's squaw, Little Rabbit, had died. Woman just seemed to perish in her own fat. All evidence of motion disappeared, leaving a mound of brown woman, mostly blubber, bound up in a variety of hides and colored cloth. So we got along. He could hunt. And I could cook. Or I damn well wanted him to think I could. Because he was what you might call a little careless in his culinary habits." He took a drink and frowned against the sliding burn of the whiskey. "An Injun sometimes is. He would just as soon cook an animal with its hide still on as to bother skinning it—unless he needed a hide. And maybe the guts still in, too. They always bleed it out, though. Something in their religion. The hair burns off, of course. And I guess you can always eat around the guts. But the idea of doing it got to me anyhow. I was brought up to be particular. And I never could get used to that."

"What about fish?" Louis broke in. "We've eaten heads and tails and all. You've done that."

"A fish is not a deer. Or a sheep either."

Louis scratched his head. A gust of wind buffeted the tent and set a pine bough to scratching against the canvas roof. It quieted. The fire popped.

"I don't believe we said ten words in all the time we was gone. And we was away close to six weeks. We just rode. We stopped at a ranch and a couple of sheep wagons to put shoes on the horses. That's all, though. Not ten words at a stretch. The farther we got, the less English Bent Tree would suffer himself to talk. He jabbered in Injun lingo of course. And I knew pretty much what he was saying—even if I didn't know enough Ute to translate it. I never went on anything like it. That trip was a whirlwind. Sometimes we would ride all day and all night. Goddam horses plodding along, covered with lather, tired, knocking us into trees. . . ." He broke off to watch Louis reach around with the bottle and refill the tin cups.

"We rode every trail I can ever remember seeing. We explored canyons. We went to the tops of mountains. I think we discovered some things nobody else ever had."

Willie remembered it himself. The old man just disappeared. A week passed, the old woman continuing to set his place, dusting the plate after each meal, refusing to even notice that he did not show up. Then, information started trickling in. Rumors. Lies. Distorted truths. Truth distorted with lies; lies distorted with truth. Gossip. One thing never varied: the old man was with Bent Tree in Wind, the ancient turncoat Ute who had lived on the corner of the ranch till it was sold out from under him, too. The accounts concerning the two of them were without end. The white man who had finally succeeded in becoming a savage. The Indian who had for years bordered on being white. Simple re-

ports became convoluted, apocryphal. A bearded white man traveling with an aged and mad Indian guide. Tales tinted with the
awesome pale colors of twilight. Wreck and plunder were often
hinted at (only there were no places for it). Rumor and confusion had them constantly spotted at at least two different distant
places at once: Taylor Mountain and Spirit Lake; Red Springs
and the head of the Dry Fork; Carter Creek and Blue Mountain
Gorge. They agreed, the stories, on one thing. The two wild
figures were always on the move—horses blowing, kicking up
sparks on a mountain trail; the two men's black hat-brims grayed
with trail dust and plastered flat against the tall crowns, a distinct look of the essence of the wilderness distilled as fire in their
eyes.

"To what purpose?" Brad was asking.

"Purpose?"

"Yes. Purpose. Why?"

"Bent Tree never did say why we went. We just sort of took off
one day. I gradually figured it out for myself. Bent Tree was
looking for the Big Spirit. Injuns call it some nonsense like that. I
guess I could say I was along for the ride—but that'd be a lie. I'd
have gone, too, goddammit. I'd have gone to the Big Spirit with
him. Only I couldn't keep up. Or maybe I wasn't ready. I don't
know. I did make it for damn near six weeks. Then it happened
all of a sudden. Bent Tree seemed to find the right trail. I noticed
him riding off ahead of me. It was like being in some kind of
crazy dream. I was beat all to hell. So was the horse. But I tried
to follow. I tried my damnedest. Spurring and whipping. But he
just kept pulling away, kept getting smaller and smaller. Riding
on up to timber line. Sitting straight—smooth on that old horse—
with two buzzard feathers stuck in his hat, one old blanket dragging off to the left, the pony never quite stepping on it. And
that's the last I saw of him. The last anyone I know ever saw of
Bent Tree. He rode right on up into the sky."

"Do you believe that?" Brad asked seriously.

"Shit!" the old man cried out, fiercely indignant. "I know it. I
saw him do it. It's a fact as big as any man's god. But I had to
stop. I could no more follow him than I could fly. I made a camp
in the first spot I could squint at and still call level and slept for

two days solid. Maybe longer. I only remember waking twice
and seeing the sun. Disappointed each time."

"Disappointed?"

"Because I kept hoping I would be seeing something else."

"What?" Brad demanded, caught up in the story, almost off the
edge of the cot.

"The obvious."

"The obvious? What does that mean?"

"The obvious. The thing nobody ever believes in, probably
don't even believe in it when it comes along and catches them off
guard."

"Ah!" Brad said. "Death. You mean death?"

"Yes." Bill Light nodded.

"So death is the obvious." Brad seemed relieved.

"Yes." Bill swirled his whiskey and took it down in one neat
drink. "Death and life."

5.   Yes. Even something as big and apparent as the sky offered some puzzles.

The old man pushed himself up off the cot and ducked out
through the canvas flap, leaving them to sip their whiskey and
think about it. He walked into the trees, crossing fresh snow to
the clearing, where the surface had melted and refrozen and
been honed by the wind until it shone in the moonlight like a
vast expanse of milk glass.

Bill Light stopped, pissed. His member felt comfortably warm
in his hand. A blank hole opened in the snow—like an empty eye
socket. He turned and retraced his steps into camp. The tent
glowed orange from the wavering light of the lantern. The shadows of Willie and Brad and Louis were cast on the wall and
warped up the slope of the roof. The old man paused. He leaned
against the trunk of a yellow pine and listened to the voices.
Strange. He felt distinctly that this had happened before. The

idea left him feeling emptied, lost. He touched the tree with his hand, fingers clawing, finding purchase in the rough surface of the bark.

Hunting, he thought. Hunting something. Yes. After all these years you hoped to find something in yourself. But you could not look for it there. You had to watch the others. And the trees. You had to observe the way the land moved in and out of its seasons. You had to feel the stones breaking down, the fallen mulch eating itself. You could speak about the others and the land with experience and certainty. But you had to guess about yourself. Always. And you had to hope for a brief glimpse of whatever you thought you had set out to do or be.

Maybe you saw it. Maybe you did not.

How could you ever know?

6.   "Could it have changed so much?"

"What?"

"The world. I mean that the lesson of experience is no longer specific. That we've lost all that."

"That there is no sky to ride off into?"

"Yes, Willie. What have we done?"

Willie caught the flash of gold in the front of Brad's mouth; something else flashed. "Well, what about that tooth?"

"Tooth?"

"Isn't that hunk of gold evidence of something? I recall some sky. I recall riding into it. Sky and mud, too."

Brad's tongue flashed across the face of the tooth. "The fourteenth of October, nineteen thirty-six," he repeated.

"What happened then?" Louis asked.

Willie looked at the boy a second, not sure whether to overlook it as impertinence or to answer. He answered. "Brad confronted reality."

Louis frowned.

"He confronted the reality of the sky," Willie clarified.

"In the form of something harder," Brad added, shaking his head.

"It was right after algebra. Sixth period." Willie grinned.

Louis blinked and looked vexed.

"Haven't you heard of algebra?"

"Yes—I take algebra."

"Sixth?"

"No. I take Miss Tottle's English."

They had taken algebra. That day, he and Brad left the classroom and raced across the lawn to the parking lot where he had left his motorcycle, a sinister machine into which he had sunk half of his summer's earnings (the rest he had invested in the Chevrolet they were beating it home to hang a truck engine in).

Willie stood and rode the kick starter down. The bike fired and took hold.

"A motorcycle." He sighed in the tent, savoring that experience.

Yes. There was something about it, something exhilarating—the feel of the twist-grip, the wind blowing cold in his teeth, whipping his shirt, drying his armpits, the ambivalent sense of being in control of it and at the same time being helplessly borne along on it—that left Willie with a jangling sense of freedom.

They roared past the house the first time, the haywire speedometer fluctuating in a wild dance between sixty and ninety-five. Momentarily (and he felt Brad tighten behind him, anticipating the turn he ought to have known he would never make the first time) he looked to see who was home. The old man pretended to ignore him from the side of his pickup where he was unloading lumber. The old woman pulled her head back from a window, the curtain dropping, so she would not let him know she had been watching, had even been concerned. Then he began easing up, letting the machine slow down enough to allow him to turn around at the next section road and come creeping back. Not a habit (which the turning in would have been). No. A pattern.

A flood bridge carried them in an arched upswing over the Ashley Creek slough. The bike grew light in Willie's hands; his stomach rose against his diaphragm. The wooden cleats, worn, shrunken away from their nails, rattled like the out-of-tune keys on a muffled xylophone. Then down in the swampy dip just beyond the end of the bridge, a wagon loaded with loose alfalfa hay loomed up like a sudden mountain. The shaggy fetlocks of the draft horses flashed in syncopation under the high bed. And at the same moment, as though it were all being set up and timed to fit some sick sense of comedy, a car appeared. A black model A. Approaching.

Which left Willie three choices. The wagon; the car; the slough. It did not take any kind of genius to figure out the easiest, the safest, and—in fact—the only way to go. Riding both brakes, he leaned the machine towards the right hand barpit. Brad, who must have calculated the whole thing differently, froze to his back and began screaming a string of meaningless pleading obscenities in his ear. The drag of the brakes ceased. It seemed they were flying.

"Yes," he said now, breaking into the telling to remind Brad, "A bit of the sky—"

The bike soared out over the slough. The cattails started slap-slapping against the wheels, footrests, leg guards, handlebars. The brown heads burst, releasing a flurry of white fuzz. It was like going down through a cloud.

Then the machine seemed to have plowed into a gigantic pond of chewing gum. It hit the swampy surface and stuck. Something from behind came along and wiped Willie off the seat. His face smarted from the sharp cattail whipping. Then it was cooled in a balm of mud and slime.

When he finally got the muck cleared away from his eyes, he saw Brad sitting up against a fence post; it seemed he was trying to talk to it. His eyes were crossed and his nose was bleeding. In his right hand he held the round rear-view mirror off the handlebars. He was looking into it—dazed.

"I couldn't focus," Brad laughed, swallowing whiskey.

The black model A was clattering across the high bridge with an insulting nonchalance—stilted, tilting away in the October haze. The horses were still running with the hay. The farmer, yelling *whoa!* at them, seemed merely to succeed in scaring them more. After a moment, he and Brad were alone.

The motorcycle stood nearly half submerged in black mud. A

blue pocket of dense smoke formed around the hot exhaust. A line of flame like a single finger, pointing in accusation, reached towards the smoke. Fire spread rapidly over the entire machine.

Brad broke in, "Willie grabbed me and dragged me up onto the road, right across it, and down into the ditch on the other side before I knew what the hell was happening."

They dived through the stiff salt grass and into the stagnant water. A bullfrog, in a display of squatty indignation, leaped away and disappeared down through a lacing of watercress.

It was like waiting for the explosion of a firecracker with a defective fuse. When finally it did go off, the earth jerked and shook. Spongy chunks of smoking mud, cattail spears, and bits of shrapnel from the motorcycle came showering down on them.

"Christ," Willie muttered. "Half a goddam summer—shot."

Brad held his eyes squinched shut; they were starting to swell, starting to go puffy and black. "What about my tooth?"

Willie looked at the upper lip twisted away from the gum. "What tooth?"

Brad's tongue poked through the hole. He moaned.

"Come on," Willie said.

Cautiously, they crossed the road. Around the smoldering skeleton of the motorcycle was a crater as big as a spud cellar. Brown slough water was starting to spill into it, the hot steel parts hissing.

Willie clasped his hands and then spread the palms to the stove. "How many times, when Bernie and I were tearing all over France, riding that goddam GI Harley–Davidson, did I think of the explosion it could make under us. Jesus. Big enough to dig our graves."

"Yes, okay. But what about the sky," Brad insisted, the joints of the cot creaking as he pressed his face towards Willie's. "Where was the sky?"

"We missed it."

"Yes—but how?"

"I think we were like the old man. We thought we were looking for our bit of the sky when actually we were running from it —though we didn't know that at the time."

"Oh. And how would we have found it?"

"We could have climbed back on that bike."
"And let it blow up under us, I suppose."
"Why not?"

7. But it was, finally, the old man's trip. Even though—and this was the first time in well over sixty years—he did not get his deer. Which was not the fault of the deer. The deer tried. Willie watched them sneak past him in the trees. And the old man knew they were doing it. A man of his experience could not help but know. He almost deliberately refused to look the way instinct was obviously telling him to look. If he had bothered to shoot, or even to allow his rifle to go off, Willie thought, a buck could at least have attempted to jump out in front of the bullet. Something suicidal, out of some kind of simple cosmic embarrassment, that would have maintained the balance of things. But no.

Willie tailed him for four days. The old man set out in a different direction each morning. He walked for miles, tireless, revisiting favorite spots, creeping down to the scenes of old and important kills. He took his rifle—its chambers empty, magazine empty too. And there was not even a click of brass shell casings when he reached in his pocket for a little something to throw to the birds.

Late in the fourth day, Willie realized (the snap of a twig, the rustle of stones confirming a vague awareness) that Louis was following them both.

Back in camp that evening, Sunday, he spoke to the old man, "Better get your gear loaded up, Pa. We can't stay up here all winter."

"God—I can't go down yet," Bill Light declared, drawing himself up, his voice stern. Somewhere in the tone there was a soft quality; and Willie almost choked on it. "Maybe it hasn't occurred to you—but I've not got my deer yet." He fished for his chewing tobacco.

"Yes. I've noticed."

"Go on down then," the old man said, opening his knife. "I'll follow you in a day or two."

"I can wait."

"No need," the old man said, looking up from the plug he was cutting into, the sharp blade shaving neatly at the outside leaf.

Willie felt the urge then to quote from Lear. He had read the play over and over in Council Tree; there was a passage Robbie Rydell had underlined in soft red pencil:

Oh reason not the need

It was frighteningly appropriate. But the impulse to repeat it was foolish. And he did not. For he recalled the one time he had quoted Shakespeare to the old man.

"Who said that?"

"Shakespeare."

The old man had leveled a look across the supper table at him that would have brought a dump truck to a shuddering halt. And the two syllables broke like a stick, "Snakeshit!"

"There ain't no need," the old man was saying. He pushed a trimmed cut of the plug into his mouth, his words growing soft, clearing. "That ought to be plenty clear by now. You and Louis been tagging me all over this goddam mountain for days. Scaring the deer off so I couldn't get a decent shot." He spit. The juice hit a seam in the stove and came alive, dancing till it consumed itself. He turned to Brad. "Jesus. If I'd walked over a cliff, those two fools would have marched right off behind me. No more goddam sense."

So Willie went down. He left the old man up there alone. But he could barely wait through the night. He got up at four and dressed. Somewhere in the dark, he heard the old woman mutter something to the wall. Something about men. He heard the flat of her hand fall on the pillow. He left the house. New frost swirled up behind the car as he sped back toward the mountains. It was still dark when he reached the summit. He did not drive right up to the camp. He parked a mile away. He took his rifle and struck out through the snow, over a ridge, climbing to a spot from which he could see clearly down into the ravine.

Yellowish lantern light burned through the heavy canvas of the tent. It was as if the walls of a house had been taken away and only the lighted interior remained. Smoke trailed out of the stove-pipe. Breakfast was probably cooked. The thought of it drew at his stomach. The old man would have done it because it was to be done and he would let it go cold and then scrape it into the fire.

A few moments passed. The lantern went down. The tent seemed to grow smaller and then almost to fade. The old man emerged. He stood in the cold, looking around him, plumes of his breath rising into the trees. He ducked back into the tent. When he pushed the canvas flap aside again, he held his rifle. It would not be loaded. He slipped away into the trees. Willie skirted the open area near the camp and followed him. The old man moved quickly, with stealth and grace. Willie stayed above him, real-izing they were headed for the spring.

The old man stopped in the cover. Downwind. He laid his rifle across his knees for support and crouched. A huge buck stood at the spring, drinking. It was a perfect shot. The old man could have hit the buck anywhere—at the base of the horns, or in the chest. He could have got his deer; he could have continued. But he did not move. And Willie knew he could not, would not shoot. He wondered if he should shoot the deer—if the token gesture would count. No. Then he wondered if he should shoot them both.

Slowly, the buck raised its head. But it did not break and run. It walked to a tree, moving with a spongy gliding step that could put it into instant and graceful flight. It rubbed its horns against the low branches of the tree. Perhaps to wear off a little late vel-vet. Or perhaps because it knew that out there somewhere was an old friend in a bad time.

And Willie, overwhelmed with his own helplessness and super-fluousness, turned and left them.

8.   "What do you suppose he wants to see you for?" Geo asked, reading the note from the office over Louis's shoulder.

They were in their first-period class, study hall, which was also their homeroom. They had just finished copying the last of Little Benny Westlake's algebra answers, which he got from Julie Volks, when one of the student secretaries brought in the note from the principal.

"It's probably about last week," Louis decided.

"Aren't you shook up?"

"Why should I be shook up?"

"Well—likely as not," Little Benny conjectured, "they'll just up and kick your ass out of here."

"Yeah. You knew about the mimeographed letter," Geo reminded. "They'll probably kick you out."

"How could I ever stand the torture?"

"Shit—that ain't the half of it," Benny added. "Then, they'll haul you back."

"It's kind of hard to understand how the system works," Geo commented seriously.

"Well," Louis said, drawing a hand with the middle finger extended obscenely across the note. "I'll bet you money old Pukus has invented a pretty good word for it."

9.   "Compulsory." Martin Lukus muttered to himself, getting clear in his mind precisely what he was going to say.

Most of the time it would be "a cold" or even only "ill." Now there was a word for you. Please excuse so and so. He was ill. They would be out of school for two days, usually the Friday and Monday of the opening weekend of deer-hunting season. The same for pheasants.

But not this one. He reread it.

To Whom It May Concern:

Please excuse Louis Light for absence Monday through
Friday of last week. He was deer hunting.
                                        Respectfully,
                                          (signed)
                                        William Light, II

What did you do with something like that? The parents knew
the policy. Mimeographed announcements had been sent out:
students were absolutely forbidden to stay out of school to go
deer hunting. This was preposterous. Couldn't he just have lied?
Like the rest of them. Did no one understand the ridiculous position this kind of stupid bullheaded honesty put him in?

Martin Lukus read the note through one more time, reading
also the attached note from Louis Light's homeroom teacher. He
dropped his feet from the top of his desk and tugged his Ivy
League vest straight. He would damn well bring this up at the
next PTA, quote a little John Dewey (Dewey must have said
something that would work out here).

"Louis Light to see you, Mr. Lukus."

He could tell from the way the girl looked at Louis that she
would listen through the partition. Damn these kids; they hung
together. Maybe he ought to send her down to auto mechanics or
somewhere. No. He let it go. He would give her something to report. Maybe he would also get Louis to admit to writing the
poem on Miss Tottle's board, a little mystery that still remained
unsolved.

"Have a seat, Louis." Martin Lukus looked sidelong out into
the clouds (something he knew was efficacious in producing pos-
itive tension) until all of the air had hissed out of the leatherette
cushion in the chair across from the desk. He realized, at that
moment, that he actually hated the boy. Genuinely, honestly,
hated him. Well, that would make it easier.

"Now," he said, swiveling in his chair. He let the word hang
ominously between them while he leafed through the papers on
his desk—as if he were not thoroughly familiar with the case.
Then, reading, he slowly let his eyebrows raise and he unfas-

tened his glasses from his ears. "Yes. Now, Louis, what's the meaning of this?"

"What?"

Martin Lukus thrust himself forward, as though to counter and block the boy's arrogance. He dropped his glasses from a meaningful height onto the stack of papers, heavy plastic earpieces clicking. "This little note from your father."

"It came about because of a little family friction."

"What does that mean?"

"My Grandmother Fulton wouldn't write one."

"Obviously she was aware of our strict regulation on the matter." He paused. "And your father wasn't."

"No—he knew," Louis said. "I told him."

"And he saw no reason to observe it?"

"He just said he thought it was a lot of bullshit."

Martin Lukus swallowed his fury. The little bastard was not going to get to him with that old trick. He would not fall for it. "That was quite uncalled for, Louis." He swallowed again.

"That's what he said—sir." There was no apology.

"Does your father have a phone?"

"Yes. He's got two." Louis seemed to sprawl more comfortably in the chair. "Private and business."

"Which one would reach him at this time of day?"

"It depends on what you want. The phones are side by side. He has an office in the back of my Grandma Light's house."

"What are the numbers?" Now he recalled the enigma of Willie Light's life. A man who had shown up after the war—years late. With money. Apparently legal—though never explained. Money that reputedly continued to grow in New York City, on Wall Street, through some magic or other.

"347 and 625."

Martin Lukus waited for the operator's "Number please," and gave her the 625.

"Mr. Light?"

"Speaking."

"Mr. Light, this is Martin Lukus, principal of—"

"Beg your pardon, Lukus, could you call me on my private line? I'm expecting an urgent call from New York on this phone." He hung up.

Without flashing a look at Louis, Martin Lukus drove his finger down on the receiver button, pressing until he felt a small circle printed in his skin. He let it up and whistled drily while he waited for the operator again.

"Lukus?"

"Yes."

"Now, then, what was it you wanted me for?"

Martin Lukus found that in his consternation he had lost sight of a considerable part of his plan of action; the words he had rehearsed had all but escaped him. He went ahead, but feebly. "Did you write this note for Louis."

"Well, I did write one—yes."

"And you were aware of our regulations on the matter?"

"I think that's a lot of—"

"Louis already related to me what you think," Martin Lukus cut in. "The fact is, Mr. Light, the rule does exist. We made the rules in order to keep things functioning."

"All right, Lukus. I believe you've established that point. What're you going to do with him?"

"To tell the truth, I haven't arrived at an appropriate punishment yet. . . . But let me say this: we could very easily expel him. We could, if we felt it necessary to carry things that far."

"Now, hold on, Lukus. Let me get this straight. You mean to tell me that you would stop him from coming because he didn't come in the first place?"

Martin Lukus swiveled his chair around so he faced the window. "Mr. Light, you're twisting my meaning." He glared out into the clouds. A single-engine plane droned above the school. Its shadow crossed the lawn, stretched up the side of a house, and was gone. He ground his teeth silently.

"Just what the hell is the meaning of the word expel, Lukus? I don't mean I want you to run through the whole etymology since god or someone invented it to describe that hurried leave-taking Adam and Eve made from the garden—since that obviously meant never to come back. No. I mean only the practical meaning you school people have invented for it in the meantime."

"We would force him to leave—"

"That's just what I got through saying: force him to leave

when you were forcing him to stay in the first place and would turn right around and force him to come back."

Smiling badly, Martin Lukus looked at Louis Light. He firmed his jaw. "Mr. Light, expel means, as it implies, that he had somehow made himself unfit to share in the opportunity of being in the school system—and we would be sending him out. But, since school is compulsory (There!) in this state until graduation or the age of eighteen, he would have to be dealt with by the juvenile authorities who would insist that he be reinstated."

"Court? He would go to court?"

The tone in Willie Light's voice gave Martin Lukus a new measure of self-confidence. "That's right. Court."

"Okay, Lukus, you can write that note off as null and void. I'll have another one in its place by morning. Now—my other phone is ringing. Thanks for calling, Lukus. Pleasure to speak with you."

For the second time, Martin Lukus was left with a dead phone in his hand.

"Louis," he ordered, trying to keep bewilderment and growing exasperation out of his voice. "Go on back to your homeroom."

The boy left. The chair cushion filled with air, erasing the depression he had made in the yellow ersatz leather. Out in the front office, a typewriter began clacking along at the jog-trot pace of the student secretary's still inexpert fingers. Martin Lukus sat quietly, raising his feet, and attempted to think through what had happened.

As promised, a new note arrived the next morning. It was on letterhead bond this time: Schwartz, Geller, Levi, Stein, and Light, Inc. There was a New York City address and a cable code: *Slight*.

Dear Mr. Lukus:

Louis Light was kept out of school Monday through Friday of the past week to undergo treatment for an ancient, in-

exorable family plague—hart sickness. I hope you can view
this absence with understanding and tolerance.

> I remain,
> (signed)
> William Light, II

Martin Lukus had his glasses yanked free of his face and had the
phone in his fist before he got together sense enough to stop and
think the whole thing over.

9

Man and Beast:

Lessons in the Shadow of Reality, Truth, and Solid Fact

❖❖❖❖❖❖❖❖❖❖❖❖❖❖❖❖❖

1956

1.   "Never can tell nothing about nothing," Lucky Jordan muttered, languishing easily against the bar. "Always sort of run my life according to that there piece of philosophy. Ain't been wrong yet. Mostly." Lucky brushed lightly at a deceptive shadow on the sleeve of his laundry-stiff white shirt—he was never to be seen in any other kind: white, a fancy-cut yoke, everything fastening with an excess of pearl snap buttons. He looked into Louis's face, then Geo's. He had deep gouges in the leathery skin below his cheekbones; his nose, moderately long, was humped in the middle; and his lips were half-opened and squared in a chapped sneer. Finally, he shifted his gaze between the two boys and came to focus on a forest of racked cue sticks lined along the wall.

Geo was nervous. He had not wanted to come in the Brown Derby Poolhall. This was no place for a Mormon. Or a minor. The place swam with lazy afternoon shadows. Beyond the pool tables, a shaft of sunlight burned onto a checkerboard over which two silent old men pored, reaching occasionally to make a stealthy move, settling back into the small-town oblivion. The bartender was smoking a Camel and listening to a cowboy music program on the radio. The orange light of the tubes fanned out onto a calender nude.

"One of you fellers got some change on you—a quarter?"

Lucky asked it, Geo thought, as if it were nothing, a simple everyday question about the weather—or, which was worse, they even owed it to him. Louis, true to form, just stood there, neither yes nor no expressed on his face. So Geo, who grew embarrassed by static confrontations, fished a coin out of his Levi's pocket.

"Yeah." Lucky grunted, taking the quarter without seeming to see the hand. "Pay you back pretty soon. I'm expecting dough. Ought to be coming through any day now. Been looking for it." Outside of casual references to his own fame, this expected money from some mysterious somewhere was Lucky's most frequent topic of conversation, which all somehow offset his most frequent action: bumming a little change to see him through. Affixing the squint that passed for wisdom and constant abysmal thinking beyond the two boys, he polished the bird on the quarter with his thumb.

"Where does your money come from?" Louis asked, without either derision or any apparent hope of an answer. "I mean—normally."

"I got a source," Lucky replied, as though that were not vague. "Waiting on my source right now, matter of fact." He sighed. "Waiting on my source."

Meanwhile, Lucky pushed the coin across to the bartender, who came away from the radio—his face falling in shadow—long enough to draw a beer. Intent (and with absolute impunity), Lucky wrinkled his brow, sniffed seriously, and slipped the dime of change into his watch pocket. He pressed the schooner to his lips, the mechanism of his throat gathering and sliding between the stiff white flanges of his shirt collar.

"I got that barrel rigged," he said. Two peaks of foam were printed at the corners of his mouth. "I strung it up down in the old man's barn. You can get in some practice there."

"So!" Old man Jordan accused sharply from the porch, where he sat with his cane. "So you're fixing to make no-counts of these two young fellers, too?" He looked them up and down, his hazy bifocals flashing in their small metal frames.

"Too?"

"Yes, *too*! I'm talking about you. There ain't nothing in that blamed head of yours but working about ten seconds a week— the weeks you work at all—to the fancy blare of some brass orchestra and a loudspeaker shouting your greatness out towards them bleachers full of folks come down to have a close look at a bunch of bona-fide fools."

"Nothing wrong with rodeo," Lucky argued lugubriously. "It's a respectable profession."

"It is if you happen to be the horse."

Lucky ignored him and turned towards the corral.

Grumbling and dragging his bum leg along through the weeds, old man Jordan hobbled after them down the path past the outhouse to the barn.

Inside, as soon as his pupils adjusted to the dark, Geo saw suspended from four ropes stretching off into the corners of the barn, a fifty-five-gallon oil drum scantily padded with a scrap of mouse-eaten quilt. A spidery man, maybe twenty or thirty or more—Geo could not tell—was doing up the latigo on a brief bareback rigging: an oblong piece of leather only slightly wider than the cinch, with an adjustable handhold that looked like a drawer pull.

"This here's Bit Johns," Lucky introduced, repeating Louis's and Geo's names, gesticulating with his thumb.

"Bit?" Louis asked.

"Yeah." Bit seemed to giggle down the word.

"Funny name."

"Yeah—it is, ain't it?" Bit grinned, a spit softened toothpick pegged between two teeth.

"Bit's a bullrider," Lucky said generally. "Rides bulls."

The statement puzzled Geo. "What else? I mean—if he's a bullrider."

"Some don't."

Bit shoved his hands into his Levi's and let his eyes flash.

"Might ought to raise that there barrel to about forty feet," old man Jordan muttered, forcing his way into the conversation.

Geo swallowed and wondered what he was doing here. He looked at Louis. Louis was already touching the barrel and inspecting the rigging. And it struck Geo that he was really serious.

"Knock it off, Pa," Lucky warned.

"Might ought to," the old man persisted. "So's these here greenhorns'll get some practice in on that there phase of things too. Unless maybe they're making britches glue a damn sight stouter than they used to. Yessiree, you two young bucks better hurry up and grab yourselves some of this famous living. Then you can wear them stiff white shirts—like Lucky here—because your ma's work with an iron won't come up to snuff no more. Course now, her cooking won't deteriorate none, likely."

"Pa. I believe I hear them hogs of yours grunting and wanting their slops," Lucky hinted firmly. Then, turning, he peered back into the shadows of the barn. "Where's that Injun?"

Geo knew from frequent allusions in previous conversations that Lucky was referring to Dog's Tree, a Ute who rodeoed with him and Bit Johns.

"Maybe he's off to the laundry after a white shirt—so's he'll be fit to kowtow with the likes of yourself."

"Pa, I told you about them pigs!"

"Injun's absent," Bit surmised.

"Looks like I'll have to help yank them ropes," Lucky frowned, gazing regretfully at his open palms.

"Yeah," Bit said. "Does."

"Don't leave me a whole lot of time to coach—the way I ought."

"Nope. It don't."

"Wish that goddam Injun'd show," Lucky muttered, out of sorts. "This's just like a Ute. Don't want him around and you're tripping on him. Need him for something and he vanishes."

"Does." Bit worked a second with his toothpick.

Lucky hung his hat lightly on a nail—so it would not get soiled or bumped out of crease. And though it seemed to hurt his pride, he yanked fiercely at two of the ropes in addition to chanting professional advice to the two new young barrel cowboys.

They took turns mounting the mechanical bucking horse. Geo felt the wide curve of the barrel between his legs, cold, hard. There was something exhilarating about it. It rose and lunged, rolled and canted. His knuckles cracked against the steel. Then the rigging was ripped out of his hand. It seemed he was hardly on, one hand clawed around the handle, feet ahead in a spurring position, before he flew off and landed on the thin layer of bedding straw spread on the barn floor, his nostrils stinging from the loose chaff.

"Christ, Louis," he puffed, picking himself up. "Do you suppose he's right?"

"Who?"

"That old man."

Louis shrugged.

"Forty feet would make it ten times as far to fall," Geo reasoned. "And ten times worse hitting. And I don't know whether I can stand that." And maybe he would have just called it quits (as though some sense of logic and sanity had been jarred into his head) but an instant later he saw Louis bounce back from the barn floor, shaking off straw—moving like an actor in a movie, the projector suddenly reversed—and shout for more.

"It's my turn," Geo insisted.

"Look, Geo. You don't have to," Louis said. "Maybe you could help Bit pull the ropes or something."

Geo moved Louis Light out of the way and mounted the barrel. After another hour the skin on the insides of his thighs was raw and his spine felt like something someone had been beating with a rock. Then, finally, Louis did not spring so suddenly back to his feet. He rolled over into a sitting position and admitted he had had about enough for one day.

Using the edge of his hand as a squeegee, Lucky Jordan slicked the sweat off his forehead. He eased his wide black hat off the nail and set it squarely on the top of his head, the abrupt upsweep of its brim adding to the chiseled look of his face.

"See you in a week," he said.

Louis turned in the path and raised his hand. Lucky and Bit Johns, the weedy bullrider, stood in the doorway of the barn, their white shirts stark against the shadows.

Getting in the car, having to sit carefully and let himself down into the cushion lightly because of his bruises, Louis said, "God, that was fun!"

Geo turned his thin, pained face and stared at him.

2. Midweek, Hartt Westlake was picked up by the State Highway Patrol, jailed briefly, then hauled off to the State Mental Hospital in Provo. This came about as the logical result of his own incongruous action against the general public: he was seen walking naked, with the exception of his red beard, a few other profusions of carrot-colored hair, and the violin he carried but refused to employ as a shield over his ample manhood (virtually unused in all the years since the Second World War and his own faulty French campaign), right down the white centerline of Highway 40.

A major part of the problem with Hartt arose out of the enthusiasm of an ambitious young officer named Sorrels. Sorrels, armed with flashlight, pistol, and handcuffs, pursued Hartt into a tall cottonwood tree and ended up with a broken arm. Hartt, his violin tucked under one massive arm, cornered Sorrels in a crotch of the tree. Sorrels fumbled and dropped his pistol. Hartt kept coming. Sorrels, a shaky silhouette against the full moon, pleaded for mercy. He tried to blind the naked musician with his flashlight. Hartt caught hold of him, handcuffed him to a limb, and kicked him backwards off his perch. He was just climbing down with the stolen flashlight and a silver whistle when he was surrounded by all the available lawmen in the immediate vicinity.

Golden Westlake, the father according to all extant county records, refused to have anything to do with the matter, drawing his lips in a thin line over his teeth and stating, "That there redhaired loon ain't none of my affair. He's an impostor. The boy I sprung from my loins and helped draw out of her belly on my own scrubbed kitchen table died somewhere over there in the

Big War—before he got tangled in with them French bastards
and their whorehouses."

So a grief-stricken Belle Westlake filled out and signed the
necessary papers to pronounce Hartt a public nuisance. So he
could be legally recommended for treatment. She came home,
climbed the stairs to the attic, and got set for a long cry, burying
her face in the lap of her cotton dress and letting her head hang
between her knees. Little mud pies formed in the floor dust.

Naturally, all this was not without ramifications of another
sort.

At the next Saturday dance, a very sad affair, since Belle's silent weeping left the piano keys glistening like wet Italian tiles,
Arnie Sikes—who had, one month earlier, stepped onto the
bandstand and asked if he might sit in (he played pretty good
banjo and fair harmonica and could solo on both instruments at
the same time, an act of pure spectacle which pleased anyone
who did not know much about music but loved a rousing show, a
category into which most of the Westlakes' audience fell)—
played all of Hartt's parts.

Arnie Sikes had his eye on Julie. Little Benny knew this and
tried his best to talk some sense into Belle's head. Arnie was an
oil-field roughneck (out of work) and one bad character. And
besides that he had a dashing way with women; not to mention
the fact that he was taller than Julie, who had already begun to
laugh at his jokes and spurts of fast-talk between numbers. But
Belle would not listen to reason in any form.

The next Friday, playing a benefit, Little Benny heard Arnie
Sikes, his voice grown suddenly earnest, ask Julie during the in-
termission break if she would ride home with him after the
dance. There was no mistaking the purpose in Arnie's mind. And
when she accepted, Little Benny was so upset that he could
hardly contain himself. He almost played the rest of the band
right off the stage. After two numbers, more than half of the dancers had ceased and were collected in a semicircle to just watch
and listen to his playing.

Then, backstage, before Julie had wiggled out of her accordion
harness and gathered up her sheet music, Little Benny cornered
Arnie Sikes at jackknife-point and told him solemnly to haul ass;
if he ever saw him again, he said through his teeth, he would cut

him to ribbons. Arnie just gave a crusty laugh. Benny made a serious two-inch slit in the man's silk shirt. Then, holding the knife
point against his skin for emphasis, he added, his voice shaking,
"If you ever show your face around here again, mister, I'll kill
you."

"Arnie?"

Little Benny (who had, that spring, ordered elevator shoes
from the back pages of a man's magazine and then had Belle let
out all of his pants an inch to cover the telltale tops) stood bent
over his guitar case, wedging his shell-colored pick between the
first, second, and third strings. Sweat was starting to make his
scalp itch.

"Where's Arnie?"

"Just saw him drive off," Golden said, coming in for another
load of electrical gear. "Can't figure that guy out. He was just
going to beat hell."

"Benny—"

"You can ride home with me, Julie." He was trying to keep his
voice steady.

Without a word, Julie spun and marched out to Golden's pickup truck.

Little Benny hardly saw her at all during the next week. At
home, she kept to her room, shooting the bolt and pretending to
study. She would not ride to school with him; she got up early
and took the yellow eight-o'clock bus. Wednesday, she came
home late. He heard her tell Belle that she had a job; it had come
about through the recommendation of her business skills teacher,
since she was the best in her class at typing and shorthand. She
would work evenings after school for Buddy Bell, a young geolo-
gist who was making it big on oil exploration. And when summer
came, she would go on full time for him. It meant, she said, she
could start saving for college.

At the Saturday night dance, Buddy Bell, recently separated
from his wife, though nothing had been done to make it legal,
showed up in the crowd, stag, and waited for Julie.

Little Benny tried to act as though nothing were happening, as
though he really did not care. He tapped his foot quietly while
he put his guitar away; there seemed to be a rhythm to his very

thinking. But he was doing everything too fast—even if it had the same deft precision of his playing. Outside the hall, he watched Buddy Bell put Julie in his T-bird (the way someone would place a valuable object in a box). Rich bastards, he was thinking slowly, rich bastards can get anything they want.

The throaty sounds of his twin exhausts calmed Little Benny. He drove a safe distance behind Buddy Bell. And when Buddy parked and ushered Julie into Jim's Cafe, Little Benny nosed his Ford out of the alley behind the post office to wait for whatever came next. His nervous hands, insensitive to the nippy April night though they usually stiffened at the slightest cold, traced and retraced every line and imperfection of the steering wheel. He was thinking. He had the jackknife; and there was a long tire iron under the seat. He thought of his deer rifle. It had a scope and he could shoot. But he could not risk taking the time to go home for it.

Half an hour later when they came out, Julie was walking close to Buddy Bell, her head against his shoulder, her arm swinging in a careless happy way. Buddy pressed her against the door of his T-bird with an earnest kiss. Little Benny watched to the end, his forehead resting on the steering wheel, his eyes leveled just above the dash, staring.

Little Benny did not crowd the T-bird. He kept his distance. Buddy drove to no place special: he simply cruised along a country road to an indefinite spot, pulled one wheel into the weeds, stopped, and turned off his headlights.

Little Benny put out his own lights, crept closer, and stopped. He tried to think what he was going to do. His pounding heart shook his whole body. He had taken care of Arnie Sikes all right. But Sikes was a drifter. No damn good to anyone. Worse. Now he had to do something about Buddy Bell. That was different. He felt frozen. His body was cold, leaden with pain. In fact, he did not make a move—his thumb and forefinger still closed on the key—until he saw the interior light flash on then off in the T-bird and Buddy Bell walked around to the back. Buddy unzipped and pissed in the grass.

Little Benny leaped out of his Ford and raced towards Buddy, calling him a no good sonofabitch, a dirty bastard. Clawing up

stones as he ran, he peppered both Buddy and the car. Buddy
sheltered his head and ran around in front, doing up his pants.
Julie jumped out.

"Benny!" she screamed. "Benny, stop it!"

Little Benny came to a standstill.

Julie reached behind her and did up the zipper on her organdy
dress. "Benny," she said sternly. "What's the matter with you?"

Benny could not reply.

"You sawed-off little so-and-so, you leave me alone. Just who
do you think you are?"

Little Benny started numbly to retreat.

"Who do you think you are, Benny Westlake?" she shouted.

3.   A few days later, Hank Withers, the famous cowboy
bandleader and recording star, came to the Imperial Hall for a
one-night engagement. The Westlakes were booked as the backup
group. Little Benny, still badly broken up about the previous
Saturday night, played as though his very soul would shatter.
Hank Withers himself came out of the dressing room and stood
right in front of the stage, a tall conspicuous figure in his white
hat and embroidered suit. When the set was over, he stepped up
and offered Little Benny an on-the-spot job as his new lead gui-
tarist and talent discovery. Little Benny was too smart to fail to
see this as a chance of a lifetime. He accepted and did not even
stay in town long enough to graduate from high school.

The Westlake family was cut in half. Hartt was off his rocker
and Little Benny had taken to the road. The band had all but
perished. So Melody Mountain did not open for the annual May
Day Dance.

Which was part of the whole failure of spring that year.

4.   "Oh, man—get a load of that stern!"

"Arf!" Geo chomped ardently.

The young student teacher, Miss Boulle, wearing patent high heels, came chipping across the room in front of the class. Mr. Lukus had just announced that Miss Tottle was in the hospital and that Miss Boulle would be taking her place. Miss Boulle wore a billowy white blouse with a lace front and a straight-cut charcoal skirt. At the edge of the lace, a jeweled pin rode her left breast like a small lighted boat. She was solid and more than moderately sexy. Ironically, her obvious attempts at hiding these facts somehow emphasized them—the frilly blouse so incongruous with the weight of her bosom, the neatly fitted dark skirt rounding and tapering over what Louis had just pronounced her stern, and the delicate pin like the symbol of some attainment, left perhaps by an admirer (though it was, in fact, merely her sorority charm).

"I've just had a premonition," Louis murmured, leaning towards Geo.

"What's that?"

"I think I'm going to like the last few weeks of English better than I thought I would."

"No kidding."

"It's going to be painful, though."

"Painful?"

"Yeah. Like having to sit back and watch an ice-cream cone melt."

"You mean two ice-cream cones," Geo grinned.

"Right."

"Hell, Louis," Geo sneered out of the corner of his mouth. "She's not all that hot in the face."

"The face has not been created that a sack won't hide," Louis argued cogently. "A sack or the dark of the moon."

Geo was ready with an insulting retort when he happened to glance to the front of the room. The slender grin wasted from his lips, his narrow face and shoulders drooping sheepishly. He stared at Miss Boulle. Hands forked over her hipbones, she had fixed them with an unpracticed and slightly overdone expression of harshness and discipline. She was visibly uneasy, visibly trying not to seem so. Really more woman than she could stand to be. More woman than teacher.

"Is there something you'd like to tell the whole class?"

The class turned and looked at them.

"No—" Louis said, adding a delayed, "Ma'am."

"All right. Please save your talking till a later time. Would you come up to the front at the end of the hour." She thrust her forefinger into Miss Tottle's perforated rubber fingertip and started leafing through the grammar text towards the assignment.

Already, Miss Boulle had given away her two worst qualities. The first, her smile, revealed large white teeth that shone like muted footlights for the play of her tongue, hinges of saliva flexing in the corners of her mouth, as she worked for an exaggerated clarity of enunciation that she obviously thought befitting her position. The second was her habit of pausing mid-thought and chewing chunks of lipstick from her lips.

"What're you going to say?" Geo asked.

"When?"

"After class?"

"I'm going to tell her what you said about her ass."

"Me!"

The bell rang and class ended. Miss Boulle, her hand trembling just perceptibly after her lecture on the basic structure of a good paragraph, smiled hesitantly at them.

"I hope you will like the class," she said in an unexpectedly friendly tone. "I'd like to keep it casual if I can. This is my first real teaching experience. It's unfortunate that Miss Tottle had to go to the hospital for this operation. But it does give me an opportunity to be on my own. I'm young. And I think I'm close enough to students to be able to understand your problems. If anything comes up that I can help with, please talk to me about it."

"I sense," Louis said, when they were out in the hallway, "that at least one of those problems is going to come up. One problem in particular."

"You thinking what I think you're thinking?"

"I'm thinking," Louis admitted.

"Man, Louis, I don't think you're going to be getting any of Miss Boulle."

"Oh? Ten dollars says I get her by the end of the next two weeks—by graduation."

"Louis, you already owe me seventeen-fifty."

"I know, Geo. We're not talking about that."

"Okay, Louis. Ten bucks. But you'd be money ahead to just forget this one and let me padlock your fly."

5.   It was probably merely the thick fill of sand and sawdust in the arena that did it. It was soft and deep and they could not get traction with their slick leather-soled boots. So, like the others, like all the old hands, they seemed to slough and swagger the whole distance along the fence in front of the bleachers. They acted totally oblivious to the fact that they were being observed, or even noticed (they might have been walking alone through Death Valley)—though they were an essential part of the spectacle. They wore Wrangler jeans, pressed to a sharp crease, and stark-white shirts with pearl snap buttons. Black numbers stenciled on squares of oilcloth were pinned to their backs. Louis was 15; Geo 28. Their upswept Panama hats offered no shade. But it was night.

"There they go," Brad Meade announced, his gold tooth showing at the edge of his grin.

"Just now strutted down from the drugstore," Bill Light commented drily. "Drugstore cowboys."

Willie Light pursed his lips, then did not say anything.

Looking vaguely up into the bleachers, both Louis and Geo lifted and caught first one foot and then the other in a square of the mesh fencing and fastened on their spurs.

"Good god! Stamping around like a couple of young cocks, parading their plumage and the bright flop of their combs!" the old man observed with disgust. "We'll see if them broncs can't straighten them out some. Unless maybe the horses they got here are of the same caliber."

"I guess a boy's got to learn to cast a man's shadow sometime," Brad interrupted. "Isn't that right, Willie?"

"I guess," Will said, neither agreement nor disagreement apparent in his voice.

"I expect those two tinhorns'll be able to measure their shadows just as soon as they hit them," the old man huffed. He spread his feet in a wide V and discharged soupy brown spit down into the darkness beneath the bleachers, hoping to hit some kid hunting for dropped nickels and pennies in the slatted shadows. "Maybe they can stop a minute and size it up. Might just decide to throw it back for something a little bigger." He drew the edge of his hand across his mouth and then tongued his cud back in place. "Something they ain't likely to set eyes on from no drugstore stool."

The horses had been drawn. Geo was to be the first rider in the first go-round of bareback broncs, riding hopefully (at least he was starting on it) a horse called Strawberries—because of its color. Following him were two out-of-town cowboys. Then Louis Light was to come out on Down Under.

The announcer called out over the loudspeaker for Lucky Jordan. He was wanted at the judges' table to settle the small matter of his entry fee.

Lucky had Bit Johns and Dog's Tree backed up against a chute. "I'll pay you back as soon as they dole out the prize money for the saddle broncs," he was promising.

"And who says you're going to latch onto a piece of that dough?" Bit charged, his reedy legs spread, his toothpick working nervously in one corner of his mouth.

"Always do. Most always, leastways. Besides, if I do draw a bum horse or fall victim to some bad judging, I can pay you in a couple of days. Just as soon as my source comes through. That soon."

Dog's Tree, the Ute cowboy who lived profusely on government Indian grant money and oil royalty checks, flatly refused to look at Lucky. "One buck!" he cried and drew the bill out of a tight pocket.

Louis slapped a sock filled with powdered resin into the palm of the tight glove he would wear for his ride.

Geo gave Lucky a dollar and climbed the chute gate for the third time. He peered down at Strawberries. "Man," he said, "I've got to pee."

A few more cowboys loosened up enough to give Lucky Jordan his entry fee in dollar bills. Then they all turned to watch the grand entry.

As the rodeo queen, Miss Spring Stampede, rode past, flying the American flag, Louis took a step forward and lifted his straw hat in a baroque salute. She smiled at him from under her white Stetson and leaned into a turn, her ass, tight in snug twill pants, bouncing softly up and down against the dished seat of her fancy tooled saddle.

"Hey, easy money," Bit Johns chortled, slapping his leg and wagging his head. "You'll have trouble enough trying to stick on that horse you drawed."

Spurs jingled. A general appreciative guffaw rippled among the ranks of the cowboys.

Geo looked again at his horse, asked again if the rigging was secure, and went out behind the chutes again to pee. He returned, but he was by no means relieved. He climbed the chute gate and took one more look at Strawberries. Louis scaled the gate behind him.

"Looks a little different than that barrel of Lucky's, huh?"

"Yeah," Geo agreed.

"You ready?"

"I guess so. Shit—I keep thinking I've got to pee, or something. But I know that if I went back there again I couldn't get anything to run this time either." He tried to brush nonchalantly at the sleeve of his white shirt and nearly fell off the gate.

"Come on. You've got to get ready."

"Okay, Louis, let's go."

"You've got to get on him first."

"Okay, Louis."

With Louis holding his belt, Geo eased down onto the horse,

finding its back surprisingly narrow. He pushed his fingers under the leather handhold, his knuckles sinking into the soft sheephide cushion. The horse seemed to freeze, crouching slightly.

"Ready?"

"I guess."

"Spurs high in the shoulders," Louis reminded, speaking now through one of the openings in the gate. "The minute you see daylight, set them in the sonofabitch."

"Yeah," Geo breathed, tightening hs hand desperately on the rigging, wondering how the hell Louis could know. "Let's have him."

The chute gate might have opened on the world. In the brief terrible fraction of a second during which the horse swelled and gathered its fury, Geo heard his father's stern voice accusing him of wasting ten hard-earned dollars (that he had even paid tithing on), ten dollars to get himself killed. Only one week before graduation. In the face of the future, his scholarship, a career. Then the horse caromed into the arena and he was snatched away from his fantasy.

For the first few jumps, he knew exactly where the rocketing horse was and exactly how it felt to have his crotch slammed down on its sharp withers. Then one of them (he or the horse) seemed to fall out of step. He was distinctly aware of being astraddle something one instant and nothing the next. Horse flesh; its absence. Mere air. And the first half of the distance to the ground seemed to take forever, as if he were tumbling weightless in a vacuum. But for the final twenty-five feet or so his speed increased and the ground seemed to draw back and come at him in a hardened onrush. Then—just as the reel of his life was about halfway through its run in his head—there was a red explosion. A wave of blackness. He took a big gritty bite of sawdust, dirt, manure.

He got up, spitting, half laughing. And for the first time in the entire evening, he sensed the crowd. He was limping.

Louis slapped a final coating of resin in his gloved palm and tested it for tackiness. Climbing the chute gate, he paused to frown at Down Under. The horse laid its ears back. Geo watched

Louis swing his leg over the top three-by-six of the gate and let himself down into the chute; his jaw was rigid with dead-centered self-confidence and careless abandon.

"Doesn't this scare you at all, Louis?"

Louis looked up. His sun-tanned skin was like a thin shadow stretched over his blood-drained face. "Jesus, I'm petrified."

Reaching, Louis got his grip on the rigging, his fingers closing, his heavily resined glove squeaking like a rusted hinge and causing the horse, Down Under, to quiver like a taut wire.

Geo had the distinct feeling that Louis's hand would remain in the rigging till the end of the ride—no matter what happened to the rest of his body.

"Outside!" Louis cried.

The gate flew open. Down Under exploded out into the air. The music in the arena stopped. The horse farted as its haunches spun and jerked. Louis's spurs flashed and flicked, clicking stiffly, insistently, the rowels driving into the bronc's spongy shoulders, springing away, driving again and again. The number 15 on his back flapped like a single poorly formed and ineffectual wing. Except for the occasional ringing stab of the spurs, the one hand in the rigging and the points of his buttocks were the only things touching Down Under. Louis was almost pried loose the moment the buzzer rang, signaling officially that the ride was over; but he managed to stay on.

In the middle of the next jump (or so it appeared from the bleachers) the boy was finally wrenched free. The horse went up and came down; Louis went up and kept right on going. He flew through the air, frozen in the forked shape of his last punching drive with the spurs, as if he could do nothing about the interminable hazard of the approaching earth.

There was a momentary whirlpool of arms and legs, the twinkle of silver steel, the hat—jammed on till then—spiraling out of it, the dust clearing. Finally leaving a heap of cowboy. Resiliently, Louis sprang to his feet and brushed off his white shirt. He stared at the spot where he had hit. Then, retrieving his crushed Panama, he started back through the applause and cheering towards the chutes. He was limping too.

After the last event, bullriding, the Light men remained in the stands, sitting there, looking as though they did not know the show had ended. Geo saw them and shook his head. This meant some kind of trouble. He waited for Louis to collect the trophy buckle and the three-hundred-dollar check he had been awarded for winning first place in bareback bronc-riding. Then they both vaulted the fence, with difficulty, and walked up the tops of the benches to where the Lights sat.

Brad Meade's smile spread clear out to both ears. "You not only made that ride, Louis," he said mostly to the two older Lights, "but you won the money too."

"Put one hell of a hitch in your swagger, though," Willie commented. His lips suggested a smile, but nothing on the rest of his face confirmed it.

"I guess he showed he could cast that shadow," Brad continued to grin.

"Yes," Bill Light agreed. "What little they was of it. Course now, that wasn't a hell of a lot of horse. And to my notion you wouldn't want to go around bragging that that there ride contained a whole lot of style. Not the way I seen it."

"No—it wasn't much of a horse," Louis said.

Geo blinked that one down. He remembered the time Louis's grandma had called him a Light to the core, as though it were something different. And it was. He was sure of that now. It implied that somewhere there was the remote possibility of some kind of perfection. Geo knew personally, because of his intense Mormon training and what little bit he had heard actually about God, that perfection was impossible for a human being. Utterly impossible. But it was, nonetheless, not inconceivable that Louis Light might just some day achieve it. Somehow.

6.   "Louis," Renee Boulle began. "I was wondering, Louis, if I could ask a small favor of you." She found herself unconsciously searching her finger for the perforated red tip. Her lipstick, she knew, would be chewed off; it always was by

afternoon. She had wanted to put on more, but there had been
no opportunity.

"Sure, Miss Boulle—anything."

"I'm moving, you know." Why was she so suddenly out of
breath? "And I have some rather large boxes. I was won—would
you come over in a little while, as soon as you can after school,
and help me carry them down to my car?" She tried—but could
not—to meet his eyes. She was disappointed at being so weak.
Still, she was amazed that she had remained as steady as she
was. Well, why shouldn't she be?

"I'd be happy to," Louis said.

Only the boxes, she was thinking. That was the only reason she
had asked. They were heavy. Just the same (and she could not
deny this—she was always entirely honest with herself) there
was something about Louis Light that had prompted her to ask
him. Nevertheless, she realized who he was and who she was;
and she reminded herself, though she hardly needed to bother,
that she only wanted him to carry the boxes. A few. Because they
were heavy. (And *no,* she had not deliberately chosen large
ones.)

Actually, she could have asked anyone. It really would not
have done to have asked Martin Lukus, who had already made
one not-too-obscure pass at her in his office—stammering inco-
herently about how all life was a poem (Martin Lukus, who
claimed to hate poetry!) and that one had to experience these
poetic things in order to be whole. . . . No, Louis Light would
merely carry the boxes. From her apartment. Down to her car.
Yes, and she would offer him some appropriate reward. Probably
a soft drink. That's right. She would give Louis a Coke for carrying all the boxes—a Coke, or something soft. After all, she did
have some respect for his talent. When the class had composed a
sketch, Louis had handed in a perfectly vivid scene. Ridiculous
and highly unlikely, but vivid nonetheless. It was a cowboy riding up to a ranch house and playing a violin solo for a girl. A
really silly scene that was supposed to be the beginning of a proposal. But the details had been good. The muscles of the horse
working tightly under its lathered hide, dust on the saddle permanently shadowing the legs of the rider. . . . She had made him

see where it was good, where it was bad. And since then he had
improved constantly. Louis was a boy with feeling and percep-
tion. So rare, so very rare indeed. She had a few boxes that
needed carrying. That was all. And she did have a Coke.

She left school earlier than usual. Louis had promised he
would be there in one hour. Which did not give her a lot of time.

She removed her make-up and put on a fresh layer. She
combed out her hair. She sprayed it again. It was silly to spend
so much time fixing up. Really silly.

She changed her sweater, putting on a white blouse; the collar
reached to her throat, the cuffs buttoned at her wrists—warm
zones. She clasped on a choker of pearls, five strands that looked
like mail. She spotted the skin behind her ears—it lasted longest
back there—with brief spurts of *La Femme Jolie*. Then, swallowing hard, she parted her blouse between the buttons and pointed
the white nozzle of the atomizer in there. The mist felt deliciously cool. Oh!

Louis had shaved. There was a dike of white shaving cream in
his left ear. He smelled of lotion: Old Spice, Seaforth—something pungent, virile.

She showed him the boxes. He carried them out to her little
VW. After the last box was loaded, he stood in the small bare living room, his hands—hanging at his sides—looking suddenly
very large and very empty.

"Coke, Louis?" Renee asked. "Wow! I'll bet you're tired."

"No—I'm not tired."

"But you will have a Coke?"

"Yes," he nodded. "Thanks."

She brought the bottle from the refrigerator, apologizing that
her glasses were all packed, and invited him to sit on the couch
while he drank it. She sat with him. There was a whole cushion
between him and her. Of course. She would have it no other
way. A whole cushion and a wall of silence.

She wished desperately for a cigarette. Then she was sorry.
She had come out here to this school, this school in a Mormon
town, and they did not allow teachers to smoke in the presence
of students. She had been brought up to hate it, brought up a
Mormon. But going on dates from her sorority house at the Uni-
versity of Utah she had often borrowed two or three cigarettes to

put in her purse. Funny how much protection there was in such a small stick of white. Oh, so many things; so many problems. It was not easy.

"Would you mind if I had a sip, Louis?" she asked. "I guess I could have opened one for myself." She tried to laugh. That was the only reason she had asked: it made her thirsty to watch him drink. She wanted a sip. That was all. Absolutely. Whatever else happened (she could not let anything happen)—well, she could not be responsible. She was, after all, a woman. Powerless, really.

Was it her fault that it worked? As though the exchange of the bottle, their lips touching the rim, had somehow been a test kiss, she felt suddenly lured towards Louis Light.

It was, of course, his fault. Entirely. She was not in control. Leaning, she aimed, she shut her eyes, she touched her lips to his lightly, then she pressed. And fastened her body to his.

"Well," she gasped. "Well, Louis Light, you've finally kissed me."

"Yes . . ." Louis seemed to have a problem with his throat. He was working it, trying to swallow.

"You like me, don't you, Louis?" she whispered.

"Yes."

"You like the way I look, don't you?"

"Yes."

There was more certainty in his kiss this time. She had awakened the male arrogance in him; and he was beginning to dominate. She had only to guide his hand onto the white mound. Clumsily (one button popped off, hit the floor, rolled away) he found his way inside, discovered the deception, recoiled, then drove his fingers down to the smaller breast beneath it. The muscles around her mouth would no longer hold to kiss. As they gave way, she thrust with her tongue. Again, he recoiled—from inexperience, she assured herself—but resumed hungrily.

When he moved his hand lower, she just knotted up, her feet coming off the floor. And they slid from the couch onto the shaggy area rug.

"Louis," she whimpered when he probed her with his fingers. "Oh—Looo—is!"

He arched over her, trying to cover her, his clothes still on.

"Carry me, Louis," she whispered hoarsely.

"Where?" he gasped.

"Carry me to the bedroom, Louis Light!"

"Where is it?"

"Oh—find it!"

Struggling like a knight to save a damsel (she thought; and she tried to call to mind every scene she could from literature) Louis scooped her up in his arms and clambered to his feet. He stood there, swaying unsteadily, as though he were having guilty second thoughts. She reached down and took hold of his member —which stood so marvelously erect. Oh! And he started walking. Easy, confident, swift.

It was dusky in the bedroom: she had pulled all the blinds before he came. He was almost running. She clung to him, as though she were holding a fiery torch to light the way. He stumbled over a pair of shoes she had not yet packed and sent them both sprawling headlong on the bed.

Then they were at each other, fighting clothing, snorting fiercely through the moisture of an unctuous, poorly suctioned kiss. Wrestling. Locked.

"Louis—" she moaned.

He recoiled but came on again. Firm. Suave. With unswerving speed and purpose.

"Louis! Louis Light!"

The beads, five strands of artificial pearls like armor around her throat, broke and went chattering onto the floor. Renee felt his mouth trying to work itself away from her deliciously pained nipple for an apology.

"No, Louis. No, Louis, darling." She clasped her free hand over the top of his head and pulled him harder against her. "Don't be sorry . . ."

7.   "I don't need to smell anything. There's enough evidence smeared all over your face and shirt to convince me."

Louis checked himself in the mirror, scraping at the lipstick on his shirt. "There's nothing on my face."

"That's what you think. Maybe you can't see it, because maybe it looks that way all the time from the inside. But I can see it."

"So? Where's my ten bucks?"

"What ten bucks?"

"I won, didn't I?"

"Won?"

"You haven't forgotten our little bet, have you?"

"I haven't. No. But I thought you might have."

"I won, didn't I? Why would I want to forget?"

"Well," Geo pointed out, "at the last count, you owed me a total of seventeen dollars and fifty cents. That bet we made about Miss Boulle was for ten bucks. So, after this win, dubious as it is, you only owe me a total of seven dollars and fifty cents. Do you want to pay me now?"

"I don't have it on me."

"I didn't think you would."

"I'm gaining on it, aren't I?"

"Call it anything you want, Louis."

8. Falling apart.

Except now it was over. Yes, thank god. Martin Lukus put his hands to his head. Over for three months. His fingers eased at his temples. Three months of peace. And quiet. He sighed. Time to regroup. Time to get yourself glued back together. In desperate preparation for another nine-month nightmare.

If he could weather it through one more year maybe he would go back for a Ph.D. Get a grant. Something.

Martin Lukus shuddered and reached for the electric percolator. The coffee steamed in his insulated cup.

School. It was sinister. Each year the kids got progressively worse. A bunch of holy terrors. Somewhere, twin exhausts blasted. His hand shook, slopping coffee onto his green blotter. Goddammit. The car—he could not tell what make it was— rolled up in front of the building. All the chrome had been stripped off its exterior, leaving it sleek as a bomb; one look under the hood, though, would be like examining the precision interior of a fine watch. But the kid himself—who the hell was it? Couldn't they leave him alone?—would be a mess: dirt under his fingernails, grease in his duck-ass hair, shoes stinking of crankcase oil. One of those kids who kept you sitting all day beside a gas pump while he fooled with some gadget on his own car.

Good god, he thought, seeing the girl he had hired for his summer secretary climb out of the car. Well, you never could tell by looking. She had seemed nice enough. Then.

Of course, she was out now. They had graduated last night. He had sent them out. Though god knows to what. A world full of communism and corruption. Red. Pink. (Ah—he still felt the ripple of pleasure that had gone through him at the last PTA meeting after he had analyzed the problems of communism and discontent in youth and seen the appreciative nods go around the room.) And what were they? What were these graduating seniors?

The hope, for christsakes, of the nation?

Ha! Hell, the very thought of the future scared him silly. These kids were fit for nothing but hopped-up cars and jitterbug. Speed and sex.

And some students were so utterly hopeless you hardly knew how to think about them—let alone classify them. That Westlake boy, for instance. Little Benny. With only one month left to go, he had run off in the company of some miserable group of tinhorn cowboy musicians. Six months and he would be taking dope. Musicians did. But the boy refused to listen. Obviously. And ten years from now—if it took that long—he would be telling people how he had cheated himself. Yes, and he would be sending in matchbook covers for finishing-high-school-at-home courses so he could finally amount to something. But fat chance. Oh, it was dismal. Dismal as hell. Little Benny Westlake slaving away at night for a La Salle diploma, when in one short month they would have given him one. To get rid of him. Still, when he thought of it, remembering the crazy brother they had to haul naked off the public highway and lock up in an asylum, it was no damn mystery.

Some of them did not know what they had when they had it. The Seagram boy, for one. Geo had won a scholarship in geology —full tuition, room, board, a book allowance. And what was he doing? He tagged that damn Light kid around to rodeos. He had seen them at the Spring Stampede. Goddam little fools. They would probably break their necks. Or at least the Seagram boy would. That was the way it was with things: someone worthwhile would be snuffed out before he had a chance to prove himself.

Louis Light was a bad influence. He knew that for certain. Although he had never been able to come up with any concrete proof, he was sure Louis had written the poem about Miss Tottle. *Pee in a bottle!* My god! But Lukus caught himself smiling. He gulped some hot coffee to hide it and scalded his mouth.

The student secretary—her name was Ardith; she had been a cheerleader—brought in the mail.

"Should I go through the letters first, Mr. Lukus?"

"No, Ardith. I'd rather do them myself." He paused—for effect. Then he cleared his throat. "Ardith."

"Yes, Mr. Lukus?"

"You are fifteen minutes late."

What almost presented itself as a sheepish smile came out finally in a look of nervous concern. "It was the graduation."

"That was over well before ten-thirty."

"I stayed for the dance."

"Yes."

"Then there was a party."

"Oh."

From the looks of her eyes, he thought she probably had never even bothered to go to bed at all. Probably not even home. Or not home to bed. And if she had gone to bed somewhere else she had not done it to sleep. That was clear. Jesus, what was he dealing with? A little whore? Eighteen years old and already they could not stay out of someone's bed or the seat of his car. He sighed.

"Don't let it happen again."

"Oh, no, sir."

Watching her walk out, tossing her hips that way, trying to be sexy, he cursed her. Cheap little . . . Then he started and sat up straight in his chair. Would they make it through the summer? Just the two of them in the office. Day after day. Alone together. The dictation. Going over records. He looking over her shoulder. She standing beside him. A signature. An error to correct.

Frantically, he reached for the phone and gave the operator the number of his home.

10

A Common Denominator

⚡❖⚡❖⚡❖⚡❖⚡❖⚡❖⚡❖⚡❖⚡❖

1956

1. Hate? Willie recoiled at the bluntness of the word. Was it? After sixteen years, could it still be hate?

Willie knew it was something. Because when he saw Leon Fulton, he felt it. But what cause, he reasoned with himself, did he have for any bitterness towards this man? Wasn't everything that happened logical? He, Willie, had been away at the war; well, at least he had been on his way to it, running towards the war; running, too, from a cold Utah stubble field, from a woman and a burning car. Yes, from Gloria. Choosing what—in his mind at the time—seemed the lesser of the two wars available for him to fight. And Gloria? Why had they finally taken Louis from her? A question he had never really thought about. God knows what her qualifications for responsibility were. Of course, Louis and Gloria had been living with the Fultons at the time the court was working out the details of the divorce. So perhaps in the eyes of the judge (and Brad had assured him over and over again that you did not question the rightness of justice) it was the logical place

for the boy to remain. It was, then, probably only an accident of
logic that Louis had ended up with Leon Fulton. Jesus, could he
actually stoop so low as to hate a man because that man had fallen victim to logic?

Whatever the cause and however strong the persuasion and
counter-reasoning, Willie nonetheless felt suddenly uncomfortable. His skin seemed a full size too small for him. He was facing
Leon Fulton on Main Street, at noon. It was June. The summer
sun was high. The sky burned a hard clear blue. And even here
in the middle of town, the smell of first-cutting alfalfa, lying
moist on the ground, curing for baler and stack, floated in on the
breeze.

Willie shook his head. He had only himself to blame. And
maybe that girl from the office. She should not have been working overtime. Both of them should not; not on the same day. The
insanity of his actions, the way it all seemed to fit a scheme, sad-
dened him. Even now, at this distance in time, remembering the
stupidity of it all, his insides seemed to fall a foot.

"Hello, Willie."

"Leon."

They exchanged greetings and shook hands—an act to estab-
lish and maintain a gentlemanly distance.

Where the hell, Willie was wondering, did Leon Fulton find
vests like that? He had always worn them—winter and summer.
Vests tightly buttoned over his stomach, that gold watch chain
draping in a neat loop on his paunch.

Leon released his breath (it was done as though by a manually
controlled valve). "Well," he said, "Louis made it through. Yes—
and graduated. The diploma was real. And the ink even held
up." He smiled. Willie, naturally, had not gone. Gloria either.
Just as well, though. Louis had sneaked out the back way so he
would not have to suffer a couple of Polaroids in his cap and
gown. Leon had seen Emma Light; he had been aware of her
and Louise ignoring each other all through the exercise and then
going out opposite exits. In the car on the way home, he had
asked Louise about it. Was there no chance of reconciliation
ever?

"What's a life for," Louise had snapped with furious stiffness, "if it's not to be spent despising people like that tribe?"

No, there was no chance for a reconciliation.

"What's Louis going to do now?" Willie was asking.

"I'm not sure that I can say." Leon was tempted to ask Willie what difference it made to him. Willie's own life had been mystery enough. Nobody asked; nobody was told.

"Hasn't he made any plans?"

"Plans? I wouldn't know. We've gotten used to living with Louis from day to day. Maybe it's not the best way—but it certainly has been the easiest. And now, with his new passion for rodeo, we sort of wait to see if he's going to show up in one piece."

"Isn't he going to college or anything?"

"If he is, it'd be news to me. Of course, now, it'd be news if he decided to stay at home, too. I've even asked. But he hasn't really said. Not that Louis's insolent. No—he always has a reply. But it's rarely an answer. But he's dependable. When he's ready to do something he usually makes an announcement. So, I figure I'll just wait until he does."

"Hmm." Willie rubbed his hand across his mouth thoughtfully. "I see in the paper that his friend Geo has a scholarship. Doesn't that mean Louis'll probably want to go?"

Leon was beginning to enjoy this. Here was Willie Light confronted with something as close to himself as anything could be —short of a mirror. And maybe even closer than that. It was, too, the first time he had ever seen Willie look even remotely bewildered. "Well, I sure hope so. I hope he goes for the sake of the Seagram boy."

"Why him?"

"That boy seems to do everything Louis does."

"You don't think he'd be crazy enough to give up his scholarship, do you?"

"Ha! Louis has been talking Geo into things and out of things for over ten years now." Leon tilted his head. "But you know of course that we're just wasting our time."

"What?"

"Now—with all these rodeos—neither of them may make it through the summer alive."

2.   After Leon had gone, Willie found himself caught up in the past. He sat in his car, unable to turn the key to start it. Main Street had settled down following the flurry of activity that always beset it at noon. Now, the only people out were a few men in front of Penney's, a few more in front of the bank. He touched the steering wheel, as if to steady himself. His mind kept reeling on. With a million good ways to begin, why the hell had he chosen one of the few bad ones? He had gone over this time after time, trying somehow to reason through the stupidity of it, the sheer lack of foresight and anything else. He found himself drifting back the sixteen years, sixteen years to where his failure had begun. . . .

Late Saturday afternoon, he sprayed a Ford coupe with a coat of black lacquer. When he finished the final panel and switched off the compressor, he saw the office girl, Norma Jean, standing in the doorway. She held a work order for him to sign. Norma Jean was no particular beauty. But she was not any slouch either. She had good features, dark hair, cut short, a coy smile. Everything considered, the light, her pose in the doorway, and the strained circumstances of Willie's family life (Gloria had rationed him for two years, since the birth of Louis) she did have a certain appeal. She knew this, of course.

Lifting the mask off his nose, Willie said, "You shouldn't be here. You'll ruin your lungs."

"My lungs," she declared, "are all right."

They were. Or, after she had shared a case of beer with him, they certainly seemed to be. On a quiet country road, beside the Rock Point Canal, a place sparsely sheltered by winter-thin willows and black saplings, her lungs seemed perfectly all right. Lungs and everything else.

"Nothing to worry about," she had whispered when he had fumbled a question. "Nothing to worry about."

He did not realize the full impact of these words until after he had dropped her back at the garage at dark and driven home, trying to sober up in the cold wind. Gloria was waiting on the porch. She was, it seemed, caught in a classical pose. The utter beauty of it shamed him. And he failed to recognize it as a pose.

Just as Agamemnon must have missed that in Clytemnestra. He was struck by her. She looked absolutely beautiful in the winter breeze, cloth coat blown against her, outlining the good curves of her body, the body which had already caused him so much despair and which he was destined never again to touch.

The whole scene, swimming slightly in his beer-hazy eyes, started clearing as soon as she flicked on a flashlight and came towards the car. The beam blinded him. He blinked, trying to clear his eyes, trying to see her. And she said, almost without pause, as though she had known exactly what she was looking for, in a voice as taut as a piano wire, "Have you been bleeding?"

His eyes cleared. He saw it: A red-brown stain in the center of the seat. An island, a small patch of earth almost to be consumed by the sea. And that was when his stomach started falling.

Gloria's voice dropped to a whisper, words spaced, contemptuous, "You . . . whoring . . . son . . . of . . . a . . . bitch!"

She flashed the light once more across his eyes, leaving an effervescence of spots. She spun and marched back into the house. He leaped out of the car, sober now, but unsteady on his feet, and started in after her. She reappeared in the doorway. In her uplifted right hand she clutched an eight-inch butcher knife.

"Gloria—" he began, not believing for a second she would listen. And as soon as he saw her arm descend and felt the point of the knife, which he himself had honed to a professional sharpness, cut through the woolen outer layer of his jacket, he knew she would not.

He turned, already running—glad, suddenly, he had not taught her to shoot. Once, he paused to look back. She was in the car, revving the engine. She whipped it around. He cut into a field. It was stubble, hard from frost, almost bare of snow. He stopped—stupidly, he decided now—long enough to swing a flimsy wooden gate against a post. And he was barely into the field when he heard the brittle boards shatter on the Chevy's grille. He cut crosswise on the irrigation corrugations, hoping to slow her down some—or at least mess up her aim.

But she came on faster than he had calculated. The old knee-action shocks, even reinforced with coil springs from a truck, plunged and shuddered with a sound like a gatling gun. The car came closer. He had never been—even in the war—nearer to death. He turned and, out of desperation, ran in a tight circle. Which threw her off—momentarily. But she was immediately back on his trail, coming faster than ever, bearing down on him. He waited till the last possible moment, registering in his nervous system the vibration of fenders and headlights; then he made one more tight turn and headed for the edge of the field.

He heard the car behind him, eating up the margin between him and her. It was so close by the time he reached the ditch and leaped that he could detect the steady suck of the carburetors and the annoying chatter of one loose tappet.

It was a ditch that caught waste water from all the irrigated fields above it. Not too wide, but cut deep by years of drainage. When he reached the other side, Willie fell, too tired to run farther. He just waited for the car to come booming over him.

There was a crash. Then silence. He looked over his shoulder. The front wheels had dropped into the ditch and lodged there. The lights continued to shine, picking out a fringe of weeds, setting the frost crystals afire.

He could not see Gloria. Had she been hurt? He rolled over, got up, and crept closer to the car, concerned but cautious, trying to see in.

"Gloria?"

He stopped at the edge of the ditch. He could make out the dents the gate had made in the finish. Then the door was wrenched open. Gloria leaped out, holding the butcher knife. She started after him, but she could not run in her high heels. She took them off and threw them at him. He caught one: her best pair. She had wanted to go someplace.

"Gloria—listen."

She replied with stones. She clawed them up from the bank of the ditch and hurled them at him. He retreated to a pile of cold boulders.

She started the car again. It had apparently come to rest on the oil pan. Because the rods were knocking. She raced the engine and attempted to rock the car out of the ditch. The tires howled; the differential snapped and banged. Willie smelled the rubber as the tires burned against the rocks and the clutch lining chewed at the steel pressure plate. The hot tires thawed the mud; the rear wheels sank as deep as the front wheels. She shut off the engine.

Clouds covered the moon and the stars. He and Gloria became two shadowy silhouettes on opposite sides of the ditch. Two shadows slowly being swallowed by a winter darkness as heavy as cloth. He could see her. Occasionally. Patrolling her ground. He waited until he thought it might be safe. He moved stealthily away from the boulders.

Suddenly, the headlights came on. She leaped out and started peppering him with stones. One caught him in the forehead. It knocked him to his knees. She continued to rain stones around him. He got up finally and staggered to the safety of the boulders.

He told himself that sometime she would have to return to Louis. But she did not. He knew she was still there by the periodic click of the door latch as she got in or out. Hours passed. His head throbbed. He shivered with the cold and with fear.

The engine roared again. She let it knock and bang. She ground the gears and jerked the transmission with the clutch. Forward; reverse; forward. She held the accelerator down for what seemed to Willie, whose very soul had gone into the building of that car, an eternity. Then it stopped. Either it quit, or she had simply shut off the key. He would never know.

The silence was ponderous.

The door opened slowly, the hinges grating, squeaking. The hood latch popped, a sound like a shot. That puzzled him.

A match flared and fizzled out. She struck a second one. Cupping it with her hand, she held it until there was a healthy flame. The yellow light caught the smooth intensity of her face. She tossed the match onto the engine.

Flames burst up, outlining the car, leaving the open hood looking like the mouth of a dragon. The fire spread. Gloria stood beside the car longer than Willie would have dared. Then, calmly, she turned and walked away. Barefooted. Just walking away into the corn field. Lost in darkness. Forever.

3.   "How long do you think it'll take us to get there?" Louis
asked, consulting his watch casually.

"Judging from the speed you went through that last town,
which I assume was Roosevelt," Geo said, shaking his head in
disbelief, "I'd say we might be there any minute. Only we'd have
to slow down in order to recognize the place. Man, Louis, I don't
get it."

"You don't get what?"

"The unfairness of life." Geo made an incomprehensible gesture with his hands. "If I'd have come through that town five
miles above the speed limit, every cop in the country'd be flat
smack on my ass. But you double the speed, almost hit an Indian, and nothing happens."

"They don't give a shit about Indians around here."

"Dammit, Louis, I'm talking about the speed."

"It's all in the way you handle yourself, Geo."

"Style, Louis?" He knew that was what Louis meant. It was a
word Louis was starting to kick around a lot.

"Yes, Geo," Louis's eyes narrowed to something in the distance.
"It's all a matter of style."

"You mean everything—even Little Benny's success?"

"*Even?* God, with Benny, style is everything."

"We'll see, Louis. Still, it was good of him to think of us and
send the concert tickets—" Geo shut his eyes as Louis passed a
truck on a hill. "Even if we don't make it."

"We'll make it."

4.   Maybe Louis was right. Maybe it was style. But Geo
found himself wondering if it was style or the lack of style that
had changed Little Benny. Benny had reserved front row seats
for them at the concert in Salt Lake City. Hank Withers, King of
Country Swing, was singing all his newest hits: "Two Rights

Don't Make One Wrong," "Lucky Break," "Tears of Ice," "You Let Me Down," and many many others. Little Benny stood on Hank's right. He wore a white suit embroidered with big blue flowers and a pair of fancy green boots with needle toes and inlaid tops.

"Little Benny's the best thing he's got," Geo observed.

"Yes," Louis agreed. "And I'll bet he won't keep him long, either."

"He sure looks different now—sort of (Geo was tempted to say something about style) sophisticated."

"Yes—in a barnyard sort of way."

"No, Louis—I'm serious."

"So am I. I meant it as a compliment."

"I don't know how you could wring a compliment out of what you just said. But I guess there must be a way—if you say so."

Little Benny's fingers fluttered over the frets with so much ease that it seemed he was pantomiming his own playing. Hank Withers sang his last song. He sang an encore, which included a long solo by Little Benny. The audience stomped and ahh-ed. Little Benny swept the Stetson off his cloud of white hair. The crowd whistled and applauded and rattled seats for a full five minutes after he had unplugged his electric guitar and trailed the coiled cord off through the opening in the pleated curtains.

"He's right in his own glory!" Geo cried, caught up in the excitement.

They got backstage just as Little Benny had finished wrapping his custom-made guitar in a soft orange cover and was lowering it with a special kind of affection into the purple plush-lined interior of a case.

Benny had changed. Geo recognized this at once in the weight of maturity that had fallen, in such a short time, on his boyish features. There was something else, too—a refinement: it was most evident in his hands. Always before, his knuckles and fingernails had been marbled with the grease from some old jalopy he had been fixing up. Now they were white as wax, which made them seem so much more slender, and the nails were manicured—pink, nicely shaped, showing traces of orange sticks, cuticle scissors, emery boards.

Seeing them, Benny immediately brightened, "Goddam! I can't

start to tell you how good it felt tonight," he grinned, grabbing them both in an anxious hug. "Just like old times—playing out at Melody Mountain or on some high school talent show. Lord, it made me feel good to see you two guys sitting down front like you was!"

"That was the best playing I've heard in a long time," Louis declared.

"Come on over here, I'll introduce you to Hank."

Hank Withers, the tall cowboy star, had a lanky stoop from years of hovering over a microphone. "Beg your pardon, boys," he apologized in a quaking voice. "Before I can say one coherent word I need me a snort." He slopped a wave of amber bourbon into a Lily cup and emptied it quickly into his wide mouth, his Adam's apple slicing up and down behind his knotted silk scarf like a hatchet blade. He batted his watery, faded eyes. "There. Whoo-ee! Hell. Whiskey tones things down some. Spreads light out into the shadows."

Benny made the introductions. Hank Withers signed a copy of his latest album, writing, *Best of luck always, Hank.* Then he tucked the bottle of Jim- Beam under his arm and said good night.

"Man, Benny," Geo commented on the way to the hotel. "You've sure got it made."

"Looks that way, don't it."

"Hell—you're the best thing on Withers' whole show."

Little Benny released a tight, childlike giggle of glee, then sobered, "But I ain't staying. After this trip to Germany to play for the armed forces, I'm quitting Withers."

"Then what?" Louis asked.

"I've got a recording date set up for November, to cut my first album. I'm going to do a few personal appearances on through January. Then I'm going to settle down somewhere and spend the rest of the winter thinking about myself and working on my technique."

"God, Benny," Louis said. "I'd say you had plenty of technique right now. If you get too much better, people'll stick about and hoot and scream about your playing all night long."

"Maybe my technique ain't all that bad," Benny admitted. "But

I don't know about myself. Some things inside me ain't quite what they ought to be. Like what I think about myself. Or what I'm going to be—ever. . . . Besides, I've ordered me a new guitar. Special made. Classical style. With gut strings."

"Benny, why can't you just be what you are?" Geo asked.

"Because I don't even know what I am."

"Then why can't you be what you seem?"

"Because I want to be more. Don't you?"

"I don't know." Geo shrugged, laughing uncomfortably. "I guess I don't know who I am either. . . . Louis?"

"What?"

"Do you?"

"Do I what?"

"Do you know who you are?"

Louis did not reply.

5. Little Benny's nerves jangled brassily all day Sunday. He had made arrangements by mail to see Hartt that afternoon. It seemed impossible that three o'clock would ever come. He moped over coffee cups. He tried to play his guitar, tried some of the fast foot-stomping honky-tonk and twangy country blues he made his living playing. But his tense fingers clawed up like dying spiders. It was like those long nights when, looking inside himself, he could find no justification for what he was doing. He would just stand there on the stage, barely able to make out the faces in the audience over the harsh glare of the hot footlights, while his being throbbed against the limits of his body—struggling, it seemed, to seep right out through the pores in his skin.

He spent one solid hour getting ready. He shaved twice, though even the first time he did it for the sake of a habit he had acquired (along with the elevator shoes he wore when he was not in high-heeled boots) to bolster his ego. Then they all went to a restaurant for lunch.

Louis and Geo had agreed to accompany him.

"Mostly," Geo joked, "it's because I think you're going to waltz in there wearing that fancy flowered suit and somebody's going to give you some static about just walking out again—unless a couple of obviously sane friends are along to vouch for your condition."

The forty miles to Provo was no problem. But the drive out to the institution was a real ordeal. The cluster of white buildings where they kept them all locked up sat in a formidable half circle against the bottom of a hill at the east end of Center Street. To reach the place, they had to pass between a pair of massive steel gates and drive along a boulevard lined with meticulously straight, spaced poplars. After the first look, Little Benny ducked his white head and stared at the dash. Not ashamed—no, he was scared.

They signed in at the desk. An attendant took them through the hallway where patients, dressed in the haphazard manner of country children, wearing their ill-fitting and unmatched Sunday best, sat in straight chairs and awaited guests—their own, anyone's. They were shown to a room in which they could see Hartt privately. Benny stood at the window, smoking a Camel and doing an unconscious nervous shuffle in his little green boots.

Slowly, the door opened. Hartt Westlake filled the space. He carried his violin pinned against his ribs. He was in a suit. His necktie was badly knotted and pulled too far back under the curling collar of his white shirt. He blinked first at Geo, then Louis, and finally he turned to Little Benny. His blue eyes began to glow and his neatly combed and trimmed full beard bristled with the rippling of the smile that spread beneath it.

"They let me have my fiddle," he explained, plucking a string, tuning it, uneasiness pitching his voice too high. He cleared his throat.

"That's decent of them," Benny observed.

"Lord, Benny," Hartt burst. "Lord, you look just fine."

"Thanks, Hartt. You've lost a little weight."

"Food's not so hot. Then I walk a lot. Sometimes I think I'm going to wear out the floor. But I can't seem to get my legs stopped sometimes. They give me pills to slow it down. But I don't trust the bastards they got here. So I push them pills in my beard and drink the water. When they're gone I give the pill to somebody who likes them. A lot of these people do."

"You're looking pretty good, Hartt."

"You never expected to see me strapped into a strait jacket, did you, Benny?" Hartt charged, thrusting with his head, unable to complete a smile.

"No, Hartt. I expected you to look just about like you do now. I never thought you needed a strait jacket. Never."

"It's damn good to finally see you again, Benny," Hartt went on, reassured. "Every time I listened to your records I'd see you the way you looked back home. And I knew that wasn't right. You've sure put on some style." He turned to Louis and Geo. "You heard Benny's records?"

"You bet."

"We even went to hear him last night," Louis added.

"He sounds real fine, doesn't he?" Hartt said. "His records are the most popular in the ward. People are always coming around asking to hear them. One guy who likes Chet Atkins a whole lot got two teeth poked out last week when he snickered and said Little Benny wasn't as good."

"Who done that, Hartt?" Benny questioned, suddenly stern.

Drawing a breath, Hartt swallowed his grin and looked out the window at the dry hill rising abruptly behind the asylum. "I guess it was me."

There was a moment of frosty silence, then Little Benny asked, "You still read?"

"Oh, yes, Benny. I read a lot. Been getting books sent up from that Mormon college down the hill. I pretty well understand what's wrong with me now—I just haven't quite figured out how to go about fixing it up." Hartt paused to chuckle through his red whiskers. "You know, there's times when I think I've got everything Freud and Jung and Adler and all those other writers have dreamed up, and there's other times when I think I'm pretty normal. And I guess I am normal—until I go off and do my trick. . . . I don't do it an awful lot. It's my fiddle that keeps me from it. If I can stand somewhere, like I used to at Melody Mountain, and just play the daylights out of things, I can usually get the feeling I crave." Sadness rolled into his blue eyes like heavy wet clouds. "Benny, I know it's a bad trick, but once it gets started on me, I can't stop it. That's the one thing they act like they don't understand here: it's not them my trick's playing anything on— it's me. I'm the one."

"I know, Hartt," Benny said sadly. "I wish I could do something for you."

"You can, Benny, honey."

"What?"

"You can send me a couple of records."

"Which ones?"

"Remember Bartok?"

"Yeah."

"When you and everybody else was gone out of the house, I used to sneak in and listen to those records you had hid behind your bed."

"I could tell, Hartt. You kept putting them back in the wrong jackets."

"That wasn't me, Benny."

"Who was it?"

"Pa."

"Pa!"

"He's the one who can't read. Pa listened to that Bartok every chance he got. I used to peek in the window at him. Hell, he'd be sitting stiff as a poker, like he was in a winged chariot to heaven. That guy talked to me, too. Lord, it seemed he could rear back and say everything there was to say—without ever saying anything."

"I'll send you some Bartok, Hartt. I'll send you every record he ever made."

Then, with the weak afternoon sunlight falling on the old scarred parquet flooring, the shadows of the mullions intersticed at odd intervals with those of the steel bars, the room grew silent.

"I suppose I've lost my mind all right enough," Hartt confessed, without provocation.

"Now, Hartt, hell—you can't go on like that."

"But that doesn't make a whole lot of difference—I mean not

about my mind. What scares me is that I'm afraid maybe they're starting to get at my soul, too."

"Hartt—"

"Benny, honey." Hartt's voice echoed in the slowly darkening room. "You know something?"

"What, Hartt?"

"If I don't get out of this place pretty damn soon I think I'm just going to perish. . . ."

6.

"Go on!" Emma Light hissed from somewhere behind the rusted square of screen door that looked blankly out onto the tent-house. "You can get out and stay out!"

Bill Light cupped his knotted palm to his ear. "You hear something just now?" he inquired of Louis, merely to show that he was purposely ignoring her.

Louis kept right on working.

"Maybe it's just the wind in the trees."

The old man was attired in an ancient moth-ruined beaver top hat—symbol of his formal acknowledgment of something: victory or defeat—and a white shirt, tieless, though fastened all the way to the throat, and a double-breasted black suit-jacket buttoned over his bib overalls. Standing beside the tailgate of the old truck, he gave a few hand signals and told Louis how he wanted everything loaded. But Louis, as could be expected, seemed to be ignoring him and putting things where he wanted them. Which was the way it was with them all.

Now and then, emerging from his shadow of scorn, the old man would lift his jaw level and spit. The stream would hit and stain down the side of the tent-house like shingle oil. One thing was bothering the daylights out of him: he seemed to have a bad plug. Because he barely got a cut balled good and set in his jaw before the taste went clear out of it.

"Hand me a fresh plug, Louis. There's something mighty fishy here. I thought that first one was bad. But this one's like having a mouthful of sawdust."

"There won't be no tears from me," Emma Light rejoined bitterly. "This isn't the first of the last forty summers you've ruined for me. But maybe it is for Louis. You ought to be ashamed, dragging him down here to waste his vacation time toting your truck and junk from hell to breakfast and back. No—not back! As far as I'm concerned, you can get out of my life for good. Cart everything away now so there won't be any earthly excuse for you to come slithering back. Sonofabitch."

Her shoes ground on the linoleum as she whirled and stalked back into the depths of the house, her fury funneling after her like a treacherous whirlpool. A door slammed.

Silence.

Louis loaded the violin—which this time Emma Light did not see—then hopped out of the truck. He slammed the twisted tailgate up into place and stuck the hook fasteners down through the matched eyes. Unrolling his sleeves, he started to climb into the driver's seat.

"Nope," Bill Light said firmly. "I'll drive."

The old man took the wheel and drew back, frowning. He had to grip it to get the little sense of the molded material he ought to have felt immediately. "Almost," he muttered, "like I was ahold of nothing."

Starting the engine, he let it roar wide open while he asserted the old beaver top hat squarely on his head; then, giving the house and yard one final glance of formal condescension and scorn, he left. For good.

"I've taken it back," he announced, without even turning his head to look at Louis.

"What?"

"The old place. The homestead. The place we bought first from Bent Tree." Bill knew he was doing it. He could see his hand automatically reaching, clawing around the knob on the gear shift, pulling back, while his foot stabbed at the clutch. But he did not feel himself doing it. He had to keep talking. "I could use a little help, a little help getting it back in shape."

"I've got a few days," Louis offered.

"Roof leaks. Leaks like a bitch. Needs tar paper and shingles.

Ain't no hinges on the doors neither. Somebody swiped them. Or else they just rotted away—screws and all. There's a couple of windows out, too. That won't bother none, though, till wintertime. Maybe stretch a little screen wire over the holes in case the flies—"

Bill Light stopped talking right where he was, in the middle of a statement. He tried to go on, ". . . get too . . ." But he could not. Because up ahead, he saw a black figure, in a shroud, standing beside an open black car. ". . . too friendly." The shroud was flowing with the whispering ease of a polished fabric. There was the smile of a woman on the strange figure's round, whitened face—female, vicious, relentless.

"Got to miss it," Bill said aloud, then shut his lips. "Got to turn a little and miss it."

"What?" Louis tilted his head quizzically.

But Bill Light could not take his gaze from the narrowing eyes of the black figure.

At that moment, a new white Continental made a slithering turn off a graveled side road and came speeding towards the pickup, making a flashing low blur on the narrow strip of blacktop country road.

"There's my dad," Louis said.

Bill Light did not hear him. Louis shouted it again. Instead of responding, the old man swerved out to miss the black car, the black figure, the old pickup truck heading directly into the path of the sleek oncoming Continental. Louis grabbed for the wheel. Bill Light, his eyes blazing, caught the boy squarely in the mouth with the back of his hand.

Willie saw it coming. About the time he was ready to raise his finger in atavistic parody of what he thought the old man would do—if, indeed, he chose to do anything at all—he saw the truck turning towards him, as if to pass something on the other side of the road. Except that there was nothing over there to pass. So, at the last moment, carefully but quickly weighing all the odds, he cut a sharp right for the barpit, the bottom of the big car thundering and jolting over a high ridge of cobbles. Good god! he thought, bracing himself back into the posh leather upholstery, the sonofabitch could have wiped out the whole male part of the family in one fell swoop.

"You ran him off the road!" Louis shouted, craning his neck.

"He's still there." The old man saw the black figure with the face of a woman leap into the black car. "He's coming. Jesus Christ, he's coming."

Bill Light tromped the gas pedal against the floor boards.

"Slow down!" Louis cried.

No, the old man told himself. No, he had never really done anything since that one bad winter, since nineteen and twenty-four. He had really never made it out of bed again.

"You're going to lose some of the stuff out of the back."

It occurred to him, fleetingly, before he stubbornly blanked the thought out of his head, that he might never need any of it. "I'll do the driving here."

The black car was gaining, overtaking at a breakneck rate. Had he been a failure all these years? Had he? Or maybe since that time he had not even done enough to fail decently. That was the painful thing.

"Do you see it, Louis?"

"What, Grandpa?"

"Do you see that black car?" He felt his voice tighten. "It's trying to pass."

Louis turned to look. "I don't see anything. What black car?"

"It's there," he said in a whisper. "It is."

The muffler on the right side of the Continental was split wide open. Willie heard it blat and started to swear. He had seen the white blur of the two faces—the old man and Louis. He shook his head. What wild nonsense was the old fart up to now? Next thing he knew, he would kill the kid. And he told himself that it had probably been a mistake to give that heap a tune-up last week. But the old man had wanted it. Plugs. Points. Condenser.

Willie whipped a fast turn, the bad muffler throbbing. He caught up with the old truck just as it made the corner and headed north towards the canyon. He did not dare pass. All he could do was sit and wait and see what would happen. The old man was holding the damn thing right at seventy-five. It was beating up dust and blowing it off into the willows. It rocked and floated high on the leaf springs, loaded with what he recognized, by one pant leg that kicked limply like a phantom dancer, as being personal belongings. He noticed the old man was also wearing the beaver top hat he had saved all these years for funerals (he had worn it first at his own wedding). And today there was something staunch in the severe curl of its hard little brim.

Willie knew the old man was heading home: they were nearing the homestead. The old man had spent the past week wheeling and dealing with the Three Bar Sheep Company to buy back the old house. . . . Just then the old truck veered into a rut, the black violin case flew up out of the back, hit on the tailgate, balancing there, and finally flipped end over end. When it struck the road, the lid of the case burst open and the violin shot out. It seemed to just stand on end for a full minute in a graceful pirouette. Then, quite suddenly, it shattered. Willie stood on his brake pedal. He saw Louis leap across the seat of the pickup. And finally, after careening crazily from one side of the road to the other, the truck came to a stop. Silence caught up with it. Dust settled off into the leaves.

Kneeling in the road, Willie collected up everything he could find of the violin. It could never be repaired. The scroll, peg box, and two loose pegs hung to the tail piece by a single string which was rapped once around the arched section between the two F-holes.

There is no hurry, he told himself, when he saw that he was trembling and fumbling with the splinters and chips. He closed the case, the lid working on one twisted hinge, and fastened the hasp. Climbing back into his car, he drove on to where the pickup sat, the dust of its flight filming its fenders and the corrugated rubber on the running board.

"Just what I figured," he murmured, barely above his breath. "I guess I knew it when I saw that violin fly apart like that. Only I still don't know why."

Louis's hands were clawed around the steering wheel and his gray eyes were fixed on something—probably, Willie thought, his own inevitability—distant in the road.

The old man was leaning. . . .

No, Willie caught and corrected himself: the old man had recently stopped leaning or anything else. Louis was doing it all now, holding up the body, though it seemed he was refusing to acknowledge having any part in it. The face was inclined in a darkly carven nod, the eyes—now glazed over with that self-contained sameness of other eyes, ordinary eyes—gathering dust under the shaggy brim of the old beaver hat. Already the old man was merely a thing, a history toughened and creased into a parchment of skin, a cryptic record of all that had happened to a rotund mass of flesh, which was now merely meat, and—cooling—was rapidly tending towards carrion: the final revision so much shorter than the original writing.

"Doesn't take long for it to burn out, does it, Son?" The word *son* felt strange on Willie's tongue. He swallowed.

Louis remained glued to the steering wheel, his shoulders frozen forward in a silent hunch.

Examining the boy's face briefly, Willie then walked around, opened the door, and dragged the already difficult, stiffening body away from the boy.

"Think you can drive him home?"

For an answer there was a scratching movement of one foot searching in the dirt along the floorboard, finding the mushroomed stub, and the starter grinding.

7. When Emma Light saw the old pickup wheel into the driveway, she knew exactly what had happened. Of course, Willie's arrival had foreshadowed it. She knew something was wrong. Because he almost stopped the first time, the mufflers (not yet one month old) on his car making as much racket as all those clunks he had dragged to the high school shop class and tinkered into a questionable state of roadability. But he had had to give way to the force of male habit. Yes, he had to go on past, slowing long before he generally did, getting back too damn soon. So even the neighbors would be wondering—probably standing out on their porches, craning to see what it was. And they would all hurry in to the phone and listen while she told

Charlie Rayburn that the old fool had not made it; that he could come and get him.

Louis just sat there. Like a bump on a log. Typical. Oh, wasn't Louis typical of the whole damn bunch. A Light to the core.

"Did you have to leave him sitting up? And his dirty mouth ajaw too?" she demanded. She yanked open the door and climbed onto the running board, her apron swishing. "You could at least have shut that. Or maybe scooped the tobacco out with your fingers." She did, shaking it onto the dirt.

She looked at Louis, sitting like a plaster statue in the seat. "Lord, Louis, you ain't no different," she lamented. "And I hoped you would be. I hoped that maybe them Fultons would raise you up into something else. But I guess there's not enough decency in any breed of woman to put out the Light in one of you. I know. You damn little shit. You're just like he was. Spit and image! Not scared of this dead man or thing, whatever it is now, because you choose to ignore it. It and anything else that might constitute a threat to you."

Louis did not move.

"You too!" she snapped, whirling to face Willie, speaking with cold asperity and furious pride. "Both of you come on. I reckon they'll still count him as my man. Somebody to blame for letting him stay around and not be buried. Let's get him laid out on the bed in the house. Then I can at least phone Charlie Rayburn to come fetch him."

"It's a whole lot closer to the tent-house," Willie said, with a sidelong look at the body.

"And it's closer still to the ditch over there. You could just dump him in and kick a little dirt on top of him!" she spat. "No! I'm not having any scandal hanging over my head. Not after all I've been through with this sonofabitch. I said in the house on the bed. That's where I want him when them people get here."

She concluded her speech with a snort of fiery purpose and authority. Then she folded her arms. A woman who had finally won.

8.   "Isn't it what?"

"Isn't it sort of hard to leave?" Geo repeated. He was trying to describe what he felt inside. The crisp September wind swirled in through the windows of the car, whipping the clothes hanging from the rod in back, snatching at a sleeve, rattling a cleaner's bag.

Louis kept both hands pushed rigidly out against the wheel. He was already driving too fast. They passed a country auction yard. A tumbleweed rolled brittlely across the highway. Geo knew from experience that Louis was getting ready to say something, so he sank down in the seat and waited.

"Do you see any evidence of pain on my face, Geo?"

Geo did not bother to look. He knew he would not. What did he ever see on Louis's face?

"I mean," he explained, "we're going off to be something totally new and different."

"Hey"—Louis gaped—"are you serious?"

"I am."

"I hope we are, Geo. I'd really like to believe that. But I doubt it—seriously."

"We'll be on our own," Geo argued.

"I wonder, Geo."

"We will! You can't deny that."

"No—I wonder how much anything ever changes. Take for instance when my Grandpa Light died last month. That ought to be the ultimate change, hadn't it? Going from life to death."

"Yes."

"Well, almost nothing happened. I swear. One minute he was there and I could feel him. The next minute he wasn't and I couldn't feel him. It was spooky. All the time I was driving him home, I kept trying to figure it out. But I couldn't see where the big change came. I think it got him, too. I think he had planned something. He was trying to make it more spectacular. But he died on the way to the location." Louis shrugged and pushed his left elbow out the window. He relaxed against the door, driving now with only one hand. "How could we expect much change?

God, we're only going from one place to another place. From one life to the same life."

"Do you just accept everything?" Geo wanted to know.

"Yes."

"Maybe that's why. Some of us do want to change."

"Oh? And how *do* some of you want to change? How do you want to be different?"

"I can't explain it exactly."

"What? Do you want to be somebody else?"

Geo was baffled.

"Do you want to wake up tomorrow a new man? Is that it?"

"I don't know."

"Do you want to be anything just as long as it seems to be different? God, take a look at Hartt Westlake. He's different."

"Hartt's crazy."

"It's sure something to think about, Geo."

"Well, Louis, I do know one thing."

"Which is?"

"One of my changes is that I'm going to give up rodeo."

"So? That won't make you any different. But it might keep you the same a lot longer. Plus maybe proving that you're chicken. Which is something I've sort of suspected all along."

"I'm not chicken! I just want to protect my scholarship," Geo argued, certain he was right. "I want to stay in school and be able to finish."

"Which means you're giving up. Right? You're chicken. Admit it."

"I'm being sensible!"

"Sensible." Louis looked at him, a smile flickering. "God, Geo, maybe you really are changing."

"Of course I am. I told you."

"But I don't think it's going to make all that much difference to the world."

"What are you talking about? What do I care about the world?"

"That's exactly what I'm talking about. People may never know."

"Know what?"

"About your drastic change."

"Why not?"

"We may never make it. And don't start giving me that look, Geo. For one thing, the earth might just open up and swallow us. Something might snuff us out. The possibility is not remote. A tree. Another car. A deer trying to cross. If not, maybe we'll go on. But that's not much of a change: we've been doing that for eighteen years already. So I don't know where you get your ideas."

Geo slumped down in the seat, determined not to say another word.

The car swayed around a turn. It started up the tan and gray hills that rose out of the east end of the valley, where the last yellow fields of wheat stubble gave way to sage and junipers. At the crest of the hill, the car seemed to hang for a moment. Then, almost insignificantly, it plunged down the other side, into the Twist, leaving the horizon empty: a line of earth, a line of sky.